Under the
Zaboca Tree

We gratefully acknowledge the support of the Canada Council for the Arts and the Ontario Arts Council for our publishing program. We also acknowledge the financial support of the Government of Canada through the Canada Book Fund.

Front cover: Boscoe Holder subject "Blanchisseuse (detail of)." © Estate of Boscoe Holder by Courtesy of Felix Rosenstiel's Widow & Son, London. Used with permission.

Cover design: Val Fullard

Under the Zaboca Tree is a work of fiction. All the characters portrayed in this book are fictitious and any resemblance to persons living or dead, is purely coincidental.

Library and Archives Canada Cataloguing in Publication

Guevara, Glynis, 1959-, author
        Under the zaboca tree / a novel by Glynis Guevara.

(Inanna young feminist series)
Issued in print and electronic formats.
ISBN 978-1-77133-329-0 (softcover).--ISBN 978-1-77133-330-6 (EPUB).--
ISBN 978-1-77133-331-3 (Kindle).--ISBN 978-1-77133-332-0 (PDF)

        I. Title. II. Series: Inanna young feminist series

PS8613.U483U54 2017   jC813'.6   C2017-900320-8
                                               C2017-900321-6

Printed and bound in Canada

Inanna Publications and Education Inc.
210 Founders College, York University
4700 Keele Street, Toronto, Ontario, Canada M3J 1P3
Telephone: (416) 736-5356 Fax: (416) 736-5765
Email: inanna.publications@inanna.ca   Website: www.inanna.ca

Under the Zaboca Tree

a novel by
Glynis Guevara

inanna poetry & fiction series

INANNA PUBLICATIONS AND EDUCATION INC.
TORONTO, CANADA

For Mommy and Daddy

1.

FOR AS LONG AS I CAN REMEMBER, I've stared at the women who've walked past me and wondered if any of them could be my mother. The week after I turned ten—as I sat next to my dad eagerly awaiting our flight—the longing for my real mom was as strong as ever. That day, despite my excitement for the changes about to take place in my life, the green-eyed monster within me poked its head out as I glared at a tall, slender woman holding a young girl's hand. I wished I were that little girl with my mother's hand clutching mine.

Suddenly, my father eased out of his seat and nudged me. I grabbed my carry-on bag, jumped to my feet, and stepped ahead of him. Dad and I were leaving the cold winters behind and heading to the tropics—sunny Trinidad and Tobago, to be exact. The thought that I'd soon be free to roam the streets all year long without a coat, woolly hat, and pairs of boots and gloves gripped me and, in my wild imagination, I felt thick beads of sweat trickle down my skin as I played and laughed and had fun with hordes of new friends I hadn't yet met. My heart thumped loudly against my chest, so I pressed my sweaty palms against my thighs and tried to calm myself; instead, a burst of energy overtook me, and I rushed even farther ahead.

"Baby Girl, wait," my father said very softly, calling me by my pet name. Back then he hardly ever called me Melody. I spun around and, as Dad stepped toward me, I heard the babbling of a nearby infant. The baby's mother's eyes caught mine, and

I saw her smile as she glided by me, the gurgling baby in her arms. I was suddenly overcome by a sense of loss as I remembered the animal sounds my dad would make when he used to play with me. He'd bark like a dog and moo like a cow; he was especially good with his trumpeting elephant noises. The first time I heard him bark, I tried to imitate him. My bark didn't sound as real, but in time—and with his coaching—I improved. Dad, however, stopped playing those games shortly before my stepmother, Charm, left us.

As we stepped onto the plane, we were greeted by an attractive flight attendant and I thought how neat it would be to find a similar job when I was all grown up. Dad shuffled sideways, allowing me more than enough room to make my way toward the window seat. After all the passengers were seated, the pilot introduced herself as Captain Raymond.

"The pilot's a girl!" My mouth dropped open in surprise. "I don't want to be a flight attendant," I said to my dad. "I want to be a pilot just like her." My father nodded and smiled.

As the flight attendants prepared us for takeoff, I imagined I was an astronaut preparing to shoot into space, directly toward the moon, just like Neil Armstrong had done so many years before I was born.

My fear and excitement got all tangled together as the plane taxied down the runway. My body jerked sideways, but my seat belt kept me secure. Suddenly, we were airborne and soaring upward. For a while I closed my eyes and imagined having a ten-foot wingspan just like the Andean Condor I had learned about on my last day at St. John's Public School in Toronto.

Using my index finger, I stroked the face of the watch my best friend, Makayla, had given me as a going-away present. *What's Makayla doing at school today?* I wondered, but I quickly answered my own question. Every Monday morning our teacher, Miss Jones, gave a spelling test, so it was quite likely Makayla was carefully writing each word in her exercise book the second Miss Jones called it out.

My father's eyes were shut when I stretched my skinny limbs across the seat, trying to hug him. His eyes opened up really wide. "Are we going to meet a lot of our relatives when we get there?" I asked.

"I'm sorry. It's just you and me, kiddo," he said, "but I'm sure you'll make a lot of wonderful new friends there."

"How come?" I stared at him, baffled by his response.

"That's just the way the cards are stacked, my dear."

"Do you think Makayla and her mom will come down to visit us like they promised?"

"Maybe," Dad shrugged.

"Makayla's mom told me that Trinidad's very green and hilly," I said. "Are we going to live on top of a big hill?"

"I don't think so." His lips curved into a smile, but he didn't show any teeth. "My parents brought me to Canada when I was barely six, but I'll never forget my grandparents' house. It was on a piece of land as flat as a pancake." Dad licked his lips. "My brother Howie and I used to race each other around it like greyhounds."

"Did Howie win all the races or did you sometimes beat him?"

"Sometimes he beat me, and sometimes I beat him." Dad waved his arms around a bit.

"Tell me more, Dad."

"What do you want to know?" Dad said. "Howie died a long time ago. I'm afraid there isn't much about him you don't already know."

"What sort of fun things did you and Howie do when you were my age?"

"We used to go to the beach a lot, just like you and I are going to do after we settle in."

My eyes widened. "Can we go to the beach every single day?"

"No, but I promise we'll go as often as we can."

"That's awesome, Dad." I smiled widely. "I really want to see the ocean, the sharks, the dolphins, and all the different types of fish."

"Sharks?" Dad grinned. "You can eat shark when you get there!"

"Oh, Dad!" I said. "I don't want to eat them. I just want to look at them."

"I really want your life to turn out better than mine." Dad squeezed my hand. "When you're all grown up, you can return to Canada to live."

"I'm not, Dad." I frowned. "I'm not going back there without you ever."

"I swear I'll never leave you." Dad's fingers circled my back. "And I promise I'll do everything I can to give you a much better life than I've had."

Moments later, Dad pulled a magazine from his pouch and began to flip through its glossy pages.

"Can we look at the family pictures?" I suddenly said, but Dad continued flipping through the magazine, ignoring me completely.

"Pleeeease." I made a face.

"They're in the overhead compartment." He hesitated for a moment before getting up and fishing two crumpled brown envelopes out of his bag.

"I used to enjoy looking at these pictures when I was a boy." He pressed both envelopes against his chest.

"Dad," I said, grinning, "you say the same thing every time we look at them."

He handed me a stack of dog-eared photos from the envelope on top. I examined a tattered picture of Dad and Howie, standing under a sprawling tree with bunches of dangling, pear-shaped green fruits. They were dressed in matching light-blue outfits, almost the same colour as the sky behind them.

"This was a special tree Mom used to rock us under when we were tots."

"What kind of tree is it?"

"It's an avocado tree, but they're sometimes called 'zaboca' in Trinidad."

"Zaboca's a funny word." I chuckled loudly, covering my mouth with one hand.

"Don't you worry, I'm sure you'll learn many more amusing words after we get there."

I flipped through the first bunch of photos. They were all snapshots of Dad and his immediate family members. I pushed the pile of pictures back into the first envelope and Dad pulled the photos from the second one. I sifted through the fresh batch. The photos on top were of Dad's parents and grandparents, but at the bottom of the pile were photos of relatives whom I could not identify. I stared at them wondering if I'd ever be able to match names to faces. I had looked at those snapshots so many times in the past that more than a few images of the unidentified people in them were stuck in my mind.

"After we get to Trinidad we'll learn everyone's name." My eyes landed on the thick blue veins on Dad's right hand. His long fingers were spread apart and plastered across his forehead.

"Dad," I said a bit louder, "what part of Trinidad did you live in?" I asked the question already knowing the answer. However, my plan was to keep him in conversation so he wouldn't slip into a long silence and forget I was there.

"I've told you before. It's a village called El Socorro."

"We're not going to live in a house that looks like this one, are we?" I pointed to a dull, whitewashed wooden house on stilts.

"No!" he said. "We're going to stay at my friend's place for a short while."

With my lips glued shut, I stared at another tiny house, imagining where I was going to sleep that night. A vision of a very big house, quite unlike any of the high-rise apartment buildings I'd lived in my entire life, filled my head.

"Let's put the photos away," Dad said. "We've looked at them enough today."

Dad went back to his magazine and before long he was snoring softly. I decided to let him nap.

I pulled out a book from my hand luggage titled *Love You*

Forever. I flipped to the first page, tracing the words, *To Baby Girl, from Charm, Happy Birthday,* handwritten in dark blue ink. The book was a birthday present from my former step-mom. She lived with my father and me from the time I was three until I turned eight.

I shuffled through the storybook, humming the first few bars of the lullaby she used to sing to me, until I came upon three photos that I had stuffed inside it days earlier. I glanced at the photo on top and studied Charm's face while running my finger along the scar on her right cheek. At that moment it seemed much larger than I'd remembered. Then I looked at a photo of Charm and my stepsister, Clara. I hadn't seen either of them since Charm and my dad went their separate ways.

I don't have any memories of my real mother—I don't even have a photo of her—but my father told me her name was Jada Shoemaker, and that she left us before I turned one. I used to ask where she was and why she never came to see us, but every time I questioned him about it he'd get upset, so I stopped.

I started to feel drowsy too so I snuggled against Dad and dozed off until I heard someone shouting. Both Dad and I woke up with a start. I don't know how long we had been sleeping.

"Daddy, I see land!" a chubby boy across from us hollered. "Look, Daddy, look!"

I sat up straight stared out the window, and, as the plane lowered, lush mountains became visible.

"A green heavenly landscape!" a muscular man next to the chubby boy said.

I peered out the window and imagined I was a giant hovering over the tiny objects below. But as the aircraft got lower and lower, the images became larger and larger. The landing was a bit bumpy, and my body jerked up and down. Then my ears popped.

We were in Trinidad and Tobago now, and my life was going to change. I could hardly wait.

2.

WITH OUR LUGGAGE IN TOW, Dad and I marched purposefully toward the door. It automatically slid open and very warm air hit our faces. "It's hot, isn't it?" Dad smiled. "Do you like it?"

"I love summer," I said, panting with excitement.

"The weather is like this all year round. You get sun and rain, but no snow, not ever."1

"That means I can play outside every single day?" I stressed the three words 'every,' 'single,' and 'day,' and the pitch of my voice was way higher than normal.

"Not until you finish your chores and your homework." Dad smirked.

We stepped toward an area overflowing with strange people who were just standing and waiting. Some of them had dark, sleek, straight hair, while others had curly or kinky hair. I was surprised that most of the people around us were different shades of brown. Some had dark chocolate complexions like my father. Some had an almond colouring like me, while others were almost as dark as the asphalt beneath my feet. There definitely weren't as many pale-skinned people as we'd left behind at Pearson International Airport in Toronto.

Lugging my backpack, I struggled to pull my lone suitcase. Meanwhile, Dad's hand luggage was snugly affixed on top of the larger of his two suitcases. The sun shone directly onto my face, and, as I squinted, my eyes felt as if they had shrunk to half their normal size. I was tempted to leave my belongings behind and prance about in the sunshine, but I knew Dad would disapprove, so I kept calm and stayed close to his side. Dad hadn't told me if anyone was coming to pick us up, or if we'd have to find our way to our new home by ourselves. But itching for an answer, I looked up at him and asked, "Is anyone meeting us?"

"Shoo!" He pulled out his phone and began typing. When he was done, I pointed to a bunch of taxis in the distance. "Are we going to take one of those?"

"No, we are not," he said abruptly, just as he usually did whenever I asked for detailed information about my absentee mother. But despite his cold response, my thoughts raced and I imagined us setting up house on a white, sandy beach by clear blue waters. A bunch of taxi drivers rushed toward us like a pack of wolves searching for their prey, but my father shrugged off every one of them. For the next few minutes I kept my lips together while he looked around like a lost soul.

"Hey, Smokey!" A woman's voice called out Dad's nickname.

I searched the throngs of people outside the airport but couldn't figure out where the sugar-coated voice had come from.

"Over here!" the voice called out again.

I scanned all around, and suddenly a woman's hand, heavily decorated with silver bracelets, rose up and waved above the heads of the people in front us. She squeezed through the crowd and a heavily made-up, pencil-slim, hazelnut-complexioned lady strode quickly toward us. Her curly, two-toned braids, blond on top with black edges, fell way past her shoulders and swung from left to right as she rushed toward my father with outstretched arms; he extended his arms in return. Their eyes locked together and her legs left the ground as he spun her around. Dad's grin was almost wide enough to split his face in two. My mouth froze half-open when I saw the word "Smokey," my Dad's nickname, engraved on the gold chain around her neck.

Is she the new woman in his life? The one I'll have to compete with for his affection? I wondered in silence.

"Hon," he said and pressed his lips against her cheek.

I was filled with dread as the strange woman and my dad began canoodling in my presence, behaving as if I were invisible. My father's face had lit up like a two hundred-watt light bulb, but neither he nor his lady friend appeared to have noticed my scowl. How I wished she would disappear and my real mother would suddenly appear. Dad eventually let go of her, and her feet once more touched the ground.

"Who's this pretty young lady? What's your name, love?" She exposed perfectly white teeth behind full lips.

"I'm Baby Girl." I was relieved. Finally, some attention.

I gave her a smile that I hoped was as bright as the sunlight we were in and stared into her dark brown eyes.

"You're a cute sweetheart with an equally cute pet name, and you've got such beautiful skin." She touched my chin as if she were a doctor examining my face.

"You've got nice hair too," she added, passing the back of her hand over my ponytails. I was amazed at the length of her fingernails, although I couldn't tell whether they were real or fake. She wore silver earrings and a silver ring on her right index finger, which matched her jingling bracelets. As she and Dad continued to chat, he held her hand. I frowned, peeved that no one had offered to hold mine. Using her free hand, she took hold of my small blue suitcase and dragged it on its wheels. I remained silent as my father pulled open the back door of her Jeep Cherokee and ushered me in. He climbed into the front passenger seat. She slid into the driver's seat, and as she steered the vehicle out of the airport, I carefully listened to every word they said while the Sherlock Holmes within me tried to figure out what was really going on. She was driving on the wrong side of the street! But so was everyone else, I soon noticed. The roads were way narrower than those in Canada. I didn't have a clue where we were heading, but as we zipped along I stared out the window with razor-sharp eyes, taking in the few unusually shaped buildings that rushed past us. I spotted a circular one, but most of them were rectangular. Some roofs were covered with tiles, but most had a sort of silvery tin-like roofing. I wondered why so many of the porches and windows were enclosed with decorative wrought iron, but I didn't ask.

I couldn't help but notice the mass of tall, thin, circular poles sticking out of the ground and the throngs of tangled wires and cables connecting them to each building. Almost every two-storey house we passed had a very long staircase running from its yard to its porch. And more than a few of these larger dwellings stood next to some puny ones. But no matter their size, most buildings were very brightly coloured in varying shades of red, green, blue, and yellow.

The wind hit my face and my hair blew in all directions.

"Roll up the windows," my father said as he glanced back at me and noticed I was trying to hold my already messed up hair in place.

"I want to feel the breeze on my face," I protested.

Dad didn't fuss but instead faced forward, continuing to chat with his lady friend. They mentioned the names of several people I'd never heard of, but I didn't dare interrupt them. Instead, I kept my eyes on the roadway, glancing at the different makes and models of vehicles moving in both directions.

A while later, when Dad lit a cigarette, I knew it was my chance to ask a few questions. "Dad," I asked, "what is the name of this street?"

He turned to face me, the cigarette sticking out of his mouth. He inhaled before exhaling sharply. The dirty smell of nicotine surrounded me, and my sinuses instantly got stuffy. "We're on the Eastern Main Road," he replied, taking another puff as I screwed up my face.

"How do you like it?" Dad's lady friend said, but even though her voice was loud and clear, I didn't realize she was posing the question to me. "How do you like Trinidad so far, Baby Girl?" she said.

"It's hot and it's so, so greeeen."

"Devilish weather," she chuckled. "Are you hungry?"

"Yeah, I'm hungry and thirsty too," I said, even though I wasn't really hungry.

She glanced at my father, raised one hand from the steering wheel, and began to tickle his neck. Then she pressed his hand between hers and squeezed gently.

"What do you want to eat, Smokey?" she asked, putting her hand back on the steering wheel. "Do you want to get some chicken?"

"That will do," my father said. "I haven't eaten since last night."

"Is it because you didn't like the food on the plane, or were you just being picky?"

"You know my issues are way bigger than that." Dad's voice dipped almost to a whisper.

"Oh! I know!" she exclaimed.

"What's done is done. I'm trying hard not to dwell on the past," he added.

"That's good to hear. You've got to stay upbeat now that you're starting a brand new life."

"Brand new life?" he repeated. "I'm not exactly a newborn."

"Well, you get my drift," she said. "Consider it a brand new start to an old life. Others may refer to Trinidad as a Third World nation, but there are lots of opportunities here."

After a few moments of silence, Dad's lady friend threw a black cell phone at him. "Call Monty," she said as it landed on his lap. Her words sounded more like an order than a request.

"We're not going there today, are we?" my father asked as she pulled a tiny book from the vehicle's front compartment.

"Look! His number is in here."

"Don't you save people's numbers in the phone's address book?" he teased.

"Yes, of course I do, but that's not my regular phone. It's a spare one."

"I see." Dad bent forward and picked up the book just as it slipped between his legs. He hesitated for a few seconds before dialling. "No one's answering." He sounded relieved.

"Leave a message, please." She spoke like a strict parent.

With the phone still stuck to his earlobe, Dad glanced at her and shook his head before speaking into the phone. After leaving a brief message, he attempted to rest the phone on her lap.

"No, keep it," she said. "Monty might call us right back, and, anyways, you can use it for a couple days until you convert to a local plan."

"Thanks," he said.

The car jerked as she swerved onto a narrower street and dipped into a hole. I grabbed the handle above the door, but as I steadied myself, she steered the vehicle in a zigzag fashion to escape a bigger dip in the road.

"Take it easy," Dad said calmly.

She immediately slowed down, but continued for two more blocks before pulling into the parking lot of a fast food outlet.

"What do you want to eat?" she asked me.

"Orange juice, please."

"No pop?"

"I hardly ever drink pop."

"Good for you. You can teach my kids a thing or two. They always choose the unhealthy stuff," she said. "But don't you want anything to eat?"

"No, thank you. I'm just thirsty."

"You're sure?"

"Yeah." I nodded.

"Smokey, do you want anything besides chicken?" She gently rubbed Dad's arm.

"I guess I'll try a soda and some coleslaw."

She climbed out of the vehicle while Dad and I remained in the car. She returned with two big bags.

"You've got more than enough food to feed an army," Dad joked.

"Mom helps out a lot, but she's definitely not my cook or my maid, so today I'm treating her and the kids," Dad's friend said.

"It must be great living with your mom when you're over thirty," Dad teased.

"I'm happy to have my mother living with me even at my age." She smiled at him.

I bowed my head and stuck out my bottom lip, thinking that I was only ten and my real mother wasn't around at all.

"What's the matter, Baby Girl?" Dad's friend asked as she handed me my drink.

"Nothing," I said as my eyes hit the ground.

"You're sure?"

I looked up at her and nodded. She smiled, and I forced a smile too. She threw a single braid off her face and turned on the ignition. Suddenly a woman stepped past the car with two screaming children at her side.

"I can't forget how hard it was to take care of my own kids when they were that age," Dad's friend commented.

"How are they coping?" my father asked.

"Quite well, actually. They both fit in as if they were born here. When I initially returned, I was the one who felt like a fish out of water. Thank God for Mom. She's been a lifesaver."

"Good for you," Dad said.

"Mom loves her grandkids, but in truth she's very, very strict. She keeps them on a tight leash. They don't like it, but she's teaching them good discipline."

"Like she taught you?" Dad chuckled.

"Sure right. She's from the old school," she said, swerving left onto Morrow Drive. She brought the car to a stop in front of a big black gate. Thin iron bars ran horizontally and vertically, creating large rectangular spaces. Attached to the upper third portion of the gate was the number 33, printed in bright red on a silver background.

"Is this where we're staying?" I asked with wide eyes, poking my head out the window and peeking through the gaps in the gate. Iron bars shaped in a curved design covered not just the windows of the lime-green dwelling in front of us, but encircled the entire porch, making it look like a very large cage. But in my mind it was an eye-catching mansion. I imagined galloping up and down the staircases and running my fingers along the jet-black, shiny railings. My eyes shifted to the paved left side of the yard, where star-shaped flowers blossomed in huge flowerpots.

"Do kids live there?" I asked, but neither Dad nor his friend responded.

I climbed out of the car, glancing at a red swing set in the unpaved portion of the yard. Dad climbed out as well, but his friend remained in the driver's seat, honking the horn loud enough to attract the entire neighbourhood. All the while, I kept thinking that if kids lived there, I definitely wanted to meet them.

The curtains on the upper level shifted slightly and a shadowy figure appeared, but I couldn't tell whether it was a man, woman, or child looking out at us. However, in a few winks, a tall, skinny man hurried down the staircase and unlocked the gate.

"You're well fortressed in," my father said as the man peered inside the front window of the vehicle.

"It better to be safe than sorry," the man said.

"You bet." Dad's lady friend climbed out of the car and stood beside him.

"Vena, good to see yuh again," the man said. I was all ears. I finally knew her name.

"Yes, Monty, I've brought someone from your long-lost past to meet you."

"Smokey?" Monty asked, as if he wasn't sure it was my dad standing next to him. Monty hugged Dad firmly, but Dad's arms stayed at his side. Then Monty patted Dad's back so hard, it sounded like three big slaps. Dad remained stone-faced, but Monty glowed.

"It's really you?" Dad said, as if he himself wasn't sure who the tall, skinny man was.

"Yes, is really me. Is yuh Uncle Monty in de flesh."

Monty's eyes caught my face.

"Come," Dad said, taking my hand. "This is my daughter."

I stood next to my father and examined Monty's tall, bony form, sunken cheeks, and dark, shiny complexion. His hair, with a sprinkling of grey, was a bit thin on top. He surely didn't resemble any of the people in my father's old photos.

"Yuh sure she's really yuh daughter? She look a wee bit too cute to be yours." Monty's lips and nose widened as he grinned, exposing his discoloured front teeth. His eyes slipped from Dad's face to mine. "Yuh sure that ugly man related to you?"

"Yeah, he's my dad," I said confidently.

"What yuh name is, sweetheart?" As Monty spoke I looked at his hairy arms and legs, which reminded me of a bear's.

"I'm Baby Girl," I said, straining to look at his neck, which reminded me of a crane.

"That can't be yuh real name?" A sudden serious expression came over his face, and for a moment I wondered if he hated my nickname.

"I'm Melody, but everyone calls me Baby Girl," I said.

"Give yuh Uncle Monty a big, big hug." Monty's smile returned.

He pulled me closer, and a whiff of perspiration filled my nostrils.

"Where yuh heading?" Monty asked Dad, but Dad looked at Vena as if he wasn't sure how to answer.

Vena spoke for him. "My place."

"On Paradise Lane?"

"Yeah," she said.

This was the first real clue I had regarding our intended destination, and I smiled because I liked the name of the street.

"Oh, I see, well, me and some of the boys having a few drinks tomorrow. Yuh want to come and lime wit' us?" Monty said to Dad.

"Can't commit, but we'll play it by ear."

"Dad," I said after we climbed back into Vena's car, "what does 'lime' mean?"

"It means to hang out," he replied.

"To lime means to hang out?" I said with surprise. "I thought a lime was a fruit."

"In this town, lime can be a noun or a verb," Vena chuckled. "Do you know the difference?"

"Yeah, a noun is a name of a person, place, animal, or thing, and a verb is an action word."

"That's right," she said. "I'm sure you'll soon master the local slang."

"Dad, can I come along and lime with you at Uncle Monty's place tomorrow?"

"I don't think so."

"Why not?"

"'Cause children aren't invited."

"Is Uncle Monty your mom or dad's brother?" I asked, since we didn't have family in Canada, and I was anxious to meet as many of our Trinidadian relatives as I possibly could.

"Monty's not my uncle. He's not related to us." Dad's blunt reply threw me for a loop and my eyes opened up bigger than an elephant's.

"But Monty said he's your uncle, didn't he?" I was genuinely confused.

"He's Aunt Mona's youngest brother. You know the story about how she took me in after my parents died. We don't have any blood relatives on this island worth an ounce of our time."

Dad had often told me about the day his world had been turned upside down. He was a boy, not yet eleven, when a drunk driver swerved off the roadway, hitting his parents' blue Toyota. His mother was killed immediately. His father died on the hospital's operating table. Aunt Mona took him in, but she died of ovarian cancer a few years later. After her death, my father lived with foster parents.

"We've got no family here either?" I felt like I was going to cry.

"What's the matter with you?" my father said in a loud, angry tone.

I lowered my head and my chest heaved, tears streaming down my face.

"She's probably missing her friends back in Toronto," Vena said calmly.

"I wish my real mom was here!" I blurted, my voice shaking.

"Huh!" Dad said.

I pulled the edge of my sleeve and wiped the tears blocking my vision and the watery mucus dripping from my nostrils. Right then, without warning, the intense sunlight was blotted out by several large, black clouds. Small drops began to hit Vena's windscreen, and in seconds the droplets turned into pouring rain.

"Close the window," Dad said.

I obeyed. And for a while my eyes followed Vena's windshield wiper as it steadily swayed from left to right. I calmed down, feeling as if I'd been hypnotized. Then, all of a sudden, bolts of lightning flashed and thunder echoed.

Vena finally brought the car to a stop in front of a row of neatly shaped hibiscus trees that formed a border separating the tiny garden of a big white house from the sidewalk. Rain continued to lash down on Vena's vehicle, and since we didn't have umbrellas, she suggested I pull apart the newspaper resting on the seat next to me and use a few of the loose sheets as a makeshift cover. I climbed out of the car and onto the water-soaked ground. The newspaper covering my head wasn't large enough to keep my bulging backpack from getting wet.

"No, no, not there! Here!" Vena said as I inched toward the long, winding staircase of the big white house. I spun around, confused for a few seconds before getting my bearings and following Vena and Dad in the opposite direction. We made our way along a paved, narrow path at the side of the large dwelling.

"Are we going through the back door?" I asked, without addressing anyone in particular.

"This way, sweetheart," Vena said.

She and Dad spun around at almost exactly the same time, and as I rushed forward a tiny bird with buzzing little wings hovered into view.

"It's a hummingbird," Vena said when I asked what it was. "Do you know that Trinidad is the Land of the Hummingbird?"

"No," I said, but stepped forward thinking it was awesome that the first bird to catch my attention was of such importance to the island. Vena explained that *Iere* is the original Amerindian name for Trinidad.

"It literally means Land of the Hummingbird," she added.

Vena, who seconds earlier had stepped ahead of Dad and me, slowed down in front of a tiny brick house. She dipped inside her pants pocket and fished around for several seconds before pulling out a bunch of keys. As she shoved a silver key from the bunch into the lock, a lump of disappointment became trapped in my throat. This wasn't what I had imagined. I pretended it didn't matter, butI desperately wanted to enter the sprawling mansion that towered like an awesome giant over this tiny house that we were about to enter instead. The wooden door creaked as Vena pushed it in. Dad took the soaked newspaper I'd used to cover my head and dumped it into a silver bin at the left side of the entrance. Then he lifted our luggage, placing the suitcases one by one next to a brown, fibre-textured mat.

Vena flicked a switch and a beam of light shone through the little house. On entering, I noticed a few basic pieces of furniture, including a small sofa bed, a television, a wooden dining table, and two matching chairs. Inside the small kitchen to our right was a two-burner stove. A miniature fridge stood a few feet away, near a sink with an old-fashioned faucet. I walked farther in and yanked the handle of a door to my left. A white toilet bowl and small shower stall stood side by side. It felt cramped with barely any room to spare.

The floor of the living area was covered wall to wall, not with carpeting but with a multi-coloured piece of linoleum. The louvre-type windows—their horizontal slats fitted with several long, rectangular pieces of glass—were covered with faded red and yellow curtains that didn't blend in with the colours in the linoleum.

I looked up at the aluminum ceiling, resting on top of thick, rough planks of wood, and only then did it hit me that this ordinary house had only one living room, one bathroom, and a tiny kitchen.

I wondered where I was going to sleep as I stepped toward the windows and pulled back the curtain. I wanted to poke my head outside, but the openings between the louvre slats were too narrow for that, so instead I adjusted several of the rectangular pieces of glass, allowing myself the best possible view of the backyard, where two big trees were sprawled in front of a high brick wall separating Vena's yard from the neighbour's. I was glad the rain had stopped and dazzling sunlight had returned.

"This is it, Baby Girl." Dad made his way toward me. "Do you like it here?"

I nodded, even though I really wished we could live in the much larger white house.

Vena threw a bunch of keys on the table. The keys and the bangles on her hand made a musical sound. She came toward us and pulled the curtains further up. "It's small, but it's got a big backyard," she said.

"This place is fine," Dad said. "We'll make the best of it until things turn around."

"You could eventually get a government house," Vena said.

"Are they worth taking?" Dad asked.. "If we got one, wouldn't I need a heap of money to fix it up?"

"Well, they're not perfect, I have to admit, but putting out a few dollars is much cheaper than buying a place on the open market."

"God knows I just want some place decent for me and Baby Girl to rest our heads."

"Tony could surely pull some strings," Vena said and headed toward the sofa.

"I know. You already mentioned that when we spoke last week, but I don't want to be a bother to him, or anyone else for that matter."

"I can tell you didn't grow up here," she chuckled. "On this island, you need someone to stand behind your back and give you a push forward, otherwise you'll be left to just pick up scraps."

"Okay, ma'am."

"Don't worry. I'll talk to him. Tony owes me more than a few favours, and it's definitely time for him to return one to his younger sister."

"If you insist." Dad settled on the sofa beside Vena.

"They're going to start building some new places in Arima soon. One of those would be ideal for you," she said.

"Let's not get ahead of ourselves. I still need to get a job before I can make concrete plans."

"But we can still look at them," she said. "Phase one is already completed and they're going to start constructing phase two pretty soon."

"We'll see," Dad said.

"Think about it," Vena said, then waved me over to her. "This is for you. It's a welcome-to-Trinidad present." She uncovered a shoebox, exposing a pair of brown leather sandals. "Try them on." Her eyes remained on my feet as I wiggled my toes in.

"They're nice," I said. "Thank you."

"They fit her just as if you measured her feet," Dad said.

"Don't give me too much credit." Vena smiled at Dad. "I had Lena try them on at the store before I bought them."

Vena got up and stepped toward the table. She separated a single key from the big bunch she'd placed on the table. She held the silver key in the air for a few seconds before placing it in the dead centre of the table, beside the phone. "I'm resting it here. Don't lose it," she said.

As soon as Vena left, Dad poked his head in our tiny fridge. He dragged out a bottle of water and put it to his mouth. He sounded like a thirsty dog as he gulped. Then he headed straight to the sofa and converted it into a bed. He collapsed on his back, and, with his hands clasped, he closed his eyes.

As the room fell silent, I unzipped my backpack, pulled out a notebook and pencil, and settled on one of the two wooden chairs in front of the small table. I flipped my book to a blank page. While Dad slept, I drew cartoons and doodled. I almost jumped out of my seat when the first few notes of Destiny's Child's "Bootylicious" came on, but it didn't take me long to realize that it was the ring tone from the cell phone Vena had left behind. "Hello," I stuck the phone to my ear. "Who's there?"

"Hey," a woman said above the backdrop of children's voices. "What's Smokey doing?" she asked. "May I speak with him?" I quickly recognized the voice as Vena's.

"He's lying down with his eyes closed."

"Is he meditating or sleeping?"

"He's resting. He looks very tired."

"Does he?" she said with laughter in her voice.

"Vena wants to talk to you," I said, giving my father a gentle shake.

Dad opened his eyes and looked at me with a blank, sleepy expression. "Vena?" he said, as if he didn't understand what I had said. I nodded, stretched forward and placed the phone in his hand. He pressed it against his ear and curled his legs as if getting ready to practice yoga. I raced to the bathroom. When I returned, he'd already hung up the phone.

21

"We're going next door." Dad leapt to his feet as if his conversation with Vena had given him a boost of energy.

"To the big white house?"

"Yeah, we're going there right this minute," he said, "so you've got to hurry."

I threw my socks and sneakers off the doormat and slipped on my brand-new leather sandals.

"You're going to sleep at Vena's house," Dad said.

"Tonight?" I looked Dad straight in the eyes, wanting to make sure I'd heard him right.

"No," he said, gathering my stuff, "not just tonight. Every night."

"You're going to sleep there too?" I questioned as he shifted his own bags closer to the sofa bed.

"No, I'll stay right here," Dad said. "I'm a big boy, I'll be fine."

Though somewhat confused and a little bit uneasy about our unusual living arrangement, I didn't press Dad for further details, since by then I sensed that, if I kept my mouth shut, the answers to all of my questions would come to light.

I threw my backpack over my shoulders and made my way out of the house. The ground was still soggy, even though the sun had long since returned. Dad picked up my blue suitcase and put it in the yard before pushing the key into the lock.

"Oh," he said, his face twisting. He rushed back in and moments later stepped out the door with the cell phone. I trailed him across the concrete path and up the rear staircase of the big white house.

Dad knocked. The door flew open and a bug-eyed woman appeared. Her head was covered with a black and white headscarf and she was wearing a dress at least two sizes too big. My eyes fell on the strands of grey hair curled up under her chin.

"I'm Nathaniel, better known as Smokey, and this is my daughter Melody, better known as Baby Girl," Dad said to the woman, whose egg-shaped face was as wrinkled as a crumpled brown paper bag.

"I is Vena mother, Wilma," she said in a husky voice, making me wonder if she was nursing a bad cold.

"Pleased to meet you, Miss Wilma," my father said.

I repeated Dad's words exactly and then I smiled at the old woman, but she kept a poker face.

"Come on in. Vena inside." Miss Wilma spoke without emotion and I didn't know what to make of her. We slipped off our shoes, leaving them on top of a stiff doormat. While Miss Wilma led us through a roomy kitchen, I gazed at the stainless steel appliances and the shiny, jet-black cupboards. We followed her into a spacious living room, and she left us there without saying anything. Dad placed my suitcase next to a wooden coffee table. After briefly admiring a bunch of red and white hibiscus flowers sticking out of a white, slim vase on the table, I loosened the straps of my backpack and rested it next to my suitcase.

Dad parked himself on a huge, black leather sofa and just as I settled next to him, Vena made her way toward us wearing a smile broader than I'd ever seen on anyone's face. She was accompanied by a boy and a girl, both close to my age.

"You guys are here," Vena said as the children eyed us curiously.

"In flesh and in bone," my father said.

Vena laughed. "I'm seeing more bone than flesh."

She and the children stepped closer to us. Dad rose from the sofa and embraced Vena.

"Baby Girl, meet Lena and Harley," Vena said as soon as Dad released her from his firm grip. Lena was a wee bit taller than her brother, Harley, but she was exactly the same height as me. The children had matching facial features, like two figurines designed from the same mould. Their complexions were slightly lighter than mine, but while I had long, curly, dark brown hair flowing down my back, Harley's wavy black hair was cropped short and Lena's puffy hair was parted and plaited in four separate braids. The two braids at the top of her head stuck out from her scalp, as stiff as an officer at a parade.

Lena stepped forward and shook my hand. "Your name is Baby Girl? You don't look like a baby to me," she said in an accent almost identical to mine. I didn't move a muscle. I was unsure what to make of them. I wasn't sure I liked them.

"Watch your words, Lena!" Vena said sternly.

Harley stepped forward and greeted me with a crooked grin. Dad and Vena shifted toward the big grandfather clock to my left, leaving me in the middle of the room facing the two children. The murmur of Dad and Vena's voices remained constant, but I was unable to figure out what they were talking about.

"Who's your favourite author, and what's your favourite book?" Lena asked.

"Robert Munsch and *Love You Forever*," I said.

"J.K. Rowling and *Harry Potter*," Harley said.

"I don't have a favourite. I like a lot of different books by a lot of different authors," Lena said. We continued to chat, and I quickly forgave Lena for poking fun at my nickname.

Dad tapped my shoulder. "I'm going to Arima. You'll be fine with your new friends," he said.

"You're going to see the houses?" I rose to my feet. "Can I come?"

"Not today, kiddo," he said.

"Mom, I'm stepping out. Lena and Harley, don't give any trouble, and be nice to Baby Girl." Vena spoke loudly enough that Miss Wilma, who'd long since hobbled back to the kitchen, could hear her.

I peeked out of the window as soon as Dad and Vena slipped out the front door. Dad held the car door, allowing Vena to ease into the front passenger seat. Then he circled the vehicle and settled into the driver's seat. The moment they sped off, I walked toward the half-moon sofa as slowly as if heavy weights had been cemented deep within my shoulder blades.

I slumped down, leaned on a bulky cushion, and folded my arms snugly. My mind drifted.

What if Dad doesn't come back? My eyes grew big with tears. I sobbed. My body shook. Lena and Harley's eyes remained firmly on my face as I gave an extra-long, sharp wail. Miss Wilma came into the room. Her right leg brushed the floor more than her left. She stood in front of me with both hands on her waist. I thought she looked like an old, cracked teapot that had seen better days.

"What wrong wit' yuh?" She gave me a long, hard look. Her arms fell to her side and she pushed her fat lips outward and downward. An agonizing silence took over the room.

"Nothing," I eventually said, my voice shaking.

"I hope so. Yuh not a baby, so don't behave like one in dis house."

As she walked away, still sweeping the floor with her feet, I tried to pull myself together.

"You want to play with us?" Lena asked.

"No," I said.

"You're missing your dad?"

"No, I'm not."

"You're missing your mom?"

"No, I'm not missing her, and I'm not missing my sister or anyone else."

"Then why don't you want to play with us?"

"I'm not in the mood," I said, wishing she'd go away and allow me enough space to brood. Lena shrugged and without another word, ran out of the room. It wasn't long before Harley followed his sister. He slammed the door so forcefully that I flinched. Both kids giggled, and the sound that followed was thunderous, as if they were both jumping from the ceiling to the floor wearing steel boots. Whatever they were doing, they were certainly having more fun than I was, and I regretted turning down Lena's offer to play. I wanted to join in the fun, but it was too late.

I heard the sound of Miss Wilma's feet sweeping against the wooden floor long before I saw the edges of the brown, frayed leather belt hanging loosely from her stubby fingers. She ignored me, moved past the sofa, and stopped in front of the room that Lena and Harley had entered. She folded the belt in two and her upper arms wiggled like a bowl of Jell-O. Then she stepped through the door and slammed it shut almost as loudly as Harley had done minutes earlier. For a few seconds, the only thing I could hear was the ticking of the big grandfather clock. Where was she going with that belt? I was suddenly afraid.

"What happenin' here?" Miss Wilma bellowed. Then I heard a sharp, brisk whacking sound. Lena screamed. Then Harley's sharp cries overpowered his sister's. With each whack, the kids' cries grew louder.

"Allyuh have no damn behaviour!" Miss Wilma yelled.

The door flew open and Harley rushed toward the right side of the large sofa. I didn't dare speak or move as Lena sprinted to my left. She landed with such force, the sofa felt like a waterbed.

"Keep yuh mouth shut!" Miss Wilma repeated several times, addressing Harley, but he continued to holler. I moved a bit, not wanting him too close because I was fearful she might aim the belt at him and accidentally strike me. Miss Wilma wagged the tattered belt, and, as her threatening eyes caught mine, I lowered my gaze. I urgently wanted to escape her presence.

"Allyuh better sit right here. If anyone move I goin' put two lash in allyuh ass!" She twisted her mouth. My eyes drifted to the ragged belt as it swayed like a pendulum in front of me.

"Allyuh hear me?"

"Yes, Granny Wilma," Lena and Harley said almost in unison. I, however, whispered my response.

"She's your grandmother?" I asked as soon as Miss Wilma stepped away.

"She's Harley's grandmother, not mine. She's a soucouyant," Lena said. Her eyes were still wet.

"What's that?" I asked.

"She turns into a fireball at night and sucks blood. She's evil. I hate her. She's always smacking us with her belt." Lena scowled.

"She's your grandmother too." Harley's face was puffed up with anger. The welts on his legs stood out like a recently created tattoo, a clear sign he'd borne the brunt of the strap more heavily than his sister.

I was glad I'd turned down Lena's offer to play and remained on the sofa instead.

3.

IT DIDN'T TAKE LONG FOR Lena, Harley, and me to become really good friends. No one could pull us apart and the fact that we weren't related didn't matter. Lena and Harley were twins, born exactly one month before I was. I was overjoyed that the three of us were in the same class at our elementary school and could walk to and from school together every day.

Dad did odd jobs to make a few bucks. "You're a damn good handyman," people in the neighbourhood would often tell him. One day he'd fix someone's leaking pipe, and on the next he'd help someone else put up a wall or dig a hole. One Friday, just as I arrived home from school, Dad greeted me with a big smile. "I'll be delivering detergent and other household products to supermarkets," he said. He explained he'd been hired by a Mount Hope-based company to drive a truck, and he promised me that we'd soon get our own place.

"Are we going to move to Arima?" I immediately asked.

"Arima?"

"Isn't that where the government houses are?" I replied.

"Oh." Dad made a brushing motion with his fingers. "Those units have already been allocated, but Vena's promised to help us get into an even better development."

"Can't we get a house right here on Paradise Lane?"

"My daughter's got very expensive taste," Dad laughed. "My measly income isn't going to be enough to pay for a house on this street, I'm afraid."

After Dad started his new job, he began to leave home in the wee hours of the morning and return at about nine o'clock each evening. I rarely saw him because on most weekends, when he was off work, he and Vena would stay out way past midnight. That meant that more often than not I was left in the care of Vena's mom, and as much as I hated the arrangement, it was beyond my power to change it.

One day after school, as the twins and I made our way up the staircase of the big white house, I moved out of the way, having suddenly lost all interest in jostling with them to get to the doorbell first. As I dawdled at the bottom of the staircase, Lena rushed ahead, pressing the bell ahead of her brother.

"You cheated! I wasn't ready!" Harley yelled, but Lena simply stuck her tongue out at him.

"Why's she taking so long to open the door?" Lena stomped impatiently.

We had been standing outside for maybe five or six minutes, a much longer time than was customary before Grandma Wilma let us in.

"She must be inside," I confidently said, since I heard the television blasting.

"Maybe she fell asleep," Lena turned around. "I'll get the secret key." She darted behind the house, and Harley and I sat on the staircase in silence, waiting for her to return.

"I've got it." Lena appeared with a gold-coloured key dangling on a round, silver wire.

"Give it to me. I'll open it." Harley tried to snatch the key from his sister, but she managed to hold on to it.

"No!" she screamed when he tried to grab it a second time.

"Stop it!" she yelled, spreading her arms to keep her balance. Harley eased off and Lena unlocked the door. "I'll tell Mom," she shrieked. Lena shoved her brother to the side and burst through the door. I calmly made my way into the house after them.

The television was on. Harley grabbed the remote and flicked through the channels, but he quickly lost interest and switched it off. "Grandma?" Harley called, following Lena and me toward the kitchen.

"She's sleeping on the chair." Lena momentarily glanced at Harley, and then at me. Grandma Wilma's head was slumped over the kitchen table, and her headscarf had slipped off her head, exposing a mass of silvery hair braided in thick cornrows. Her eyes were shut tight and her arms drooped at her side.

"Grandma, wake up." Harley nudged his grandmother while Lena gently patted her head. I stood a few feet back, waiting for Grandma Wilma to open her eyes, but she didn't, so Harley nudged her a bit harder.

"Let me try," Lena said, grasping her grandmother's right hand, but there was still no response.

"Let's call the neighbour, Mrs. Elliot," Lena eventually said, glancing across the room at Grandma Wilma's address book. Harley's fingers trembled as he grabbed the tiny black book from the kitchen counter. The book slipped and hit the floor. Lena squatted and picked it up.

Within minutes of receiving Lena's telephone call, Mrs. Elliot arrived at the house.

"Where's Wilma? " Mrs. Elliot asked as soon as Harley unlocked the door.

"Grandma's in the kitchen," Harley replied.

Mrs. Elliot rushed ahead of him.

"Grandma isn't dead, is she?" Harley asked as soon as Mrs. Elliot stepped within arm's reach of Grandma Wilma.

"No, not at all. Yuh granny very much alive," Mrs. Elliot said, adjusting Grandma Wilma's scarf.

"But her hand feels really cold," said Lena, who had remained at her grandmother's side.

"No use in calling for an ambulance because they're going to take donkey years to reach," Mrs. Elliot mumbled to herself. Instead she summoned her husband, who took Grandma

Wilma to the Eric Williams Medical Sciences Complex in his pick-up truck.

The following morning, tears ran down Vena's cheeks while she shared the news of her mother's passing. Grandma Wilma was the first person I had ever personally known to die, but I didn't believe she was really dead until I saw her body lying in the casket.

Grandma Wilma's funeral took place three days after her death, and during that time a host of Vena's relatives swamped the house. I was envious of how many cousins, aunts, and uncles the twins had, especially since the only person I could depend on was my dad.

After Grandma Wilma's death, Vena took several weeks off work, and, during that time, she and Dad didn't go anywhere without us.

Several weeks after Grandma Wilma's death, Vena and Dad promised to take us to Manzanilla to visit Vena's sister, Collette, and her three children. The twins and I were anxiously counting down the number of days as we waited for the long weekend of our visit to finally arrive. I had met Vena's sister and her kids at Grandma Wilma's funeral and really liked them, but I was even more eager for the weekend to arrive because Dad had promised to have a really big surprise in store for us.

So on the Friday that marked the beginning of the three-day weekend, the twins and I hurried home, dripping with sweat. Vena had informed us days earlier that we should be prepared to leave Paradise Lane very early on Saturday morning. She'd also scheduled our return for Monday evening. As we rounded the bend, making our way along Paradise Lane, I caught sight of Dad as he dipped a large, yellowish piece of sponge inside a bucket and wiped the top of Vena's car.

"Dad!" I shouted from a distance, trying to catch his eye. I was surprised he'd gotten home ahead of us. He waved, and big droplets of soapy water trickled from the sponge, down his arms and onto his clothes. He jumped backward, spread his arms apart and stared at his soggy T-shirt.

"I'm glad you're home." I ran forward, stretching my arms as far around his waist as they would go. It didn't matter that the dampness from his T-shirt was all over me.

"Look, the surprise I promised you guys is over there." Dad pointed to an emerald-green Toyota Camry parked a few feet from us. "We'll christen it on the way to Manzanilla," he said as the twins and I stepped closer to examine the vehicle.

"That's it?" I said under my breath. I'd thought his big surprise would have been a gift for the twins and me and not just a new vehicle for himself. Harley sped off like a cheetah, his feet pounding noisily as he made his way to the top of the staircase. Lena and I followed, vying for second place.

"No pushing, shoving, or shouting!" Vena's voice carried from the kitchen as we scampered into the house.

"Thank God, Auntie Hattie's coming to give me a hand," she said. "God knows I need some time to myself."

"Who's Auntie Hattie?" I asked Lena. "Was she at the funeral?"

"No, she didn't come. She lives in Tobago. She's my mom's cousin," Lena replied.

After we'd eaten dinner, Vena insisted we complete our homework.

"We've got all weekend," Harley pouted.

"Remember we're going away," Vena said, "and we aren't going to be back until very late on Monday evening."

"I can do my homework in Manzanilla," Harley insisted.

"You want to taste your Grandma's belt?" Vena said sternly.

For the next hour or so we kept our mouths shut and tackled our assignments. We went to bed around ten that evening. I woke up around two a.m. when Harley cried out, complaining about pain near the area of his belly button. Vena appeared able to soothe his pain, and his cries died down, but I didn't fall back to sleep for a long time. I woke up again six-thirty, and even though I was still tired and sleepy, I raced to the bathroom, anxious to get there before the twins got up. When I got to the bathroom, our neighbour, Mrs. Elliot, suddenly appeared in front of me. Before I could ask her where Vena was, she explained that Harley had taken a turn for the worse. She said the pain had shifted to the lower right side of his belly and was accompanied by nausea, vomiting, and diarrhoea. Our trip to Manzanilla was cancelled, which didn't matter since the big surprise was just another old car. As for Harley, he had been diagnosed with appendicitis. Everyone was happy that it wasn't more serious.

Harley was feeling a lot better and was catching up on some homework. "May I get some water, Mom?" Harley asked, chewing on his pencil's eraser as we sat around the kitchen table each of us completing a different assignment. Harley's pencil slipped to the floor and rolled beneath the table. He bent forward to pick it up but accidentally kicked it further away. I slid off my chair and finally got it back for him.

"You just had a glassful," Vena scolded. "Stop fidgeting and start writing." Just as she spoke, the doorbell rang.

"Who's that?" Lena turned to her mother.

"Never mind, don't any of you move an inch. Just keep doing your homework." Vena disappeared along the hallway.

"I'm going to peek." Lena jumped off her chair; Harley and I giggled.

"Shhh." Lena motioned us to keep quiet. Harley and I climbed out of our chairs too. We tiptoed down the hallway and positioned ourselves directly behind Lena. In silence, the three of us craned our necks around the bend. Just then Vena pulled the door open and a large woman decked out in a long, floral-patterned dress stepped in. We dashed back to our seats in the kitchen and bent our heads over our work just as Vena and the woman entered the kitchen.

I placed my pen on top of my notebook and looked up at the big woman beside Vena. Her eyes were sunk deep in her face, and the large pleats on both sides of her cheeks dragged her face down a bit. As she smiled, her nose, which sprawled from the left side of her face to the right, seemed to get even broader. A hint of blue reflected off her oily face, and several blotchy marks covered a large portion of her neck and arms. I wondered if her legs were as unevenly coloured, but her long dress kept that information hidden. She wore a pair of oversized earrings moulded into the shape of the island of Tobago. The earrings swung with the tiniest of motions.

"They sure getting big." The woman's angelic voice was a surprise. Lena and Harley flew off their chairs and sped toward her like bullets.

"Auntie Hattie!" they screamed with delight. Each appeared intent on embracing her before the other. As Auntie Hattie tilted to hug the twins, the weight of her chest pulled her down a bit and her butt looked much larger than that of most women. The twins remained in her arms for more than a minute.

Then Auntie Hattie pointed in my direction. "Who is that pretty little one?" she asked Vena.

"She's my boyfriend's daughter."

"Mr. Smokey?" Auntie Hattie smiled.

"Yep, that's the man."

"Come here, sweetheart." Auntie Hattie smothered me with her hefty arms.

As we parted, Vena's eyes made the rounds.

"Auntie Hattie's in charge for the next eight weeks, so you'd all better be on your best behaviour!"

A week after Auntie Hattie's arrival, the twins and I accompanied Dad and Vena to Maracas to scope out several acres of land where the government planned to build a new housing development. Vena invited Auntie Hattie to come along, but instead she chose to attend a church function.

"Yuck, this place looks like the countryside," Lena said when Dad parked in front of a vacant piece of land. A big sign stuck in the ground read, "Ministry of Housing, Government of Trinidad and Tobago, Future Site of Maracas Housing Development."

"Dad, are we going to move here?" I questioned.

"Maybe yes, maybe no. We don't know yet," he shrugged.

"If you don't get into this project, you'll surely get into the next one. Tony promised me that much," Vena assured Dad.

"We'll see," Dad said.

That afternoon, we arrived at Paradise Lane at exactly three-thirty. Auntie Hattie greeted us at the door. "Anyone hungry?"

"I'm starving," Lena announced and followed Auntie Hattie to the kitchen.

"Me too." Harley said, stepping behind his sister. I trailed him and Dad and Vena walked behind me.

"Well, allyuh just in time." Auntie Hattie uncovered a large pot and a strong smell of onions, garlic, peppers, tomatoes, and other spices filled the kitchen. It was the first time I tasted Auntie Hattie's callalo soup. And every Saturday after that she prepared this dish. It soon became my favourite.

"Time for bed kids," Auntie Hattie said to the twins and me at nine that evening. We followed her to her room and she read us a Bible story. Afterward, she told us to kneel and then she taught us a new prayer. Then she tucked us into our beds. This became our routine before bedtime, except for Thursday evenings when Auntie Hattie attended a weekly prayer meeting at a nearby church.

On school days, Auntie Hattie insisted that the twins and I finish our homework before switching on the television. She often watched cartoons with us while we ate snacks like mango chow and tamarind balls that she made herself.

Not long after Auntie Hattie's arrival, Dad began spending more and more time with us at the big house, and on Saturdays I tagged along with him to run errands. Gradually, and without any formal announcement, Dad moved into the larger house.

"I'll need full-time help after you're gone. I can't allow the kids to come home to an empty house after school," Vena said to Auntie Hattie one Saturday morning. My heart sank as I listened to their conversation, wishing Auntie Hattie could remain with us forever.

That evening, I pulled up a chair and sat facing the computer next to Auntie Hattie. Days earlier I had taught her how to log onto the computer. Minutes earlier I'd helped her to log onto Skype. I stared at her son on the screen, amazed at how much he and Aunt Hattie looked alike. "You are the one who made my mom into a computer expert?" He smiled broadly. "I've been trying to get her to use a computer for months and she always turned me down."

I moved away, allowing her the opportunity to speak in private while wishing the days would slow down.

A couple of weeks later, Lena barged into my bedroom. "Get up!" she yelled.

"It's Saturday. I want to stay in bed." I pulled the bed covers over my head.

"She's here. The woman Mom might hire is here," Lena whispered, pulling the covers off me and motioning for me to follow her. "Come and take a peek at her."

"No," I said.

"Get up, Baby Girl." Lena refused to give up, so I finally climbed out of bed and followed her out of the room.

"I hope Mom doesn't hire her," Lena whispered as Vena led a tall, thin woman into the dining room.

"Why don't you like her?" I asked as Vena shut the dining room door.

"She's skinny like a whip." Lena covered her mouth to muffle her giggles.

Vena and the woman remained behind closed doors for barely fifteen minutes before the woman left.

"Yuh eleven o' clock appointment here," Auntie Hattie said to Vena an hour later when the second candidate for the housekeeper position arrived.

"What do you think of her?" Lena asked me.

"I don't know." I shrugged. "She seems sort of nice."

"But she walks kind of funny," Lena said as Vena led the second woman toward the dining room.

"I can't hear anything," she added, pressing her right earlobe against the dining room door.

"Let me try." I shoved her out of the way and jammed my ear against the wooden door.

"What are you two doing?" Dad, dressed in freshly washed blue jeans and a bright blue T-shirt, approached us. He looked like he was ready to go out on his usual Saturday errands.

"Nothing," I said, easing off the door.

"Get out of your pyjamas and take a shower. If you're not ready in ten minutes, I'm going to leave you right here."

"Don't leave without me, Dad," I cried and rushed to the bathroom.

"Tell me about the others when I get back," I said, following my father out the door.

A few days later, the twins and I sat on the bottom staircase at the back of the house. I bit into the green, rubbery skin of the fruit in my hand, and, as the tough covering fell apart, I tasted the sweetness of its clear, yellowish flesh. I had ten chenetes on a paper plate. Lena and Harley had roughly the same.

"This is Petal. She'll be in charge after Auntie Hattie leaves next week," said Vena, looking down at us.

A woman with large eyes and a big smile stood atop the staircase next to Vena. Petal waved at us, a big forced smile on her face. "I expect nothing but respect toward Petal," Vena warned us.

"I like her. She's young and pretty with nice dimples," Lena said after Vena and Petal moved away. I wasn't so sure.

Exactly eight weeks after Auntie Hattie's arrival, I stood in her room watching her pack. My face remained grim as she tucked several cotton dresses into a big black suitcase. "Don't be sad," she said when she noticed my gloomy expression. She circled her right palm behind my neck before guiding me toward her bed.

"I don't want you to go." I felt a jab in my chest, as sharp as that which had struck deep in my gut when my stepmother, Charm, had left. That day, Dad had picked me up from school, and as soon as I saw him, I had known something was wrong.

"Where's Charm? Why didn't she come to meet me?"

"Charm's gone away. She's gone for good," Dad had said calmly.

"Gone where?" I hadn't believed him at first.

"She's not coming back, Baby Girl. She's no longer living with us."

"She can't do that! She didn't even say goodbye." I had started to cry.

Dad had shrugged and hadn't even tried to explain why she'd left so suddenly. I'd hated that so much.

Thoughts of my absent mother came to me now, just as they had then, too. And, as always, it hurt to think about her as I always wondered why she left us. I didn't even know what my mother looked like, even though Dad had once hinted that she was pretty.

"Will I ever see you again?" I asked Auntie Hattie, tears filling up my eyes.

"Sure, love, I not dying yet."

"When are you coming back?"

"God alone know, but I going to keep yuh in my thoughts. I promise yuh dat," she said. "Look, I got a lil' granddaughter name Madeline, and every time I see she, I going to remember you." She tangled her fingers with mine. I looked at her blankly, but a big frog filled my throat. I was suddenly jealous of Madeline.

"I have something fer you." Auntie Hattie strode toward the dresser and picked up a tiny item. She clutched it tightly in her palm. "This going to give yuh good luck, but yuh have to believe." She dropped a key ring made out of coconut shells into my palm. "My son does make all kinda things wit' coconut shell," she said. "Yuh like it?"

"It's really nice." I admired the gift before shoving it in my pants pocket. Then I buried my face in her chest, unaware that I would feel the stinging pain of her departure more acutely when I got home from school the following afternoon, and her absence became real.

4.

NOT A DAY PASSED without Auntie Hattie seeping into my mind, but at that moment I wasn't thinking about her or anyone else as I tried to slip past Lena, who had already made it halfway up the staircase, way ahead of Harley and me. Lena, Harley and I were racing up the staircase like usual, pushing each other out of the way, and trying to be the first to get to the doorbell. We never tired of racing up those stairs and trying to beat each other to the door.

"Allyuh got no manners," Petal said gruffly as she shifted out of the way and let us slip through the door. By then we'd grown accustomed to her icy reception.

Even though she'd been working at the house for almost a month, Petal hardly ever smiled. But lately she seemed to have changed a whole lot. It wasn't a gradual transformation. It happened overnight. She went from someone who mostly had a grim look on her face all the time, to someone who seemed more relaxed and happier even.

Something really good must have happened in her life to have brought about such a remarkable change. I'd heard Vena whisper those words to my dad a few days ago. That made me think about the day Petal had offered to help me memorize my vocabulary words.

"Why yuh staring at me like dat, Baby Girl?" she'd said as our eyes locked.

I'd thought about running out of the kitchen without responding, but instead I blurted, "How come you're so nice all of a sudden?"

Petal eased into the same chair that the twins and I had found Grandma Wilma slumped over months earlier. She arched forward and propped up her head on clenched fists. "I worry about meh family, Baby Girl, but I swear things gettin' better." She paused for a moment before adding, "Gawd alone know how much I been struggling to get by."

"You've got nice dimples," I told her.

"Is a family trait. Meh boys also have it." She smiled broadly and her cheeks suddenly seemed much plumper.

"Your boys?" My eyes widened.

"Yes," she said, "I got two sons."

"What are their names?"

"Drew and Warren," she said. "Warren is four and Drew is two." When she'd said their names, her smile had gotten really big.

I sat on the staircase and read a letter my friend, Makayla, had sent from Canada. In it she told me about her family's recent move from Toronto to a brand-new housing development in Oshawa. I stared at the photo she had enclosed of herself, her younger brother, and her parents for a long time, trying to figure out if she had changed in any way. I decided she looked pretty much the same as she did last time I saw her. Then, after admiring the colourful stickers she'd also sent, I tucked everything back inside the envelope and placed it on the staircase. All of a sudden, I remembered a time long ago when Makayla and I used to have sleepovers. Maybe she hadn't changed much, but my life had changed a lot since we moved to Trinidad.

I wondered if my former stepmom, Charm, or her daughter, Clara, ever thought of me. *Does she have a new husband? A new child? Does she remember my birthday, or think about me at Christmas?* That made me think about my real mom too.

A sudden heaviness rushed to the tip of my spine and oozed into my arms and legs. My entire body went limp and I buried my face in my palms.

"Don't hide yuh pretty face," Petal said. She stood in front of me and gently pulled my hands from my face, exposing my tears.

"I wish I could meet my real mom," I sputtered. The smell of avocado oil filled my nostrils as Petal pressed my face against her chest.

"I know, Baby Girl. I lose meh mom when I was real small too. I lose she de same day meh baby brother born, and eight years later, I lose meh dad too."

"Oh, I didn't know that." I lifted my head off her chest. The whites of her eyes seemed much whiter than before. I saw the pain in them and, in that instant, I felt more pity for her than for myself.

"It okay. I survive de whole ordeal and yuh goin' to survive too." Petal sat down beside me and started to tell me about her father. "He was de best dad in de world, but all dat change de day Tantie Irene come into meh school and give meh de news.

"What news?"

"The principal call meh outta de classroom, and as soon as I see how she face get white like a ghost, I did know right away something was wrong. Tantie Irene just grab on to meh real tight and said, 'Petal, yuh father dead. Somebody kill him.'"

Petal bit her lip and remained silent for a few seconds. "Baby Girl," she paused again, "meh father get kill when I was in high school, and I lose interest in school after dat. Sometimes when I think 'bout him, I want to cry because I cyah believe de police never hole nobody fer killing him."

Petal glanced at her watch, then grabbed the railing and pulled herself up. "Come and eat something 'cause it getting real late," she said and led me up the staircase.

As the weeks went by, Petal and I grew close. When she let it slip that her two sons didn't live with her, but with their dad, my tongue got as heavy as lead. Why weren't her boys living with her? I was itching for an answer, so I built up the guts to ask her.

"Why yuh asking dat?" Petal's face got stiff as the words left my lips.

"You said I could ask you anything," I reminded her.

"Baby Girl," she paused, "it real hard to talk 'bout dat," she said. "You see, de children father had money to hire a lawyer who went to court and lie big time. De judge believe what he say, and he get custody of de two boys, so I does only see dem on de weekend. Dey grandmother does take real good care of dem in de daytime when dey father working, so dat is meh consolation."

"You spend more time with Baby Girl than with Harley and me," Lena interrupted us, pouting and pulling at Petal's sleeve.

"Baby Girl don't have no mother. You and Harley have Vena," Petal said, patting her head absentmindedly. Then she gave us a big smile. "Allyuh want to bake a cake?"

"I guess so," Lena said, happy now. "Can we bake a marble cake?"

"Where's Dad?" I asked Vena one Saturday morning. I hadn't seen him all week and hoped he'd take me along to run errands. I hadn't accompanied him on his Saturday trips for a whole month and I was desperately missing our father-daughter time.

"His boss called him to work on short notice," Vena told me. "Do you want to go to the beach with us?"

"I guess," I shrugged. I would have preferred to spend the day with my dad, but the beach was always fun.

When I saw him, I pestered my dad about going with him on his Saturday errands, but Dad made excuse after excuse about why I could no longer accompany him. "What you want me to do? I've got to work to pay the bills," he said irritably one Saturday morning after I'd asked him for the umpteenth time.

Another time when I asked him again, he simply said, "I've got to help Monty do some work on his house and you'd be in the way."

"We could do stuff together on Sundays instead," I cried, but Dad ignored my suggestion. We'd been on the island about ten months and it seemed, since we'd arrived, that I saw my dad less and less.

One Tuesday evening, I felt under the weather. I didn't tell anyone. I didn't want to risk missing school the following day because our teacher, Miss Hill, had organized a field trip to the Pitch Lake, which was located in La Brea, a town in the southern part of the island. Earlier that week at school, I had learned about the ninety-five acre tar lake, discovered by Sir Walter Raleigh way back in 1595. It fascinated me that the lake's surface would yield just slightly when stepped on by a human, but something as heavy as a car would quickly disappear under its surface. Our teacher also mentioned that the forty-by-forty-foot hole completely refills itself within three days, and that it constantly pulls things into itself and spills things out.

At the dinner table I didn't have much of an appetite and played with my food, but to prevent attracting attention, I forced down a few morsels of rice and a tiny piece of baked chicken.

Suddenly Lena's large eyes opened wider. "Baby Girl, what's that in the middle of your forehead?" she said.

"Baby Girl's got a third eye," Harley teased.

"Don't be mean," Vena said, giving him a stern look.

I rushed to the bathroom and cringed when I saw the huge zit on my face. I fingered it, but it didn't hurt.

"You can hardly notice it," Vena assured me. She provided some cream, which I spread all over the blemish.

The following morning, I climbed out of bed much more energetic than when I'd slipped under the covers the previous night. I was looking forward to munching on the snacks Petal had prepared for the school outing. I examined my face in the full-length mirror facing my bed, and, to my horror, spotted more than a few raised bumps. I took several deep breaths when I realized the blemishes had also spread to my hands.

"Vena!" I yelled, dashing toward her and Dad's bedroom, "my skin's all messed up!"

"You want some more cream?" she casually asked from behind the door.

"I've got a whole lot more of them," I said.

She must have sensed the fear in my voice because the door immediately flew open. "It looks like chickenpox," she said. "Smokey, come here quickly!"

I squirmed, feeling like a weirdo in a freak show when Lena and Harley joined Dad and Vena, and the four of them huddled together, examining my messed-up skin. Vena urged Dad to take me to the doctor. I couldn't figure out why she kept insisting he should take me, especially since only a short while earlier she'd seemed one hundred percent certain of her diagnosis.

Dad and I barely said a word to each other while waiting to see Dr. Seepersaud, our family doctor. Dad was mad at himself for having forgotten his cell phone at home, and I was distraught at missing the school trip. When the receptionist eventually called out my name, Dad accompanied me to the examination room, and the doctor instantly confirmed Vena's diagnosis.

"Don't scratch your skin." Dr. Seepersaud scribbled a prescription. "Just use this lotion, and it will ease the itching."

On the way home from the doctor's office, I tried to convince myself that the Pitch Lake wasn't anything special and that it probably looked like a big parking lot. When Dad pulled up in front of the white house, it was one o'clock. He entered the house, leaving the front door wide open. I lingered behind.

"Honey, what yuh doing home?" Petal asked Dad cheerfully. "Like yuh come back to spend the day wit' me."

"Shoo," Dad said, as if trying to quiet her.

"I'm home too." I announced my arrival as I stepped inside. Both Dad and Petal wore strange expressions. It was a weird moment, which left me awfully confused.

"Y-y-y-yuh here, Baby Girl?" Petal stuttered. I guess she thought I'd gone to school and was on the trip.

Meanwhile, Dad disappeared along the corridor without saying anything.

"What happen' to yuh skin?" Petal's voice quivered. But I sensed she was much more stunned that I wasn't at school than at the sight of my blotchy skin.

"Chickenpox," I said, making my way to my bedroom.

Not long after I'd returned to school following my bout with chicken pox, Dad and Vena started arguing about things a lot. Often, on the weekends, Vena, the twins, and I would go on our little outings without Dad. By then I'd accepted the fact that my Saturday outings with my father were a thing of the past, and I had stopped bothering him about that.

On a bright Sunday morning while the twins and I watched cartoons on television, a loud thud came from the direction of Vena's bedroom. It sounded as if someone had thrown a heavy object onto the hardwood floor. Harley and I jumped off the couch and hurriedly followed Lena to Vena's bedroom.

The twins and I arrived at Vena's bedroom door just as she hurled a big, red book at Dad's head. The book bounced off his shoulder and hit the bed. It sprang up and down before going limp. Dad's lips formed a lopsided smile as he scooped the book off the mattress, strode to the bookshelf, and skipped over several magazines and a wooden ornament before shoving the thick book back on the middle shelf.

"You're never home!" Vena, shouting and breathing heavily, charged toward Dad.

"Please calm down," Dad said, but Vena threw more than a few wild punches at him.

"Stop this shit!" Dad's smile turned into a scowl. Suddenly, he shoved her and she staggered, but quickly regained her balance. She lunged forward; Dad grabbed her arms.

"No, Dad, no!" I slipped between them.

"Go to your rooms!" Dad said, letting her go, which made her fall back onto the bed with a loud thump.

"This doesn't concern any of you!" Vena, jumping up, screamed at the twins.

I slowly and warily backed out of the room. I was fearful that Dad might do something silly and that the police would take him away.

I remembered one time that Dad had hit Charm and bloodied her face. She had called the cops and they had arrested him. He'd been gone for two whole weeks and, during his absence, my stepsister, Clara, had often jeered at me. "Your dad's a jailbird! A jailbird! A jailbird!" she'd say mockingly.

"Don't say such hurtful words to your little sister ever again," Charm had said when she heard. The next time I saw my dad, he'd lost some weight and his skin and arms were covered with red blotchy spots.

"I'll never leave you again," he'd promised me the day he returned home, but I never asked, and he never explained exactly where he'd been for those two whole weeks.

The ugly brawl ended the moment Dad and Vena ordered us kids to our rooms.

"Your Dad doesn't like my mom anymore. He's got a new girlfriend," Lena said as we made our way along the corridor.

"That's not true," I insisted, but, right then, the time I had chickenpox and Dad and Petal had acted strange when I got home from the doctor, came back to me.

Vena and Dad continued to fight a lot, and I often wondered why they didn't just go their separate ways. I hated the screaming, shouting, and bickering, not just because their ugly brawls made me fearful that I'd have to move, but because the constant squabbling also affected my friendship with the twins. Dad and Vena's relationship eventually deteriorated to the point that they barely spoke to each other any more.

One Sunday morning, Dad knocked on my bedroom door. "Sweetie pie, I think it's best that I move back to the little house."

"Do I have to go live there with you?" I asked nervously.

"No, you're staying right here. Whatever happens between Vena and me has nothing to do with you," he said.

The mood in the big white house improved after Dad moved out. Dad and Vena acted civil to each other and, for the most part, lived entirely separate lives.

The end of the year was fast approaching, and despite being a girl, I was offered the part of one of the three wise men in our school's annual Christmas production. Harley got cast as Joseph, but Lena didn't have an acting part. She chose to join the choir instead.

On the last day of school, the twins and I shed our stiff school uniforms for regular clothes.

"The party was really good this year," Lena said on our way home.

I was especially excited at the likelihood of spending the two weeks' school break in the company of my father. One week earlier, he had assured me that his boss had approved his request for time off during the Christmas holidays, and he had promised to make up for not spending enough time with me. Would he keep his promise or would he offer more excuses? I was a little bit anxious that he'd let me down again.

By the time we arrived in the yard of the big white house, I held a commanding lead. I rushed up the staircase and rang the doorbell first. Vena stood in front of the wide-open door.

"Where's Petal?" I stared at Vena.

"She's not working here anymore," she bluntly said.

"She left without saying goodbye?" I pouted.

"Baby Girl, she was only our housekeeper." Lena brushed past me, heading to her bedroom.

"Sure right, only a damn maid." Vena wore a long face.

"I really liked her." I set my face up to cry.

Vena looked at me as if she wanted to say something mean, but instead she just shook her head and walked away. I locked my bedroom door, climbed into bed, and pulled the covers over my head. It couldn't have been more than ten minutes later when Dad hollered out my name. I ignored him, staying put under the covers, hoping he'd just go away. But he stood in front of my door yelling out my name again and again. "Open up!" he bellowed, manoeuvring the door handle as if intent on breaking it. "I know you're in there! Don't make me have to tear this door down!"

"I don't want to talk to you!" I said.

"Open the damn door!" he yelled. Since Dad had moved out of the big house, he'd usually phone and ask me to meet him at the little house whenever he needed to see me. So why was he making such a hullabaloo in front of my bedroom? Puzzled by his strange behaviour, I unlocked the door and faced him. Dad shoved a cardboard box at me.

"Pack your clothes right now!" he ordered.

I kept my arms at my side and Dad brushed past me. He dropped the large box at the side of my bed. I looked up at my father; I felt as if my soul had left my body.

"Hurry up! Put your clothes in your suitcase and the rest of your stuff in this box!" My dad's tone was as gruff as that of an army commander ordering his juniors. I grabbed Dad's wrist just as he stepped into the corridor.

"I don't want to move!" I sobbed, following him. "You promised me!"

Just then Lena and Harley peeked from behind Lena's bedroom door. They stared at my dad suspiciously and at me pityingly. Vena appeared out of nowhere.

"Go to your rooms!" she said to the twins.

"We're moving right this moment. Your antics aren't going to help!" Dad yelled.

I rushed back into my room, spinning like an out-of-control cartoon character. "I don't want to move!" I shrieked.

Dad's heavy footsteps threaded the floor as he darted into my room, looking as if fire was about to escape from his nostrils. He threw my suitcase on the floor and unzipped it with such force, I was sure the zipper would rip apart. Then he dragged my clothes out of the dresser and the closet, dumping each piece into the suitcase. My clothes were all rumpled and bunched up like junk. Next he grabbed a handful of the Barbie dolls I'd displayed so beautifully on the top of my dresser and aimed them toward the cardboard box he'd placed on the ground earlier. He missed his mark, and most of the dolls hit the ground.

"You'll break them!" I whined, but he didn't respond. All I could hear was his deep breath.

"We've got to get out of here!" He glanced at his watch before lifting the cardboard box overflowing with my belongings. He carried the box as if it were filled with feathers and stormed out the door. I followed him, dragging my feet and my suitcase, my backpack slung over my shoulders.

"Here, Baby Girl," Vena said softly, shoving a neatly wrapped Christmas present into my free hand. "Put it in your backpack and don't open it until Christmas morning, okay?" she said, looking at me with as much compassion as the twins had done earlier.

I grimaced, searching for an answer to the question *why me?* Vena shrugged as if she could read my thoughts, but she obviously didn't have an answer. Or maybe she thought the answer would be too painful for me to bear. I wasn't sure.

"I'll never forgive you!" Vena said at the top of her voice. "Not just for disrespecting me, but for what you're doing to your own child."

"Leave my kid out of this," Dad snapped.

In silence, Vena disappeared along the corridor, leaving me

in the company of my father. His face was red with anger. I was fearful that he would turn his rage on me if I didn't do as he requested, so I accepted defeat and stifled my tears while tucking the Christmas present inside my backpack. He led the way and I followed. But before stepping through the front door, I turned and caught sight of Lena and Harley, who were once again peeking at Dad and me. At that moment there was only stillness and silence as the twins and I exchanged a fleeting goodbye.

As I climbed into the back seat of my father's Toyota Camry, he slammed the door shut before easing into the driver's seat.

Vena, her face contorted, screamed from the uppermost stair, "You're a dog, Smokey! What sweet in goat mouth does sour in its backside!"

A group of kids playing cricket in the yard across from Vena's house looked up at her as if she were crazy. Dad offered a fake smile and then started the car.

"I don't want you phoning! You hear me!" Dad yelled.

The car sped off, and I buried my face in my hands.

5.

I CLASPED MY HANDS WHILE STARING at my feet and hoped Dad would somehow come to his senses, turn the car around, and take me back to Paradise Lane. Instead, he swerved around the narrow streets and headed deeper and deeper into alien territory. As if hypnotized, I lost all interest in the chaos around me, including the honking horns, deafening music, and shrill sounds, which on a normal day would have thrilled me.

Dad drove for what seemed like forever, but was probably no more than half an hour. Then he suddenly stopped. *Where are we?* I wondered, but I didn't ask. Dad climbed out and opened the passenger door. For a moment he stood still, looking at me in complete silence. "Get yourself together and take out your backpack!" he eventually bellowed. He seemed so cold and uncaring. I remained seated, still too shocked to respond.

"Hurry up, girl. We don't have all day!" he said, still holding the car door open.

I shifted very slowly. My legs felt heavier than my backpack, and my knees buckled the instant they touched the ground. I circled my surroundings and caught sight of several barefoot children kicking a soccer ball in a rough, uneven yard, covered with stones and rocks. Domestic chickens cackled and pecked at scraps in the yard. A bunch of kids began to throw pebbles at each other and the chickens flapped their wings and ran for cover.

Dad dragged my suitcase out of the trunk before moving the cardboard box full of my possessions and a few other boxes to one side. He then pulled out one of his own suitcases.

"We're heading this way." He pointed to a rugged, narrow stretch of roadway. There were no street signs identifying where we were; it didn't look like a real road, more like a dirt trail. I sighed, not wanting to walk up the unpaved, narrow path, and lingered stubbornly behind. Dad turned and looked at me. The distance between us had grown. "Come on!" he yelled impatiently, but he waited for me.

Houses stood on one side of the bumpy pathway, and, on the other, like a miniature forest, was a mass of greenery. The dense bush was shaded by numerous bamboo trees with thick, green canes that sighed in the wind. Before long we came to a pale blue house. A string of colourful flags flapped noisily in the breeze. Each triangular flag was attached to its own bamboo pole, firmly planted in the ground in a row in front of the house. We trudged past that house and suddenly reached several tiny, wooden houses positioned where the trail should have continued. Instead, the track shifted to our left. It seemed obvious that the houses had been constructed first, and that the roadway was only an afterthought. As a result, the pathway twisted and turned in a zigzag fashion eventually leading uphill.

A torn, black garbage bag flew by. Then a brown, mangy dog with an open sore on its back began to sniff through the trash that was piled on the ground. Flies hovered over the dump, and a horrible stench filled the air. As we continued, someone began to blast a Jay-Z song, which got louder and louder. By the time we came upon a small house stripped of its windows and doors, the stench had died down. A bunch of shirtless young men were sitting on a brick wall in front of the house, chatting noisily while passing around a rolled-up cigarette.

Don't they have anything better to do than to glare at us? I thought. I inhaled a sharp scent somewhat similar to burning leaves, but not quite the same. It was a distinct odour that I found hard to describe. I flinched when a large lizard slid across the narrow path. It was as green as the grass around us, and had loose skin under its throat, as well as pointed spines running from its neck all the way to the base of its long, tapering tail.

"Look," one of the young men posing on the wall shouted, "is ah iguana!"

"It run over there!" Another youth pointed in the direction where the reptile had disappeared.

"They're trying to catch it." Dad observed my confused expression as the young men jumped off the wall and headed toward the bushes. I couldn't figure out how a lizard could have gotten them so worked up.

"People eat that?" I twisted my face in disbelief when Dad said it was a delicacy.

"But it's only a lizard?"

"They say it tastes like chicken," Dad smiled.

"Yuck."

"Maybe they'll be lucky next time," Dad said as the youths emerged from the bushes empty-handed.

Not far from the windowless house, a woman positioned a plastic bucket under a standpipe. Several others, waiting in line to fill their own colourful containers, gazed at us inquisitively. I felt self-conscious and out of place, like an uninvited guest.

"Smokey, what's up?" a woman with a very big voice asked as she stepped out of a tiny shop positioned on an incline.

"Everything's good," Dad said, giving her a quick wave.

Next to the standpipe, a half-naked toddler stooped directly in front of a brownish house and beat the ground with a skinny, dried-out stick. Knee-high bush swallowed the front of the chocolate-coloured dwelling. The silver handle on its wooden front door was entwined with a bulky iron chain, and pieces of ply board formed big X's across its two large windows.

"Watch your step!" Dad did a jig to prevent his feet from

stepping in fresh dog poop. The higher we climbed, the more dogs' feces we saw, but most of them were stale and had almost dried up. I played hopscotch, wary in my movements. The music grew louder and louder the further up the hill we went.

We walked past a tidy blue-and-white duplex with a low wooden fence surrounding its well-kept lawn. I thought it was out of place, and then I wondered who lived there.

My father finally stopped in front of a cream-coloured dwelling, much smaller than the blue-and-white house we'd passed moments earlier. It was the house the music was coming from; inside, someone was blasting Rihanna's umbrella song at full force.

My legs were tired now, and sticky perspiration trickled down my armpits and the length of my back. With my face tilted downward and my back slightly curved, I clutched the fence, panting.

"Hello!" my dad hollered above the music.

I thought we'd have to remain outside forever, or at least until the music stopped, since it seemed unlikely anyone would hear Dad's voice above the noise. As we waited, the leaves on several huge trees in front of the house swayed in a powerful current of air, and for a moment the staircase of the house, which was painted a bright red, came into view. In spite of the large trees, the well-kept yard was a welcome sight.

A river of wobbly, erratic butterflies fluttered aimlessly around us. I had never before seen such an abundance of colourful creatures in one location. Some of them dipped forward and landed on the flowerbed behind the fence.

A petite woman dragging a flimsy pair of flip-flops inched toward us. Her hands swayed to and fro as she balanced a white plastic container filled with what I assumed was water, even though she wasn't one of the women I'd seen earlier at the standpipe. I was amazed as she approached us without losing a single drop from the container she was carrying on her head.

"Good to see yuh, man," she said. "Yuh waiting for Boyie to open the gate?"

"Yeah." Dad gave her a weak smile.

The woman tapped Dad's back several times. Then she continued to tread effortlessly along the winding track. Soon she was out of sight. The music was still blasting, and, once again, Dad hollered Boyie's name. By then his voice had grown sharper, more impatient. Suddenly, two large Doberman Pinschers rushed from the side of the house toward the gate, prancing and barking, not at my dad, but at me. They were barking ferociously. I flinched and hastily lifted my fingers off the wire fence.

"I coming!" a woman shouted from behind the trees.

First I saw her legs and then the edge of her skirt. My lips formed a big round circle, and my eyes almost fell out of my head when I saw the deep dimples on her cheeks. I barely noticed the two-year-old child she was carrying in her arms.

"I didn't expect allyuh so early. Excuse de clothes. I cleaning de place all day. Martha Carlin and she hard back children up de hill still throwing their garbage in any direction dey feel. Dey not just throwing it on their side of de fence no more, but dey throwing it on we side of de fence too. Is a damn disgrace I have to clean up dey mess." Petal adjusted her colourful headscarf. She seemed slightly embarrassed at her soiled clothes. "Baby Girl, yuh 'fraid de dogs?" Her broad smile returned.

"Yes," I said, first looking up at Petal and then at Dad, while the dogs continued to bark. "Do I have to go inside?"

"Don't worry, I going an' put dem in dey house," Petal said. "Moxley, Spider, scram!" She spoke firmly, ordering the dogs to follow her.

"Are you okay?" Dad inched toward me just as Petal and the dogs disappeared behind the house, but I instantly stepped out of his reach.

"Are you so angry with your poor daddy?" he asked, a big sheepish grin on his face.

The odd moment I'd witnessed between Dad and Petal on my return from Dr. Seepersaud's office flashed again in my mind. I had forced it out of my thoughts, but all of a sudden I felt like an accomplice who was facing the penalty for her inaction.

What could I have done differently? I wondered.

A coffee-coloured man with hair cropped short and wearing a pair of gold hoop earrings flew down the staircase. The top of his white underwear was in plain view and the crotch of his jeans almost touched his knees. The words *Soca Warriors* were printed on the front of his red T-shirt, above an image of a man kicking a soccer ball.

"Boyie, what's up man?" Dad asked.

"Everything cool." Boyie unlocked the gate. Then he exchanged a playful punch with my father before stepping aside and allowing us to go up the staircase ahead of him. The loud music vibrated the house like a mini-earthquake, so I buried my ears with my hands while inspecting the lily-white curtains covering the windows, which fluttered almost as vigorously as the butterflies I'd seen earlier. I didn't ask for Dad's help, nor did I want it, but when he removed my backpack from my shoulders and placed it on the shiny wooden floor, I didn't resist.

"I'm going to the washroom," Dad said, leaving me beside my luggage.

A boy of about four sat on the spotlessly clean floor. He was playing with a black-and-white cat, tugging its tail. The cat darted toward me, but I quickly moved out of its way.

"Allyuh inside?" Petal's eyes sparkled as she came toward us from the rear of the house, still carrying the toddler. She tenderly placed the child on the floor. The little boy glanced at me shyly before scooting over to his older brother, who was by then playing with a miniature police cruiser.

"Welcome to Flat Hill Village," she said with a smile. I forced one in return. I was too confused to speak.

"Those is my two boys," Petal said, "and dat's my lil' brother Boyie, who not so small no more."

Boyie tinkered with a bunch of CDs, ignoring us completely.

Both kids sped toward their mother; the younger boy clutched her leg while the elder child stretched his arms as far as they would go around her waist. "Dis is my big boy Warren, and dis is lil' Drew." Petal dropped onto her knees, holding her children and pointing at me. "Dat is Baby Girl. Shake she hand."

The older boy came forward, but the younger child clutched his mother's leg even tighter.

"Allyuh, I have work to do, so go an' play," Petal said. The children ran toward their pile of toys, which were confined to one corner of the room.

"I got to talk to yuh in private." Petal tapped Dad's hand the moment he returned. She glanced at Boyie. "Throw an eye on de kids fer me."

Boyie mumbled his response while continuing to fiddle with a bunch of CDs placed on top of the stereo system's mahogany stand. Petal headed toward the corridor. My father lifted his suitcase and followed her, leaving me standing there awkwardly, a few feet from Boyie. The room fell completely silent for about thirty seconds while Boyie changed CDs. Soon the music was as loud as before and he began to mouth the words to a 50 Cent song. As the minutes ticked by, I wasn't sure whether to remain standing or to sit on the sofa. The noise began to hurt my ears, but Petal's boys didn't seem at all fazed by it. I was too scared to ask Boyie to turn the music down, so I walked onto the porch and counted the birds as they flew by, hoping Dad and Petal would return soon.

From a distance, a man's grainy voice shouted, "Number ten play, monkey play!" He raised his voice as if to ensure that the entire neighbourhood would hear him. I shifted position several times until I saw the man. He had a shiny, bald head, a square jaw, and a cropped beard. To my surprise, he stopped in front of Petal's gate.

"Tell Boyie, number ten play!" he said, looking at me. "Then tell him to come and get his money."

I turned and instantly collided with Boyie, who'd stumbled out to the porch and down the stairs.

"Your number come. Ten play today!" the man said to Boyie.

Boyie's eyes gleamed; he made a fist and pumped his right arm up and down. He rushed toward the fence and the man dug into his pocket, pulled out a stack of bills, and handed them over. Boyie counted the pile, after which he shoved it into his pocket and made his way back inside the house.

"Number ten play. Monkey play!" The man continued up the hill, shouting even louder than before. He swung around the bend so I could no longer see him, but I was still able to hear his voice clearly. It eventually faded as well.

As I lingered on the porch, a girl dressed in white, an older man carrying a small child, a woman clutching a big cardboard box, a little girl dressed to the nines, an old man with one leg shorter than the other, and two boys and a woman lugging large buckets of water on their heads passed by Petal's gate. Most of them made their way uphill, but a few stepped down the trail.

Suddenly, a man wearing a sleeveless, white T-shirt with arms as thick as a body builder's rattled the iron gate. His eyes landed on my face. "Tell Boyie I have something fer him," he said. I pulled back the curtains draping the front door and peeked at Boyie as he fiddled with his music system.

"Somebody at the gate is asking for you," I said as he dusted the stereo with a soft cloth. I thought I'd spoken loudly enough, over the din of the music, but he didn't respond. I wondered if the loud music had already cost him a sizeable amount of his hearing.

"Someone by the gate is asking for you!" I shouted this time. Suddenly Boyie brushed past me.

"Come, I have the thing, man," the muscular man said to him.

"Oswald, I coming." Boyie made his way down the staircase and unlatched the gate. Boyie pulled out the stack of money he'd shoved in his pocket earlier. He counted one, two, three, four, five, six bills and handed them over. Oswald slipped a tiny package wrapped in brown paper to Boyie, who shoved the parcel into the opposite pocket. Boyie then shut the gate behind him, and headed down the trail alongside his friend.

Even after Boyie had left, I remained on the porch and continued my examination of the neighbourhood. The white duplex to my left, built on as high an incline as Petal's house, was shut tight, but I could still see some of its white walls through a drape-less window.

A portion of the roof covering the brown house to my right, which stood on a lower level than Petal's, was somewhat visible, but an ugly aluminum wall, way taller than any human I'd ever met, obstructed a wider view of the dwelling. It wasn't until I climbed on top of one of the chairs on the porch that I was able to spot a small dingy window with a piece of plywood nailed over it.

I lifted one leg, lowering my body to the ground, but the chair shifted, making a grating sound. My arms flapped around as I tried to keep my balance. Luckily, my two feet landed safely on the ground.

"What yuh doing?" Petal's older boy looked at me strangely, but moments later he smiled genially.

"Yuh wanna play a game?" Warren took my hand even before I'd responded. "I have a police car, a fireman truck, and a firehouse too."

Just then his baby brother, Drew, ran toward us. The two boys romped around the chairs. Drew tripped, banging his head on the floor. He bawled and I tried to quiet him, but I couldn't. Petal, now wearing a bright red polka-dot sundress with two large, square pockets, dashed toward us.

"What happening here?" She scooped up her younger boy and rubbed his head in a circular motion. But the young boy closed his eyes and hollered even louder. "Where Boyie?" Petal asked.

"He left."

"Gawd man!" she said. "He couldn't wait a lil' bit?"

Petal shifted her son from one arm to the next and made her way toward the living room. Suddenly the music stopped.

"You're enjoying the lovely view?" My father stepped onto the porch, dressed in a short khaki pants and cream sleeveless top. "I bet you've never seen so many birds and trees on Paradise Lane. It's nicer here, isn't it?"

"I don't like it here!" I hissed. I kept my eyes to the ground, but still felt his stare.

"You'll get used to it in no time, just as you got used to Paradise Lane." He inched closer.

"I don't want to live on a big hill," I said.

"You've got to behave like a big girl, not a little child." Dad plunked himself down on the bottom of the staircase and lit a cigarette.

After he'd finished smoking, Dad went back to the car to collect the rest of our baggage. A few minutes after he left, I heard a loud bell ring. I looked up and noticed the big square clock on the wall. It was exactly six o'clock. I couldn't tell where it was coming from. Who was ringing this bell so loudly, and why? I climbed up on the same chair I'd almost fallen off earlier, but I made sure to be more careful. I craned my neck and peered over the old, rusted aluminum fence, but I couldn't see anyone, so I swiftly climbed down.

"Yuh hear de bell?" Petal asked as she came toward the porch. I nodded.

"Who's ringing it?" I asked.

"Is de neighbour, Mr. Arthur. He does ring dat old bell at six o'clock every morning and in de evening too."

"Why?"

"He ringing it since I was a lil' girl," Petal smiled. She rushed toward her younger son, who had once again started to cry. She tucked him into her hip, and he stuck his thumb in his mouth while pressing his cheek against her chest.

My legs and arms started to itch. I rubbed all over to ease the itch and noticed that several big blotches had suddenly appeared on my skin. "Ouch," I said, as the irritation spread to another spot.

"The mosquitoes eating yuh?" Petal examined the red, swollen areas. "I going and get something fer yuh to put on it." She returned with a long, thin tube. "Put it all over yuh skin. It going to stop de stinging," she said. "Is de nasty Carlin and dem up de hill causing so much shitting mosquitoes in dis village."

After I'd rubbed the ointment all over my limbs and the itchiness stopped, Petal walked ahead, carrying Drew while Warren trailed me. We entered a bedroom with two tiny windows and two single beds. The bed to my right was covered with Superman sheets. The one to my left had ordinary white sheets. Two big boxes overflowing with children's toys stood beside the left bed.

"Yuh going to sleep here," Petal said and stepped toward the bed with the white sheets.

"Dis is my big bed," Warren said.

"Is Baby Girl bed now. Yuh have another big boy bed at yuh father and granny house." Petal dragged the white sheets from the bed and replaced them with pink flowered ones.

"Put yuh clothes in dere." She shoved a bunch of hangers overflowing with the boy's clothes to one side of a tiny wardrobe, making room for my clothes on the other.

"Yuh father going to have to get a desk fer yuh to do yuh homework on," she said and walked out of the room with her two sons following closely behind her.

Flat Hill Village, with its shabby yards, unruly trees, and assortment of odd individuals, compared to Paradise Lane, with its regular hardworking folks and neatly kept trees and flower gardens decorating the front of each house, was hard for me to take in. I sat on the bed and stared at the walls, wishing I had the magical power to make my absent mother reappear. Just then a gecko about five inches long scurried from one edge of the ceiling to the next. I rubbed my palms together as if I were lathering soap all over them. I was too shell-shocked to holler.

6.

THE NEXT WEEK, I SPENT hours on the porch inspecting the trees, bushes, and the hilltop in the distance. Despite the lush green surroundings, I felt like a prisoner under house arrest. The worst thing about this feeling was that I didn't have a clue how long this unjust sentence was going to last. The dogs contributed greatly to my problem. More often than not, Moxley and Spider had free rein to prance about the yard while I, scared stiff of them, had no choice but to remain on the porch.

I woke up early on Christmas Eve plagued by thoughts of Lena and Harley. I missed them. What had they been doing over the holidays? I hadn't spoken to either of them since I'd been forced out of Paradise Lane. I was still confused and couldn't understand why my father had forbidden me from contacting my friends.

The neatly wrapped present Vena had given me remained tucked away in my backpack. I had planned not to open it until Christmas Day, but my curiosity got the best of me, so I eased the gift out of its hiding place. I massaged the wrapping paper, fingering its edges cautiously and quietly guessing its contents. The urge to find out what was hidden inside was overwhelming that I tore off the red, green, and gold wrapping paper. It was a red iPod Nano. It was exactly the one I had wanted.

My father was out running errands. I, on the other hand, spent most of Christmas Eve in my room. Earlier that morning,

Petal had asked me to help her to mix a batter of eggs and sugar for a sponge cake, but I lied, saying I had a headache and needed to rest. I'm not sure whether she believed me, but she did all the chores by herself.

Will Lena get an iPod Nano just like mine? Will Harley get the new bike he wanted?

The smell of freshly baked cake, bread, ginger beer, and sorrel filled the air, but it didn't make me feel any better. I was lonely for friends my own age.

Petal's young sons always spent the weekends with us. The boys' father brought them over on Friday evenings, and on Sundays, after dinner, Petal usually took them back to Chaguanas. This year, Christmas Eve fell on a Thursday, so the boys weren't scheduled to come over until the evening of Christmas Day.

My very first Christmas in Trinidad and in Flat Hill Village turned out to be disappointingly ordinary. I spent long hours on the porch and in front of the television. Several of Petal and Dad's friends came to visit, but nobody came specifically to see me. When the boys arrived, they opened their presents and I played with them for a bit, but I was still bored.

I was glad when Christmas was over and the first day of school arrived. My father made arrangements with a man named Mr. Wellington to chauffeur me to and from school each day. I'd never met him and didn't know if he was old or young, or fat or thin. Petal offered to escort me down the hill and introduce me to my new driver. "Good morning, Mr. Arthur. How yuh doing?" Petal said to a very old man who was walking down the road with the aid of a black cane.

"I still battling like a giant," the old man replied, his voice as wobbly as his hands.

"Yuh sure better dan Brian Lara," Petal responded and exchanged nods with a grey-haired woman clutching the aged man's upper arm.

Days earlier, while peeking through one of Petal's old family albums, I'd seen a photo of a much healthier and younger-looking Mr. Arthur. In that old snapshot, he was sitting next to Petal's now-deceased father holding a bottle of Vat 19 rum high up in the air and sporting a wide smile. The image in the old photo did not resemble the frail man in my presence. I was sure that if Mr. Arthur tried to walk down the trail without assistance, he'd topple over and knock his face on the ground.

"What's wrong with him?" I whispered to Petal. "His back looks like a big letter C."

"Don't be rude," Petal hissed, and tapped the back of my head. She moved forward quickly. I stepped up my pace to keep up with her. Mr. Wellington had timed things well. He drove a red Ford Escape and he arrived at the spot where Dad usually parked his vehicle at the same time as us. He was balding on top but he had a mass of salt-and-pepper hair at the back of his head that curled up into kinky little knots. I couldn't spot a single crease on his stiff white shirt.

"Dis is Smokey daughter, Baby Girl," Petal said to Mr. Wellington.

"Sit in the back," he said, barely glancing at me.

I did as he ordered and climbed in alongside two girls both decked out in red overalls and cream blouses. The girls' short, tightly curled hair was heavily adorned with pink ribbons. The older girl, who appeared to be close to my age, acknowledged me, but the younger girl kept her head down, preventing even the slightest eye contact. I guessed she was scared of strangers. Later, I learned that the older girl's name was Cherise, the younger, Jasmine, and the bald taxi driver, Mr. Wellington, was their dad.

As time passed, I got to know Cherise and Jasmine better, but we never became best friends. The girls' mother lived in the United States, and Cherise often boasted that she and her sister would soon move to Houston, Texas, to join her.

The drive to school didn't seem to take as long as the initial drive from Paradise Lane to Flat Hill Village two weeks earlier.

I was excited because I knew I would finally get to see Lena and Harley again at school.

As I made my way into the schoolyard, I spotted Lena right away. "Where's Harley?" I asked. The twins were always together, so it seemed odd to see Lena alone. Lena didn't answer. Instead she spun around and grabbed me from behind.

"Where's Harley?" I repeated.

"Harley's gone away," she replied, and abruptly let go of me. Her face was grim but right then peels of laughter echoed from behind me. As I spun around, I spied the top of Harley's head. The rest of his body was partly hidden behind our classmate, Satish.

"Where are you living now, Baby Girl?" Harley asked as he stepped forward. I looked at Lena and she was laughing too. They had played a joke on me.

"I'm living with my dad," I answered, but I was too embarrassed to share the details of our new home with Petal.

"Why don't you ever come to see us?" Harley continued.

"Her daddy doesn't want her to," Lena butted in.

Harley's questions and Lena's response put me on edge, so I decided to change the subject and asked them about their Christmas. Then we all got talking about our presents.

The following Saturday, I peeked from behind the curtains in my bedroom and observed several men lugging household items into the light-coloured duplex to the left of Petal's house. A fridge, stove, cream leather sofa, two flat-screen televisions, and other furnishings were being painstakingly carried in. Two big-bellied men waddled like ducks as they carried an oversized box between them. The box slipped, but both men managed to grab it before it hit the ground. I remained at the window for another ten minutes or so, but eventually moved away when I didn't see any children, and sat on my bed sulking for a while.

Later that afternoon, I noticed a very short woman with straight jet-black hair in a single braid standing outside the gate. She was one of the people I'd seen entering the duplex earlier that day. The dogs rushed ahead of Petal and charged at the visitor.

"Scram!" Petal shouted at the dogs, shooing them away. She chatted with the woman for a few minutes and then trotted up the slight incline toward the house. When she got to the halfway point, she looked up at me as I stood on the porch, and said, "Bring de hammer and screw driver set. Dey in a box under de kitchen sink." Petal waited at the top of the staircase until I returned with the tools.

"Thanks so much," the woman said in a high-pitched voice when Petal handed her the tools. "Shiva don't have a clue which box he put we tools in," she added.

"Stop sending your shit down here. I'm warning you people!" Dad roared.

He was behind the house sweeping up the junk that the Carlin family constantly threw over the fence bordering Petal's house and theirs. The Carlins' three-bedroom house stood on a very high incline behind Petal's, and the wire fence separating both properties leaned forward due to the mounds of garbage pressed against it. Disposable diapers, detergent boxes, beer cans, empty bottles, soft drink cans, milk cartons, batteries, plastic bags, and loads of other stuff were a terrible eyesore.

Martha Carlin, two of her three sons, her teenage daughter, her grandson, and her nephew lived in the house. Martha's eldest son, Carl, had been in custody months earlier for drug trafficking. Her second born, Oswald, was also well known to the police. Her daughter, Marlene, had a baby at sixteen and, at nineteen, was due to give birth to a second child at any time. Theo, Martha's youngest son, had dropped out of school and usually hung out by the abandoned house close to the standpipe with the other neighbourhood youths. Martha's nephew Claudius had moved in a few weeks earlier, and the gossip circulating throughout the village was that he'd moved into Flat Hill Village because someone in his hometown had threatened to murder him.

"You want to help me plant a tree?" Dad wiped the sweat off his brow as I stepped behind the house.

"Yeah." I nodded and followed my father to the front, where he dug a medium-sized hole and transplanted a tiny avocado tree from an earth-coloured pot. Dad watched as I watered it carefully. We made our way behind the house again, but as soon as we got there an empty soup can tumbled down the hill and landed at Dad's feet.

"You idiots up there! Stop throwing your crap down here!" Dad yelled as he picked it up.

"Is me yuh talking to?" Martha Carlin poked her out of her window.

"Yes, it's you!" Dad shouted.

Martha slammed the window shut and found her way to the fence.

"Shame on you," Dad said as foul words poured from the woman's mouth.

"Yuh coming?" Petal asked a few days later. She was going to visit our new neighbour, Meena Ramsingh.

"Yes," I said, slipping on my sandals. As we set foot inside Meena's house, Mr. Arthur rang his daily six-o-clock bell and it immediately became the topic of conversation until Meena's husband, Shiva, and their two children, Suri and Samuel, walked in. It was a pleasant surprise to learn that Shiva and Meena Ramsingh had kids. The children had been staying at their grandparents' home in Central Trinidad and had only moved into their parents' new home the night before.

It wasn't long before Suri broke the ice. Her unusual giggle seemed so familiar that I wondered if maybe we'd met in a previous life. We sat on the carpet in her bedroom next to her four-poster bed discussing our favourite television shows, actors, and singers. The conversation shifted to our favourite writers, and then she invited me to inspect her mini-library.

Trips to the Ramsinghs' became the norm, but, besides accompanying Petal there and being chauffeured to school by Mr. Wellington, no one took me anywhere else. Except, that is, for Sunday evening trips with Petal and Dad to drop Petal's boys at their dad's home.

Several months later, I was introduced to Dahlia, a seventeen-year-old girl who lived about ten houses up the trail from us. "She going an' come over to stay with yuh dis evening," Petal said, introducing me to a pretty girl with the smooth, dark complexion. Later that day, Dahlia lugged a backpack to our house. The spines of several books busted through the seams of the bag, and I wondered if the weight of the books caused her back pain.

"I brought my books to do a little bit of studying," she said as I stared curiously at her bag.

"But you could have just picked out one or two books to bring over," I said.

Dahlia smiled and exposed thick braces. "Sometimes I'm not sure which one I want to read 'til the last minute. This way I can decide on the spur of the moment." Dahlia sank into the sofa, where she remained for almost an hour watching cartoons with me. Then she found a quiet place in the kitchen to study.

Moments later, Boyie appeared in the living room sipping a bottle of beer. He smirked, eased into an armchair, and reached for the remote.

"I'm watching *The Simpsons*!" I raised my voice, but Boyie switched the channel anyway and began to watch an action movie.

One Saturday, Dad, Petal, and I sat on the porch shelling the green peas Dad had harvested earlier that day. A big, yellow plastic container filled with the peas we hadn't yet shelled lay on a tiny wooden table, and a black bag overflowing with the shells rested on the ground.

"Mr. Arthur invite us to de Thanksgiving party he having," Petal said to Dad.

"I'm not going and Baby Girl's not going," Dad said in a firm voice.

"I use to go when I was small, and it didn't do me no harm," Petal said.

"He rings that bell morning and night, and now he's sacrificing animals too," Dad said. "What kind of strange religion is he following?"

"He does celebrate his birthday by feeding people and praying. What is de big deal, Smokey?"

"I don't feel comfortable with Baby Girl going over there," Dad said, "and that's that."

"Mr. Arthur invited me to his party," I said to Suri as we stood on Petal's porch watching visitors heading to his house.

"So why you didn't go then?"

"'Cause Dad said I couldn't." Just then I took a second look at a girl who was dressed in purple and looked a lot like my Canadian friend, Makayla. *Could she have come to Trinidad to surprise me?* I dismissed that thought as she hurried past our gate and made her way to Mr. Arthur's place.

Suri and I climbed on top of individual chairs and craned our necks to see what was taking place over the towering fence.

"It's a Thanksgiving birthday party he's having," I said to Suri. Her brother, Samuel, poked his head out the door. Earlier that evening, he had parked himself in front of the television to watch a movie alongside Boyie.

"He does ring that evil bell to call dead spirits," Suri said as Samuel disappeared inside the house. We both almost lost our balance when we heard a loud blast coming from behind the house.

"Martha, house on fire!" a big voice bellowed, and a bunch of panicky people screamed, "Fire, fire, fire!"

Numerous popping sounds way louder than firecrackers filled the air one after the other.

Suri and I scampered to the back of the house. When we got there, the Carlin house was filled with mounds of thick, black smoke. Like a world champion hurdler, Boyie jumped the wire fence to assist the neighbourhood men. They doused the burning structure with bucket after bucket of water, but the house burned to cinders nonetheless.

7.

THE CARLIN FAMILY LOST ALL of their possessions, but fortunately no one was killed. Rumours about a man who'd been seen lingering in front of the house shortly before the fire started to spread quickly.

"I don't believe none of dat shit!" Petal screeched. "If someone in dis village did see something fishy, dey woulda give a good description to de police."

"Talk to the police?" Dad huffed. "You really think anyone wants to get mixed up with the Carlins' gangland problems? They keep on throwing garbage down the hill as if they don't have no common sense. It's good for them." Dad sat on the front staircase with Petal and Boyie while I remained on the uppermost stair, observing.

"I know Marlene since I was in primary school," Boyie said, referring to Martha Carlin's teenage daughter. "Me and she brother Oswald does still go down real good."

"Well, she may be your pal and that criminal, Oswald, your buddy, but don't bring them here when I'm around," Dad said.

"She not dat kinda friend," Boyie chuckled.

"I hope so," Petal said. "But I real sorry dey house burn down and now Marlene two children don't have a decent place to rest their lil' heads."

"You want to take them in?" Dad's voice went up. "Marlene's two children are going to turn out as criminal-minded as their no-good relatives."

"Smokey, have a heart. Dey is poor people, and de fire take everything dey have."

"A little fire softened you?" Dad scoffed.

Petal sucked her teeth so loud, I was sure a skinny man walking uphill toting a crocus bag heard the sound.

It was unusual for Boyie to sit on the staircase and talk to anyone. He was rarely home, especially on weekends, but whenever he was, he'd usually park himself in front of the television, or play deafening music while bobbing and weaving his head and mouthing R&B, reggae, soca, or rap music.

"Dahlia's coming over tonight," Dad said as he made his way toward me, his eyes firmly on my face.

"Tonight?" I said.

"Yep."

"But you said you weren't going out this weekend."

"Well," Dad paused, "something came up."

"But we not staying out late," Petal interjected. "I promise we going to be back by ten fer de latest."

"You always say that," I moped, "but you always come back way past midnight."

Neither one responded, and for the next couple of minutes I remained on the porch with my arms tightly folded.

When Dahlia got to the house, she poured me a glass of orange juice and then made some popcorn. We were planning to watch a movie. But shortly after Dad and Petal left, Boyie came into the living room and switched the channel. I'd resigned myself to watching another action movie, but before it was halfway through, I must have dozed off, because I woke up just as a high-ranking U.S. army officer yelled at one of his subordinates. I'd lost track of the storyline, so I headed to bed.

By nine I'd fallen fast asleep, but I woke up around eleven thirty, very thirsty. I climbed out of bed, intent on getting a glass of water. As I made my way along the corridor, silly laughter seeped out of Boyie's slightly open bedroom door. I held my breath and peeked through the tiny opening. My eyes grew large as I saw Dahlia climb off Boyie's lap. I backed away, turning quickly, only to smash my elbow against the door.

"Ow!" I cried out, rubbing the spot.

"Why yuh spying on me?" Boyie came toward me with flared nostrils. His hands went up, as if preparing to strike me. "I going to hurt yuh real bad!" he shouted.

I tried to slip out of the line of fire, but he stepped closer, pressed his hands on my shoulders, and violently shook me. I went to and fro for what seemed like forever. When he let go, I staggered, and as I caught my balance, he kicked my shin. I went down on all fours like a frightened animal. He raised his right leg and I scrunched into a ball, trying to protect myself.

"You crazy or what?" Dahlia yelled. "You can't kick she like that!"

Boyie spun around. He stomped into his bedroom and slammed the door. Colour drained from Dahlia's face "Promise me you not going to tell nobody," she whispered as she helped me to my feet.

I swallowed hard. "Okay," I mumbled. I ran back to my room, jumped into the bed, and pulled the covers way over my head. I finally fell back asleep.

The following morning, I sat at the kitchen table listlessly stirring a bowl of porridge. I just wasn't hungry.

"Yuh should be in Africa where children starving," Petal said. To get her off my back, I forced down a few spoonfuls, but, as soon as she left the room, I dumped the rest down the kitchen sink. Then I ran the water at full force to destroy the evidence. I was of two minds. Should I tell Petal about the incident, even though I'd promised Dahlia I wouldn't? If I did tell, would Boyie get mad and seriously hurt me?

By the time I'd made my way into the bathroom and begun to braid my hair, I'd decided to keep the incident to myself.

After styling my hair, I inspected a bunch of tiny bumps all over my forehead and cheeks. Then I noticed a big, red, juicy pimple on the right side of my face. I closed my eyes wishing it and all the smaller ones would vanish. But when I looked again, they were still there, except the largest one seemed even larger. I studied the girl staring back at me. Would I always have these average eyes, this too-large nose, and this unattractive mouth? I walked out of the bathroom, convinced I was really ugly.

Why doesn't my mom try to find me? Is it because she's ashamed of me?

"Auntie Hattie came back," Lena whispered as we strolled toward our classroom.

"You can't fool me," I said, turning to face her; I was certain she was playing games.

"We're not lying," Harley said during recess, but his boyish grin wasn't convincing.

"She came back last night and she's staying for three whole weeks. Cross my heart, Baby Girl." Lena clutched my arm.

"She asked us how you're doing," Harley said.

"Our new housekeeper had a baby, and that's why Auntie Hattie's back," Lena explained.

By the time I'd settled in at my desk after our morning break, Lena and Harley had succeeded in persuading me that Auntie Hattie had indeed returned to Paradise Lane. I stared at the squiggly marks printed with blue ink on the surface of my desk, my mind in a far-off place.

"Melody," Miss Howard, the teacher said, "please pay attention."

I picked up my pen and began to copy the vocabulary she'd written on the chalkboard, but with each stroke of my pen the deep longing to see Auntie Hattie kept growing. *Will Dad let me visit her?*

Deep down inside, I knew there was no point in asking him. After lunch, my thoughts strayed even more and nothing stuck in my head. Tears welled up in my eyes. I sobbed softly at first, but my cries soon got louder. Suddenly I felt fifty curious eyes staring me down.

"Melody, what's the matter?" Miss Howard asked as I wept like a colicky baby. Most of my classmates remained silent, but a few snickers wafted from the back of the room. I couldn't manage to spit any words out, so Miss Howard walked me to the office, and told me I could lay down on the couch there until I felt better.

The following day, Thursday, I kept my intentions to myself. Not even Lena or Harley knew of my plan to sneak out of the schoolyard during our midday break. The moment the school bell signalled lunch time, I slipped out of the gate and trotted down the road, slowing only once or twice to catch my breath.

When I arrived in front of the big, white Paradise Lane house, I stepped under masses of silvery-bluish flowers peeping out of hanging baskets that I couldn't recall ever being there before. The whole neighbourhood seemed more beautiful than I remembered. I rang the doorbell, my heart vibrating like a drum.

"Is you, Baby Girl?" Auntie Hattie's gentle voice greeted me as she opened the door. Her genuine smile sent a warm rush through my body and I felt safe and happy as I buried my face in her chest.

"Chile, let me look at yuh real good. Yuh growing real nice." She held me at arm's length. Her eyes ran from the top of my head to my sneakers. Then she led me along the corridor and into the kitchen. The smell of highly spiced food hit my nostrils.

"Yuh hungry?" she said.

Even before I responded, she began to dish out a plateful of steaming hot stew chicken, fried plantains, spinach, and rice and peas. "Sit down here, chile, you need to eat something." She dragged out a chair and kept guard as I ate.

"Yuh better get back to school. I don't want Smokey to come over here an' act crazy," she said as soon as I'd swallowed the last mouthful.

"My dad's not going to do that." I quickly bit my bottom lip.

Then a chubby little girl almost the same height as Petal's younger son, Drew, appeared in the doorway. When she saw me, she immediately hid her face behind Auntie Hattie's dress tail.

"Madeline, talk to Baby Girl." Auntie Hattie picked up the child and brought her to me, but she kept her head bowed, refusing to speak

Auntie Hattie slipped Madeline's hands off her face. But she immediately rubbed her eyes with her knuckles. Then she wiggled, as if wanting Auntie Hattie to put her down. When Auntie Hattie did as the little girl wished, she disappeared along the corridor.

"It getting late. Go on now." Auntie Hattie glanced at her watch, and then placed the dirty plate in the sink. An uneasy feeling took hold of me.

"Please don't cry." Auntie Hattie touched my cheeks as she led me to the front door. But before I got there, my eyes were big with tears.

With a heavy heart, I headed down the staircase and walked briskly down Paradise Lane. The road was bare except for two cars parked a few houses from the big white house. I picked up the pace but almost stopped breathing completely when Boyie appeared out of nowhere and blocked my way.

"What yuh doing here?" He looked at me as if I were a criminal and he a police detective whose job it was to interrogate me. He dug his nails, as sharp as claws, deep into my shoulders. I twisted my face and opened my mouth as wide as I could, but no sound escaped.

"Where yuh going?" Boyie's tone was harsher than before.

"Am ... am," I stuttered.

"Yuh could get a good cut arse for dis, but I in a good mood today, so I not going an' tell nobody." Boyie's face formed a mischievous grin and then he walked away without looking back.

My knees felt weak and I was barely able to move as an image of my father with an extremely angry expression on his face flashed in my mind. What would he say if he learned I'd come to Paradise Lane? I suddenly felt the urge to puke, so

I stooped and opened my mouth really wide, but only a big burp escaped. I jumped up, fully aware that if I arrived at the school gate even a minute too late, I would possibly have to face detention, and then my secret rendezvous would surely be exposed to Dad and Petal. Even though my stomach hadn't completely recovered, I ran and luckily made it back to school just in time.

At the crack of dawn, I was still under my covers when Petal yelled, "Yuh hand swinging like yuh fielding in a cricket match." She wasn't shouting at me, but at her brother, Boyie. "I struggling to buy all yuh school books and everyone of dem sitting in yuh room just catching dust. Yuh not going to get one shitting ordinary level pass wit' de stupid choices yuh making!"

Boyie didn't ever react to any of his big sister's angry outbursts, and that morning was no different. Still feeling some measure of discomfort in my chest, I pulled the covers up to my neck and curled into a foetal position.

"She probably have a stomach bug," Petal said to my father, who gave his okay for me to skip school that Friday. Boyie didn't go to school either. His attendance at school had already started to rapidly drop off, and, in a matter of weeks, he stopped going completely. Petal eventually stopped pestering him. It was as if she'd given up hope that he'd ever go back.

Dahlia never returned to our house after I caught her in Boyie's bedroom. A couple of days after that incident, her mother informed Dad and Petal that Dahlia needed to concentrate on her upcoming examinations. Dahlia's mother, however, gave Dad and Petal the option of sending me to her house whenever they needed to go out.

A couple of days later, Boyie entered the house with his heavy boots on. "I just finished mopping, so yuh better take those off." Petal pointed to her brother's shoes.

Boyie bounced toward his sister like a *badjohn*. "I own half dis place jus' like you!" he yelled.

"I is yuh big sister. I clean yuh arse when yuh was a baby and since Mammy and Daddy dead, is I who cooking and washing fer yuh."

The room fell silent and I tried to imagine what Petal could possibly be thinking. "Boyie," Petal dropped her voice somewhat, "dis is de payment I getting fer everything I do fer yuh?"

Boyie spun around with his chest held high, and it was only then I noticed his bloodshot eyes. He remained in his bedroom all afternoon, but in the evening he swung a bulging duffle bag over his right shoulder and barged out of the house without saying anything.

Boyie didn't return that night, or the next, and after a couple of days Petal's concern was showing.

"Maybe he staying by he girlfriend." Petal stuck both elbows on the table and propped up her chin with open hands.

"Which girl's going to want him?" Dad quipped. "Boyie's seventeen going on twenty-eight," Dad continued. "He's going to do what he wants to do. He thinks he's a big man. He's not going to listen to me, you, or anybody."

Days later, Boyie returned home, but he soon left again. After a while, we all got used to his constant coming and going.

On a bright sunny Friday afternoon in the school yard, Lena turned to me and said, "We're moving to England."

"You can't be serious." I was certain it was another one of her wisecracks.

"We're leaving at the end of the school year," Harley confirmed.

Vena, an employee at the Ministry of External Affairs, was offered a promotion and had to go to England to take up her new position. But to ease the transition, she had made arrangements for the twins to remain at Paradise Lane until the end of the school year.

"Auntie Hattie's going to stay with us for a while and we're going to join Mom in England in the middle of July," Lena said. I couldn't believe it, but it was true, they were going.

On the last day of the school year, my driver, Mr. Wellington, pulled up in front of our school, but, despite the rather loud toot-toot his horn made, I lingered in front of the school gate chatting with the twins.

"Girl, hurry up!" Mr. Wellington craned his neck out of the window. I had no choice but to step away from my friends, but I kept looking back as they headed in the opposite direction. Would I ever see them again? I didn't know.

8.

THE WORDS "TOWER BRIDGE, London, England," were printed in big blue letters at the bottom right-hand corner of the postcard I was holding. I turned it over and inspected Harley's scribbles. Lena's words, written in slanted letters directly below her brother's, weren't any easier to make out. The twins and their mother had settled in London, and, during the past months, I'd gathered a sizable collection of picture postcards, thanks to them.

By that time, Boyie had unofficially moved out. I say unofficially because, even though he hadn't come home for several months, he'd barely taken any of his stuff. Earlier that week, Petal had asked Dad to pry open the lock on Boyie's bedroom door since she couldn't find the spare key and wanted to give the room a thorough cleaning.

"I ask yuh almost a week now, and yuh still haven't done it!" Petal's voice rose as I placed the postcard inside the box where I kept the others.

"You know I've been busy with work," Dad replied. "I'll get it done over the weekend."

I headed to the living room, and as I got there, Dad eased onto the sofa and slipped on a pair of socks. "You've got five minutes to get ready," he said, looking up at me.

Petal came toward us decked out in an outfit covered in so many sequins that it reminded me of a well-decorated Christmas tree, but without the flickering bulbs. A woman named

Margot had spent hours the previous day styling her long, thin braids, which she'd kept covered with a multi-coloured scarf all morning. She shed the colourful head covering, allowing her braids to fall down her back.

About ten minutes later, Petal stood in the middle of the roadway. She kept an eye on me as I strolled under the sprawling branches of a breadfruit tree on my way to Dahlia's parents' house. The family didn't have any dogs, but their talkative parrot was far noisier than Moxley and Spider put together. I knocked, and Dahlia appeared at the doorway sporting a broad smile. "Come in," she said and welcomed me inside.

"Good day, good day, good day!" The emerald green parrot with large patches of yellow above its beak flapped its wings almost as briskly as a hummingbird. Dahlia's two younger sisters waved at me as they sat at the dining table with their mouths stuffed. I sat on their living room sofa and Dahlia's mother, Mrs. Arlington, approached me.

"Yuh want some passion fruit juice?" she asked.

"No, thank you." I kept my hands on my lap.

"Yuh sure?" she enquired, holding the ice-cold drink in front of my face.

"I'm full," I said, silently reminding myself why I'd decided never to eat another morsel of food or take another sip of water at the Arlingtons'. I'd made that decision a few weeks earlier. On that day, I'd accompanied Dahlia's two younger sisters behind their parents' home, where the leaves of a passion fruit vine, deep green and glossy, clung to their chain link fence. We'd picked the yellowish fruit and placed them in small baskets. Mrs. Arlington had then made a jug of juice, and, from the first sip, I was in love with the drink.

It was Dahlia's youngest sister Constance's ninth birthday, and, to celebrate the occasion, Mrs. Arlington had baked a pineapple upside down cake. She'd also prepared several other dishes, and I had my fill of almost everything. But barely one hour later, my stomach churned and I threw up bits and pieces of a multi-coloured substance. Even after I'd vomited, I wriggled in discomfort for a long time afterward.

"She frighten to go in," Constance said to her slightly older sister, Emma, as I lingered in front of their outhouse. Dahlia, hearing the hullabaloo, poked her head out the door.

"What she so 'fraid of?" Dahlia rolled her eyes at me before pulling her head back in.

I'd felt as if a family of mice were nibbling at my guts, and, having no other option, I reluctantly pulled open the outhouse's wooden door and climbed in. I felt trapped between its four walls, which had been slapped together with a few rough planks of wood. Cautiously, I squatted over the hole, holding my breath. I gasped as my body weakened. After easing my bowels, I stepped into the fresh air inhaling deeply, but, to my horror, a small amount of fecal matter had smeared my little finger.

"Throw water!" I'd frantically begged Constance.

She'd dipped an empty milk can into a large barrel and tossed the water over my soapy hands. I rubbed my palms together like a doctor scrubbing for surgery. Even though the water bounced off the shallow concrete drain and sprinkled my legs, I ordered her to throw some more. For the rest of that evening my fingers had felt disgustingly filthy.

Mrs. Arlington finally gave up on offering me the juice. After dinner, Dahlia grabbed the remote and climbed into a brown armchair. A short while later, Constance, Emma, and Mrs. Arlington also settled in front of the television, waiting for *Without a Trace* to begin.

"Dey does always find de person who missing," Constance said as if she was the only person in the room who'd seen the show.

"But sometimes dey does only fine a corpse," Dahlia added.

Suddenly, Mrs. Arlington's eyes fell on me. "Petal hear from Boyie recently?"

"She doesn't know where he is," I shrugged.

I remained in the same chair until around ten thirty, when Dad came to the Arlingtons' to meet me. I was in such a mad rush to use our bathroom that only after I'd relieved myself did I notice the door lying flat in front of Boyie's bedroom, as well as the hammer on top of it. I poked my head through the doorway and scanned the four corners of the fusty room he'd left in a muddle of untidiness.

Wearing a simple housedress, Petal was rummaging through a large box. The clothes, books, and garbage strewn all over the floor were as much a contrast to the rest of Petal's particularly tidy house as Flat Hill Village was to Paradise Lane. Memories resurfaced of the day when my father had uprooted me from an orderly life with Vena and the twins and brought me to this dusty village with its crude inhabitants. It was hard to explain the odd feeling I had when I realized that I no longer felt out of place in this village and that Paradise Lane, just like Toronto, seemed like ancient history.

"Yuh want to help?" Petal asked with a blank expression.

"Yeah," I replied, but my energetic response was motivated more by a deep curiosity to sift through Boyie's life than any genuine desire to dust, sweep, or mop.

"I going an' get a garbage bag to put dis mess in." Petal scanned the disorder in the top drawer of Boyie's night table. I examined a stack of papers Petal had instructed me to sort. I pulled out a few unmarked sheets, mostly filled with page after page of unreadable scribbles and cartoon-like drawings. Boyie's birth and baptismal certificates were bunched in with those loose sheets. I pulled a firm, flat object from the untidy drawer. It was a small red book. The scribbles on nearly every page were hard to read, so I shoved it in my pants pocket and adjusted my top to cover the bulge. I planned to snoop through Boyie's little red book later that evening in order to get a few chuckles.

"Yuh come here to play or to help?" Petal said as I skimmed through Boyie's Language Arts textbook.

"I'm here to help," I assured her, putting the hardcover textbook on top of the large pile of books in the corner of the room. Minutes later, I pointed to the textbook.

"May I borrow that book?"

"I don't see why not, Boyie sure don't want it," Petal said. "He make me waste a whole set of shitting money to buy every one of dem." Petal's eyes were practically glued to the stack of dusty and hardly-used books. She was shaking her head.

"I guess I could make a few bucks if I sell them," she said as I shoved Boyie's baptismal and birth certificates inside a big brown envelope, along with some other documents she had indicated were important.

"They can't all fit," I said as the envelope got all puffed up. Petal slipped me a brand-new envelope, after which she swept the mounds of dust into a corner of the room. I pulled some empty soda cans from a box at the side of the bed and dumped them into the garbage bag.

"What's this?" I asked, holding a magazine with a picture of a skimpily dressed blonde lady on its front page. It was in the box with a bunch of other magazines. I opened it and peeked at the centrefold.

"Oh!"

"Gimme dat!" Petal grabbed the magazine and flung it in the garbage. "I going and clear dat box mehself," she stressed, as if she thought there might be other stuff inside it she didn't want me to see. I stood still for a few seconds, wondering what to do next.

"Stop wasting time and clean de mirror," she said.

"Jesus, what dis boy have in here?" Petal held up a clear plastic bag half-filled with some sort of brown dried-up stuff and tucked it inside her brassiere. That evening, Petal and I went to bed way past midnight.

A couple days later, I sat on my bed scanning through a stack of old magazines Boyie had left behind that Petal had deemed acceptable for me to look at. These magazines didn't have any naughty photos; mostly they had pictures of folks in the entertainment business, big stars like Jay-Z, Madonna, Rihanna, Nicki Minaj, Lady Gaga, and Mariah Carey.

"I coming!" Petal yelled when Moxley and Spider began to bark loudly. I peeked out of my bedroom window, but the sprawling branches of a guava tree blocked a clear view of the gate. I heard an unfamiliar female voice. Then a man spoke. His voice was a bit rough, but young and interesting. Petal and her guests giggled almost as loud as a bus full of school children.

"Baby Girl, come an' meet someone!" Petal hollered.

I stepped toward a large woman dressed in a drab, dark-brown outfit; she had mounds of flesh hanging from all the wrong places. I thought that if her body were a road, every driver who took their car on it would be in for a rough ride.

"Yuh father Smokey is a real nice fella." The woman eyed me from head to toe. Petal introduced her as Sandrina, her cousin from Point Fortin.

"Meet my son, Colm." The woman's eyes shifted to a slender man who was staring at me from behind owlish glasses. I stepped forward to shake his hand; I wobbled and felt myself suddenly tripping over his bags.

"Excuse me. I'm sorry yuh tripped," he said and grabbed my arm.

Petal explained that Colm was starting an apprenticeship program at an auto mechanic shop in Port-of-Spain the following week. "Colm going to be staying in Boyie's room 'cause it too far fer him to travel from Point Fortin every morning."

9.

I AWOKE TO AN OMINOUSLY grey sky. It was after ten o'clock when I poked my head out of the window for the umpteenth time to stare at the heavens, hoping the weather gods would let the sun come out. But the sky was as dark as ever and just then a bolt of lightning flashed. I spun around and banged my elbow hard on the windowsill. I cried out, the funny bone in my elbow throbbing.

"Yuh afraid of a little lightning?" Colm grinned.

"No! I'm not!" I raised my voice, not in anger, but to stress my point. Colm had been staying with us for just over a month. He loved cars. Within days of his arrival, he'd offered to wash my father's car free of charge, and since then he continued to give it a thorough cleaning every weekend.

We were in the living room. Colm was sitting on the armchair across the sofa, where Dad was watching television. Colm's eyes lifted up from the notebook on his lap. "I gonna give the car a good washing when it stops raining," he said to Dad.

"Great!" Dad replied.

"Can I help?" I asked Colm. I didn't have anything planned besides attending Monty's daughter, Roxanne's, birthday party, and that wasn't due to start until five in the afternoon.

"Sure, the more the merrier." Colm's eyes returned to his notebook, writing something in his big loopy scrawl. When the rain finally stopped, and a milky sun started peeking through the clouds, Colm and I trekked along the rough gravel path toward the standpipe. Colm filled the bucket with water and we made our way to Dad's car.

Dahlia saw us and walked toward us, her red flip-flops slapping the rough earth. "Hi, Dahlia," I called out.

"Hi, Baby Girl." She barely looked at me but she waved energetically at Colm.

The next afternoon, Colm sat on the uppermost stair of the porch with his eyes shut tight. He suddenly opened them, and several tiny ridges that had formed across his brow disappeared. "What are you doing?" I asked as he scribbled furiously in his notebook.

"Something important."

"How come you're always writing?"

"This is what I do to relax." His smile seemed effortless. "Yuh want to hear one of my poems?"

"Poems?"

"I write poetry."

"You do?"

"Yeah, yuh want to hear one?"

"Sure."

"This one is called 'Create Your Own Dreams.'" Colm closed his notebook. As the first few words left his lips, his voice croaked. He pressed his hand over his neck and cleared his throat. At ease, he began again, his voice relaxed, proceeding at a natural pace.

"What kind of sissy thing are you doing, man?" my father smirked as he stepped out of the house. Colm stopped in mid-sentence. We moved over to allow Dad enough room to get to the bottom of the staircase. Colm said, "This is poetry. Maybe yuh should try it."

"Thank you very much," Dad said, "but I'm leaving that to you."

"Aren't you going to finish?" I asked as Dad stepped out of the gate.

"Later," Colm said. I wondered if Dad's words had hurt his feelings.

The steady rhythm of a bass guitar drew me toward Colm's bedroom. I stood behind his door, quietly listening, as his voice got harsher, smoother, and then louder. He recited four poems, one after the other. When he finished, I clapped enthusiastically. Colm opened the door. "Why yuh making such a commotion?"

"I didn't know you played the guitar." I smiled.

Colm lowered his chin as if he didn't think he deserved the applause I continued to give him.

"Is only a bass." He positioned the instrument at the foot of his bed. "I've been toying with it since I was about twelve. My mother couldn't afford to pay for no lessons so I practically teach myself."

"Where'd you get all of those poems?"

"They all mine."

"Wow! How did you come up with so many different ideas?"

"The truth is there's no secret. I jus' sit in a quiet place and let my thoughts flow."

"Then you write them down? Like you were doing on the staircase last week?"

"Yep, well ... there's nothing to it. It comes naturally. I've been writing poetry since I was a young boy."

"I wish I could read poetry like that."

"Yuh sure could if yuh tried," Colm said. "Just imagine I not here. Find one of the poems in my book that yuh like." He positioned his notebook in front of me.

"Wow! I can't believe you wrote all of these," I said. "There are at least a hundred of them."

"Not quite. Is closer to fifty, but I also have about fifteen in my other book." He pointed to a black binder on the bed.

"You're sure I'm not a bother?"

"Not at all!"

I read slowly at first, but with a bit of coaxing, I started to hear and read the rhythm of the words and, as I did, Colm grabbed his guitar and started to strum. "Colm, do you think I can learn to write poems too," I asked shyly.

"Sure, yuh could," he said, and he continued to play his guitar.

It was three weeks before I was ready to share my first poem with Colm. When I finished reciting it, he eyed me with a serious expression. "You hate it?" I said. My confidence was rapidly fading.

"No, that's not it at all. Is just that I had no idea. I thought, well, I thought she was dead. I really sorry yuh mom left yuh at such a young age."

Every day after that, I'd set aside a small amount of time to write, but most days it didn't come easily. "I wish I could write like you do," I said glumly one day when my thoughts were all jumbled up. I'd been staring at a blank sheet for more than half an hour.

"Don't worry. Yuh going to become a master poet. Consider this yuh apprenticeship. But let me tell yuh this," Colm said, "don't be too hard on yuhself. Yuh need to take a little break when yuh can't concentrate."

I started to dedicate a lot more time to writing poetry, but before long my schoolwork started to suffer and I got a failing grade on an important project I hadn't completed on time. "Yuh gotta learn how to prioritize, Baby Girl," Colm said. "I not going to help yuh with any more poetry if yuh don't complete yuh schoolwork on time."

It was the first time I'd seen him angry, but I learned my lesson quickly. I'd been writing a lot of poems about my mom's absence and, it was hard to explain but, in a strange way, writing seemed to ease the pain I felt at her loss.

"Yuh wanna enter a spoken word poetry competition? The theme of this year's event is stopping crime," Colm said to me one Saturday night.

"Me?" All of my poems were about loss. I'd never before tried to write about anything else before. I didn't know if I could do it. Plus, Colm was the only person who'd ever read any of my work.

"Stop doubting yuhself," Colm said. "Yuh can do it. So, do we have a deal?"

"I guess so."

"Let's do it." Colm and I shared a fist bump, and he hurriedly left the room. He was back in a few moments. "This is the third year the competition is on," he said, handing over the instructions for the Young Writers' Spoken Word Competition. "The contest not on for several months yet, but the entry deadline is fast approaching, so if yuh don't want to have to pay a late entry fee, make sure that yuh Dad signs it quickly and give it right back to me."

We were outside on the porch, the two Dobermans lying and panting quietly beside us. Colm had patted Moxley for a long time, and then Spider, and out of the blue Spider licked my toe. "That's how it's done," he said. "Yuh gotta show them who's boss."

"You know how to fix cars, how to write poetry, and how to train dogs," I said, unable to disguise my growing admiration for Colm's many talents.

"I'm no dog trainer. I'm a dog lover." Colm eased into his ever-present smile. "Let's sit outside and practice. We gotta be ready to beat the competition." Colm walked ahead of me, clutching his black binder and notebook.

"He's ringing it again," Colm said, as Mr. Arthur started ringing his bell. He closed his notebook and stared for a while at Mr. Arthur's ugly fence as we waited for the ringing to stop.

Colm shut his eyes and squinched his mouth, as though he was thinking hard about something. "I got it." He looked at me and smiled. "I going to write about an old fence fer this year's competition."

"What does a fence have to do with a poem about crime?"

"I going to write about a crooked fence." Colm snorted. "And it's not going to be about Mr. Arthur's fence, silly," he teased. He explained that a fence is slang for someone who handles stolen goods.

The following weekend, Colm and I were on the porch again, working on our poetry. The porch had become our usual meeting place to discuss our work. "Allyuh hear de news?" Petal asked as she stepped out to join us.

"What news?" Colm said as we looked up at her.

"Mr. Arthur dead," she said. "The lady who does help him out just phone."

I tiptoed to the edge of the porch and tried to get a view of Mr. Arthur's house, but, as usual, I was only able to see a fraction of the dwelling's tightly shut windows.

That same evening Dad asked Petal if she was going to the wake. "I guess so," she said. "You coming?"

"Nah, I don't think so." Dad closed his eyes and rubbed his forehead.

"Can I go?" I asked as Petal cut a medicated disk to size and pressed it onto her big toe.

"It not fer children and furthermore yuh have school tomorrow."

As darkness arrived, the narrow roadway leading to Mr. Arthur's house bustled with pedestrians. Many of the women heading to his place wore long gowns and big, bulging head ties. The streetlights flickered for a while and then dimmed, but I stayed on the porch, keeping watch on the roadway, even though I was unable to identify anyone's face. Petal, dressed in blue jeans and a T-shirt, slipped on her sandals. *She looks out of place compared to those women in their fancy outfits*, I thought. "Can I come for just an hour?" I pleaded, as she stepped toward the porch.

"No means no," she frowned and headed down the staircase.

After the wake, three loud bangs jolted me out of a deep sleep. I glanced at the clock. It was two o'clock. I switched on the corridor lights and made my way to the kitchen. "Get back to bed," Dad barked.

"I need a drink of water," I told him.

"That sound like gunfire." Petal said, coming toward us.

"A g-g-g-gun?" I stuttered. "Dad...?"

"Go back to bed," he insisted. "It's nothing."

But it was something. After that night, the sound of gunshots in Flat Hill Village became a regular occurrence. It usually happened on weekends and especially during the wee hours of the morning.

"The boys playing the fool up the hill," Mickey, one of the villagers, said after Dad asked him if he knew who the culprits were, but Mickey didn't identify any of the perpetrators.

"What's up?" Colm said as I skipped through our gate, just back from school.

"I got ninety-nine percent on my English test," I told him.

"Good fer you!" Colm said. "I'm proud of yuh!" He then pointed to Mr. Arthur's property, which had been stripped of its ugly fence. "Yuh enjoying the view?" he asked.

I inspected the newly exposed area, and for the first time a lone poinsettia tree, its branches spread like a huge umbrella, came into view. "New owners buy the place, and they going to renovate it," he added.

I took a few steps toward the house, but then stopped. I turned around. "Do you know who's moving in?" I asked.

"No, I don't have a clue."

I spun around and continued toward the house, crossing my fingers and wishing whoever moved in had kids my age.

10.

IT WASN'T LONG BEFORE WE had new neighbours. One evening, we were greeted by a pint-sized woman with an awkward grin. "I'm Arlie," she said, standing on the left side of a newly constructed fence as Dad unlatched the gate. We'd just gotten home following a long drive in the country.

Arlie's round face caught my eye. She had a big voice for someone with such a tiny frame. A pudgy boy and a girl half the boy's size edged closer to the woman. The girl had a lighter complexion than the boy and the woman, but all three had the same oddly shaped nose. Where the bridge of the nose should have started, it was as flat as a pancake, then it steadily rose like a tiny hill, flaring somewhat at the edge, and creating a broad frill.

Dad didn't stop to chat, but waved politely. He made his way up the staircase carrying Drew in his arms, who was fast asleep. Petal, Warren, and I stepped closer to the fence.

"This is my daughter, Carrie, and my son, Dante," Arlie said, nodding to the boy and girl at her side. Petal introduced Warren and me, and then I rushed inside to use the washroom.

About five minutes later, Petal entered the house, her cheeks ballooned like a bullfrog's. "If Miss Prim and Proper have such a big government job, why she not living in some fancy place like Valsayn, Blue Range, or Federation Park?" she asked.

"Look, the woman can live wherever she chooses to live," Dad said. "And as long as she ain't throwing stuff over the fence, it shouldn't matter to you, me, or nobody else." He snatched a pack of cigarettes from the table and marched outside. I followed him, leaving Petal inside muttering to herself.

Within days of her arrival, Arlie became a major topic of conversation for the neighbourhood women. "I saw dat horse-haired woman yesterday," Petal said and pressed the receiver to her ear. And even though she didn't disclose a name, I was sure she and Meena were discussing our new neighbour, Arlie.

On school days, Arlie and her kids would leave home at roughly the same time as me, and, despite the rough terrain, Arlie always moved as speedily as if she were a participant in a walking race. Carrie usually kept up with her mom, but on most days Dante lagged behind. When they were home, Dante and Carrie always called to me from across the fence, and gradually we became friends. One day, Dante told me that he liked to compose melodies to songs, and to write lyrics as well. This impressed me, and I told him I liked to write poetry.

About six weeks after our neighbours had moved in, I asked Petal if I could visit them.

"Why yuh want to go dere?"

"Because Dante and Carrie are my friends and they invited me," I replied.

I wanted to tell her, *You always go to Meena's house. Why can't I visit Dante and Carrie?* But I stuffed those words back down my throat.

"Be back by six." Petal's face remained expressionless, but I broke into a smile, surprised at how easily she'd given the go-ahead.

"Not a minute later dan six," she added as I looked back.

After I'd visited Dante and Carrie for the first time, I was very surprised when Petal announced that she was stepping over to Arlie's house.

"How come?" Dad's head popped out from behind the *Trinidad Express* newspaper. "Since when you two are friends?"

"Maybe she could help me get a job." Petal's lips thinned out as she smiled. Before long, Petal invited Arlie and her children over to our place, and soon Arlie's visits to our home became a regular occurrence.

"It's a good thing you don't like her," Dad said one day, "otherwise she'd probably have moved in by now."

I was in awe when Arlie let it slip that she had two university degrees. This was an accomplishment I doubted anyone else in Flat Hill Village could match. Using my fingers, I tried to count the number of people in our village who I knew for sure had successfully finished high school. I stalled when apart from Colm only a couple names came to mind. Even in our household, Dad, Petal, and Boyie had all dropped out.

Besides both being mothers, Arlie and Petal didn't seem to have anything in common. In my presence, they usually engaged in small talk, but I couldn't imagine their friendship surviving for long on petty exchanges such as those about Martha Carlin and her children, the weather, and who was shooting up the neighbourhood on weekends. But one evening, when Arlie came to our house clutching an envelope, things dramatically changed.

"What's dat yuh carrying?" Petal said.

"It's a petition," Arlie said. "We're going to form a women's group."

"A women's group?" Petal said. "Fer what?"

"Here, take a look." Arlie pulled out a stack of papers and showed them to Petal.

"We've got to be our own advocates," Arlie said as Petal skimmed through the pages.

"Advocates?" Petal settled next to Arlie.

I wasn't sure what "advocates" meant, and from the look on Petal's face, she seemed as confused as me.

"We need to brainstorm and to come up with solutions that would benefit our community, especially our children. The youths in Flat Hill Village are getting more and more involved in petty crime. They need more stimulating activities to occupy their time."

"De women 'round here won't want to join no organization," Petal remarked.

"Don't underestimate your neighbours," Arlie said. "There's a whole lot of work to be done. We've got to look at the big picture and break our goals up into meaningful chunks. But first we've got to ask every villager of legal voting age to sign the petition you're holding." Arlie looked directly at Petal, but Petal didn't seem convinced.

"Look, Petal, don't we need better roads, a reliable supply of pipe-borne water, and the removal of the foul-smelling garbage, not to mention the stray dogs and cats, in this area?" Arlie asked.

"Yuh sounding like a politician, and yuh know I don't trust none of dem."

"Let's get serious here. An election is imminent, and that is going to give us some leverage. We've got to forward a petition to our Member of Parliament demanding better road conditions and a reliable water supply."

"I guess we could give it a try," Petal eventually said, but she didn't look convinced.

Later that evening, Petal shared Arlie's plans with Dad.

"You're dead serious?" Dad paused. "You've signed up to be Miss Junior Activist now?"

"I done give her meh word," Petal replied as Dad tried to discourage her from joining the women's organization.

"You barely know that woman," Dad continued, "and you've agreed to join some sham organization just because she promised to help you to get a job?"

Petal left the room without saying anything.

Colm and I got together at least two evenings a week to prepare for the upcoming Spoken Word Competition. Our practice sessions seemed to be going fairly well, until one day when

Colm grimaced right after I'd read one of my pieces. I lowered my head, avoiding eye contact. The truth was, all day long I had been totally obsessed with thoughts of accompanying Petal to the very first women's meeting due to take place at Arlie's house that evening, and my lack of concentration had made me botch my lines. "I'll do better next time," I assured him.

"Don't worry." He patted my shoulder. "We still have lots of time to prepare fer the big event."

Later that evening, Arlie's hair extensions were securely held in place with a white headband that matched her outfit. "Glad you could make it," she said to Petal.

There was no one else on Arlie's lime green porch except us. A brand new iron-framed table and four matching chairs filled up the space; it seemed way smaller than when I'd previously visited.

"You guys are number one," Arlie smiled.

"Yuh know," Petal said, "a lot of dese women going to listen to their silly men and not turn up."

"Even if only a few women come today, I'll share my vision for change with them." Arlie's lips twitched as she led us inside.

"Why didn't you invite the men? Don't men need good roads and water too?" I asked.

"Children speak when someone ask dem a question," Petal said.

"It's fine. Let her speak," Arlie said. "Baby Girl, do you think we should include men in a women's organization?"

I nodded.

"The men are going to feel left out. I think my dad is jealous because he wasn't invited."

"You think?" Arlie giggled, exposing big gums and tiny white teeth.

Dahlia's mother, Mrs. Arlington, arrived next, followed by Suri and Samuel's mother, Meena Ramsingh. Then a bunch of other women trickled in, and soon there were nine people, including me, sitting around Arlie's dining table.

"Can I stay? I promise I'll be quiet," I said after Petal ordered me to join the children who'd gathered behind the house.

"Sure, you can be an honourary member," Arlie said.

At first the women chatted about all sorts of things, including their husbands and their children. But then, Arlie called for their attention. "Ladies," she shouted. "Let us begin our meeting." The chatter stopped completely, and for a few seconds it was so quiet that you could have heard a pin drop.

"Do you mind taking the minutes until we elect a secretary?" Arlie shoved a pad and a pen at Petal.

"I'm sorry I'm late." A big-boned woman I'd never seen before rushed in carrying a sleeping baby. I couldn't help but notice her teeth, which resembled Bugs Bunny's.

"Charmaine," Arlie said, "I can put the baby on the bed."

"Thanks, but she going to be okay right here wit' me." The woman rubbed the child's bald head and tucked her tidily into the crook of her arm.

Soon all eyes were locked on Arlie's face as she explained the benefits that a women's group could bring to the people of Flat Hill Village. She talked to them about all the things she had explained to Petal that day: better roads, reliable access to water, removal of trash, and crime prevention.

"Any questions?" she asked, but the women glanced around the room as if they'd all lost their tongues. After a bit of prodding, however, the room got as noisy as a fish market as the women started to share stories of all the problems they faced in the community. Arlie tried to restore order. "We need to speak one at a time."

The women calmed down, and Meena raised her hand. "We need to choose a name," she said.

The women were animated as they tossed around possible names for their new organization. It didn't take long before Arlie's suggestion, Women's Action Committee, was agreed upon. "We can call ourselves WAC for short," I said with a serious face, but inwardly I was smirking.

"I going to give yuh a whack on yuh head," Petal said.

Someone snickered, and then I felt really silly. I tried to make myself invisible.

"This is our time. This is our moment," Arlie stressed as she presented her vision for change. "We can't do this alone. We need the support of all of the women in this community." She then spoke about power in numbers. "If we are united, we're sure to be a powerful force."

"The water company don't care if we have water to bathe we kids, to wash we clothes, or to cook we food." Dahlia's mother jumped up on one foot, waving a handkerchief.

"Could I say something, please?" Charmaine asked.

"Of course," Arlie replied.

"All of las' week and las' night too, water didn't come in the standpipe till late in the night and meh little sister, Kelly, who move in wit' me after we mother dead, does have to stay up and help tote water after midnight. She does be real tired when she have to get up in the morning fer school, and it not fair to she."

As Charmaine spoke, I was thankful we had four big tanks that filled up whenever water came. I couldn't imagine getting out of my bed in the middle of the night to bring water from the standpipe.

"Some thief break into meh husband car last week, but he don't have no choice but to park in the same dangerous spot," Meena said. "We desperately need the roads widened and paved so we can drive we car right in we yard at night."

Everybody nodded at the same time.

"You wouldn't believe Trinidad have a pitch lake, man, we shouldn't have to suffer like we doing in dis oil-rich nation," Petal said.

"What you planning for the children?" Charmaine muttered. "Is true you planning to form some kinda sports club for them?"

"Yes, I've toyed with that idea, but we'll put that on the agenda at a future meeting," Arlie said. "And ladies, think about what position you'd like to hold in our organization, or maybe you'd like to nominate one of your friends?"

We jumped up, clapping and chanting, "Women of Action, yes, yes, yes." It took about five minutes before everyone settled down again.

11.

ABOUT TWO WEEKS AFTER the women met for the first time at Arlie's house, Dad sat on the edge of my bed and gently patted the mattress. I rose from the chair facing my desk and made my way toward him. He was staring at me as if he hadn't seen me in ages. "How you doing?"

"I'm okay," I said.

"How's the preparation?" Dad said.

"The preparation?"

"For your poetry competition, silly."

"I know my two poems by heart." I sat on the mattress and leaned toward him.

"Good for you!" He paused briefly. "Baby Girl," he paused again, "I've got some news."

"We're not moving again, are we?" I sat up straight and looked him in the eye.

"No, no, we're staying put. The news I have is good." He squeezed my hand, and I giggled.

"Here's the deal," he said, "you have to stay at Monty's house for a week."

"What?" I rose from the bed.

"But Dad," I whined, "I don't want to stay there."

"Please don't act like a baby."

"It's not fair that I have to stay at a stranger's house."

"Look, Baby Girl, Petal and I are going to St. Vincent. We're going to get married there."

"Married?" I sighed. "What about me? Why can't you get married here?"

"It's our special time together. Don't you want your daddy to be happy for once in his life?"

"But why can't I stay here with Colm instead of going over there?"

"Have you thought about what you're asking? We can't leave you alone with him." Dad's voice rose. Then he told me that he and Petal would be leaving in a couple of weeks.

"You always make decisions without telling me," I pouted.

"Please don't make the situation harder than it needs to be. I've already made arrangements with Monty."

When Dad walked out of my room, my hands were clasped and my head was bowed, but I wasn't praying. Images of Vena on the day she picked us up at the airport and the quick stop at Monty's house came back to me. Even though Dad and I had lived in Trinidad for what seemed like forever, I'd only seen Monty a couple of times. Most recently, it was as a guest at his daughter Roxanne's birthday party.

When I'd arrived, Roxanne had been chatting with two friends on the porch. "I need to use the toilet," I'd said to Roxanne's mother, Marnie, as she let me in the house.

"Show Melody where the bathroom is," Marnie said to her daughter.

"She can find it herself," Roxanne had snapped, and continued to chat with her friends. I was stunned because neither my dad nor Petal would have allowed me to get away with anything like that.

After I had used the bathroom and came back into the living room, I watched as Roxanne tapped her two girlfriend's arms and said, "I've got a secret," loud enough for me to hear her. Then, she'd scooted closer to them and whispered something very softly into both their ears. Afterward, the three of them had giggled uncontrollably. I had been sure they were laughing at me, and I'd felt humiliated.

Now, I was worried that when Dad left me there, she would be nasty with me some more, and there'd be no one to protect me.

"Don't let anything distract yuh," Colm whispered, as I sat in front of the house with a long face. The fact that I was due to go to Monty's house the following week was upsetting and I hadn't stopped pouting since Dad had given me the news.

"One week sounds like forever." My voice cracked.

"It is really not a long, long time." Colm peeked above his glasses. "Yuh going to be away fer only seven days and seven nights."

"I wish Dad would let me stay home by myself."

"The time going to come and go before yuh know it," Colm said. "Now, let's get ready for the competition." The day had finally come and the competition was starting at three in the afternoon. We were going to practice a bit before leaving.

Then Petal, Dad, Colm, and I had left home a bit later than originally planned and got caught in a traffic jam. I was in jitters. After all the hard work Colm and I had put in, I didn't want us to be disqualified from the poetry competition because we were late. When we finally got there, I entered the hall alongside Colm, clutching his hand tightly. Petal and Dad made their way into third-row seats while Colm and I continued up the aisle

"Don't worry." Colm glanced at his watch. "We make it just in time."

I peeked at the dirty brown ceiling and then surveyed the stage, fully aware that I'd be standing up there all by myself in less than an hour. Colm led me toward a wooden door and pulled the handle. We entered a tiny room where all the competitors were gathered. Colm nodded at a pretty girl standing in the corner to our right, wearing a red-and-white outfit. She also sported a black-and-white baseball cap. "Who's that?" I asked.

"Alison. We've competed against each other a couple of times before." Colm made his way toward her, leaving me stranded in the middle of the room.

A short, stocky man stepped through the door, clutching a stack of papers. "Good to see so many young faces here," he said in a husky voice. He handed out the program. My heart fluttered when I saw my name listed as the second performer in the under-sixteen category. "Good luck," the stocky man said, and led us out the door. We took our seats in the front row of the packed hall.

"He's Johnny Smiths, and he's the best in the business," Colm whispered as we sat down.

My palms were sticky with sweat. "What if I'm no good?" I said, my hands clenched.

"Yuh going to be fine," he replied.

When Colm was called to the stage, my heart just about jumped out of my throat. It was pounding so loudly that I could hardly hear him. When his performance ended, the crowd erupted in applause. He bowed, shared a sunny smile, and confidently walked off the stage. Loud drums rolled and Johnny Smiths, the master of ceremonies, returned to centre stage. The audience laughed boisterously at his comedy sketch.

Identical twin boys, the first contestants in the under-sixteen category, performed next. Their performance seemed flawless until they bungled the last few lines of their second poem.

"Is almost yuh turn," Colm whispered moments before the master of ceremonies called out my name. Then he mouthed, "Good luck!"

Butterflies fluttered in my stomach. The walk to centre stage was the longest of my life.

Later that evening, I stood beside the master of ceremonies along with the other performers. I couldn't believe I'd won third prize! I stepped forward to collect a cheque for two hundred and fifty dollars.

Colm was declared the joint first-place winner in the over-sixteen category. He shared the honour with Alison, the girl he'd greeted earlier. "I going to collect my laptop and printer first thing on Monday." Colm patted his pants pocket as if to ensure the thousand-dollar cheque and the store voucher he'd been awarded were safely tucked inside it.

I awoke at seven in the morning to the sounds of Petal and Dad's voices, as well as heavy raindrops lashing against the rooftop. I looked out the window and was amazed at the amount of water gushing down the dirt trail. The water had poured into our yard, covering over a third of the gate. I giggled when it crossed my mind that if the rain didn't stop soon, Dad wouldn't be able to take me to Monty's house later that day.

"At least no one going to have to bring water today," Petal said to Dad as water poured from our neighbours' eaves troughs and flowed into their barrels and tanks. I stared at a bunch of children at the top of the hill.

I didn't realize Petal had noticed them too, until she said, "Me and Boyie use to play in de rain when we was small just like dem." Petal bit her nails and her smile faded. It was the first time in a while she'd mentioned Boyie's name, and she appeared to be emotional. She wiped away a few tears that had leaked from the corner of her eyes.

"You need boots as high as your knees to trek through that mud," I said staring at the fast-running water, and then at my father. He sort of half-smiled, but didn't respond.

The heavy downpour turned into a light drizzle and the sun eventually crept out from behind the clouds, attempting to dry the wet earth. "Time to go." My father lifted my suitcase. I held a bag of my clothes in one hand and my backpack filled with schoolbooks in the other.

"Be careful." Petal waved at Dad and me.

Colm rushed forward. "This is fer yuh." He shoved a folded sheet of paper deep inside my pants pocket. Then he closed the gate.

I hesitated before stepping onto the sludgy track that was our roadway. I made my way around a large hole filled with dirty brown water. Mud seeped onto my sneakers, making them look as if they hadn't been cleaned in months. My father, a few steps ahead, shifted my suitcase from one shoulder to the other. He didn't dare pull it on its wheels on the mucky ground. Dad stopped in front of an even bigger crater.

"This is real bad," he said to Mr. Ramsingh, who was inspecting the gaping hole the rain had created. Two other village men were studying the damage as well.

"We going to have to fill it up wit' gravel and stone." Mr. Ramsingh wiped sweat off his brow. All present nodded their heads in agreement.

Dad pulled up in front of Monty's house. "I'm running late," he said, climbing out of his vehicle. "So please speed things up, Baby Girl."

Monty stepped out of his gate and took my suitcase. "What yuh got in here?" He seemed surprised at the weight of the bag.

"Books and clothes," I said.

"She's well prepared for the entire week," Dad said. My father hugged me, but I was sullen and my arms remained at my side.

"I'll bring back something really nice for you if you turn that frown into a smile." Dad showed his dazzling white teeth, then jumped back into the car before I could say anything. He was out of sight by the time I got to the top of the staircase.

"Baby Girl, you're here!" Marnie, Monty's wife, spread her arms wide to greet me.

"You're going to stay wit' us?" Benny said.

"Give Baby Girl a chance to unwind," Marnie said to her children. "She's going to be with us for the entire week."

Monty carried my suitcase into Roxanne's room and placed it next to a bunk bed.

"Make yuhself at home." He walked out the door, leaving me in the pinkest room I'd ever seen in my entire life. It felt surreal.

The curtains, walls, and bed sheets were almost entirely pink, with only a smidgen of white. I was immediately drawn to a collection of dolls, each wearing a sash identifying its country of origin. The dolls, which looked like tiny mannequins, crowded two shelves. I stepped closer, admiring them and wondering how long it had taken Roxanne to collect them. I stretched my arm, preparing to touch a dress made from blue-and-white fabric that a blond doll from Finland was wearing.

"Don't touch them!" Roxanne growled. I looked over my shoulder, stunned she'd been observing my every movement like a security guard.

"I was only looking at them," I said, and then pulled my notebook full of poetry from my backpack and darted out of the bedroom.

Roxanne trailed me as I entered the living room.

"You're settling in?" Marnie asked. I could see she was helping Benny with his homework.

I nodded.

"You need to finish your homework too," Marnie said to Roxanne.

"Oh, Mom!" Roxanne threw herself on the sofa and stuck in a pair of earbuds. "I'll do it later," she said, tapping her feet on the hardwood floor.

"You'll never become a registered nurse like me if you don't take math and science seriously," Marnie warned. For an instant, I stared at Marnie and then at Roxanne, knowing full well that there was no way Dad or Petal would have allowed me to get away with such awful conduct.

I stepped out of the front door and stood on top of the staircase enjoying the light breeze as it stroked my cheeks. A while later, I put my notebook on the bottom staircase and eased onto one of two swings, quietly observing people and cars moving up and down the street. As the swing carried me to and fro, I wished Petal and Dad could have afforded to move to a better neighbourhood where we wouldn't ever have to trek through mud and grime when it rained. I closed my eyes just as a strong gust of wind hit my face. I opened my eyes when Roxanne bellowed, "Get off my swing!"

"You may be taller and bigger than me, but you're a spoiled brat!" I yelled.

"I was here first. You can sit over there." I pointed to the empty swing beside me. For a moment she shifted sideways, but then she stepped closer and blocked my view of the street.

"Don't!" I said as she snatched my arm.

She dragged me forward, and I found myself lying face up on the ground. "Take that!" Roxanne's fist landed on my chin. It hurt a lot; I thought she'd broken my jaw.

"No, don't!" I cried, blocking my face when she raised her fist again.

"What going on out there?" Monty was halfway down the staircase, but Roxanne continued to pound my face with clenched fists.

"What the heck yuh think yuh doing?" Monty said as Roxanne put both hands around my neck and squeezed tighter. I was just about to pass out when Monty dragged his daughter off of me. I coughed, trying to catch my breath.

"You're okay?" Marnie appeared out of nowhere. She picked me up and held me close to her.

For a while, I was unable to speak, but I eventually said, "Yes."

"Yuh cross de line dis time!" Monty grabbed Roxanne's wrist and dragged her up the staircase.

"Monty!" Marnie hollered.

"Hell, no!" He eyed Marnie with a dreadful expression. "She not getting away with dis!" Monty's face was the angriest I'd ever seen it.

Marnie bandaged three cuts, one on my chin, one on my neck, and one on my hand. Then I examined my battered face in the bathroom mirror, gently touching the dressing on my chin, hoping it wouldn't leave a scar as noticeable as the one on my former stepmother's cheek. Then I thought of my father's absence, and my stepsister Clara's taunting words: "Your father's a jailbird, a jailbird, a jailbird." I began to sob but swiftly wiped my eyes since I didn't want Roxanne or Benny to see me crying.

"You're okay?" Marnie seemed concerned as I strode out of the bathroom.

"I'm fine," I said, even though I really wasn't.

I remembered the folded sheet of paper Colm had shoved into my pocket, so I fished it out and silently read a brand-new poem he'd written especially for me.

"I'm working a twelve-hour shift tonight," Marnie announced. An hour later, she backed her car out of the driveway and headed for work.

After dinner, Monty, Benny, and I sat in the living room watching *Deal or No Deal*. I plastered my hand over my eyes when a pretty young female contestant got down to the final two cases.

"Not that one!" Benny yelled as the woman geared up to make her selection. I spread my fingers slightly and peeked through them for barely a second. But I covered them again as the cute model opened her case.

"Oh no!" Benny screamed.

I shifted my hands from my face when Monty said, "She got two hundred and fifty thousand dollars. So, why allyuh complaining?"

The three of us grinned, but my smile evaporated when Roxanne entered the living room.

"Hell, no, I already warn yuh!" Monty hollered at his daughter.

Roxanne darted to her room, and Monty rushed after her. For a while he was shouting and Roxanne was bawling.

"She's getting a good whipping." Benny seemed pleased at what was happening.

Monty marched out of his daughter's room carrying all of my stuff. "Yuh going to sleep in Benny's room tonight."

"In my room?" Benny pouted, but Monty ignored him.

"Come and get yuh nightclothes so de girl can go to bed," Monty said.

After Benny had gathered his possessions, I stretched out on his mattress, grateful that I didn't have to sleep in Roxanne's room that night.

"Yuh going to be late for school." Monty knocked on the bedroom door early the next morning. But I didn't climb out of bed until he pounded on the door again. On my way to the bathroom, I almost knocked over Benny, who was already in his school uniform. I showered and, as I came out of the bathroom, Roxanne brushed past me. She smiled, and I spun around to see if anyone was standing behind me, but no one was in the corridor besides the two of us.

Roxanne and Benny's school was a five-minute drive from their house. My school was a bit farther away, so Monty dropped Roxanne and Benny off first and picked them up before driving east to meet me. I spent most of my free time after school doing homework and writing poetry and the week flew by, as Colm had said it would.

On Sunday morning I got up early. I was excited and relieved that Dad and Petal's flight was due to land within the hour. Dad had promised to drive up to Monty's house before noon to meet me. I sat on Benny's bed clutching my notebook. Then I scanned through the pages. I was extremely proud of my week's work.

At around ten thirty, Marnie called everyone to the breakfast table. But less than five minutes after we'd sat down, Benny started to fuss. "Yuh can't have everything yuh want," Monty yelled at his son.

"Take it easy." Marnie tapped Benny's hand. After breakfast, Marnie invited me to go with her and the kids to her cousin's place. She suggested I put all of my stuff in her car, and she'd have my Dad pick me up there.

"I'd rather stay here and wait for Dad." I settled onto the

porch and watched the passing cars. A while later Monty called me to the telephone.

"Honey, my flight's getting in much later than expected." Dad explained that he wouldn't be able to pick me up before eight o'clock that evening.

"You might as well come along with the kids and me," Marnie suggested. "No point in sitting here and doing nothing."

"Okay," I said, and headed to the bedroom to get dressed. But as soon as I entered Benny's room, I realized that my notebook was not on the bed where I'd left it earlier. I dumped my clothes and books on the floor and carefully searched through each item. Then I got down on all fours and scanned under Benny's bed. But only a few pieces of a jigsaw puzzle, a screwdriver, and a tiny flashlight lay beneath it.

"You're not coming?" Marnie poked her head in.

"I'm looking for something," I said.

"For what?"

"My book of poems is gone." My eyes welled with tears.

"It couldn't have just vanished. Maybe you put it in one of your bags."

"No, I'm sure I left it right there." I pointed to the bed.

"What's the commotion going on here?" Monty appeared at the door.

"I can't find my book with all the poems I've written."

"I'll take care of this," Monty said.

"Where's Baby Girl's book?" he asked his kids.

"They probably haven't even seen it," Marnie answered.

"You're their lawyer?" Monty said. "Dey got tongues. Let dem speak for demselves."

"Where's de book?" Monty turned to Benny and then Roxanne, but they both shrugged and denied having touched it.

"I going to get to de bottom of dis," Monty told the kids. "I'm going to turn dis place upside down. Allyuh better tell me where it is before allyuh regret it!"

Despite Monty's threats, Roxanne and Benny continued to

deny taking my book. A while later, Marnie rushed out of the house with her children, leaving Monty and me behind.

Even after several hours had passed, I still couldn't find my notebook. I sat on the porch as still as a mannequin, hoping Dad would come to meet me before Marnie and the kids returned. I tried to recite some of my newer poems, but it was hard to concentrate. Then I tried to write them out in one of my school exercise books, but I couldn't remember most of the words.

"You're happy I'm home?" My father swallowed me in his arms and gently rocked me.

"I'm really happy, Dad." I craned my neck to look at his face. We shared an enormous grin, but he completely ignored the bandage on my chin. Then I settled on the sofa and watched *Jeopardy* while he spoke to Monty.

"We've got to get going. Baby Girl's got school in the morning," Dad said after he'd chugged down the two beers Monty had given him. Just as we stepped through the front door, Marnie's car pulled up and she parked next to Dad's vehicle. I secretly wished Dad hadn't stayed back to drink beers and to chat.

Marnie embraced me, almost squeezing the air out of my body. When she eased off, I clumsily stepped back and found myself next to Roxanne.

"Bye, Baby Girl." Roxanne's voice was stuck deep down in her throat. She awkwardly pressed her lips together and offered a faint wave. Then she moved forward, hurrying up the staircase.

"Goodbye." Benny used his full lung capacity.

I climbed into Dad's car, and he shut the door. "Monty phoned me." Dad gently touched my hand and my chin. "He told me everything. Is it hurting?"

"It's nothing." I shifted his hand from my face. I didn't want to discuss the details about my clash with Roxanne. I was a little embarrassed I hadn't been better able to defend myself.

"Did Monty tell you what happened to my poetry book?"

"No." Dad paused. "What?"

"It went missing." My voice dropped and I lowered my head, wiping the tears that had begun to cloud my eyes.

"Did you find it?"

"No! Roxanne or Benny might have destroyed it."

"You think?"

"Monty threatened them, but they didn't admit it."

"I'm sorry your week ended like that, but you're a smart kid, you can rewrite them." My father looked at his watch. "It's late. We've got to get going."

"This is serious, Dad. I can't remember them all. I can't remember all the words of the new ones." I was dying for more sympathy from him, but I wasn't surprised since he'd never shown any real interest in my work.

"Don't worry, you'll be all right," he said, turning up the music.

Dad parked in his usual spot. I climbed out of the car and trudged along the trail, walking slightly ahead of him. I entered our house and headed straight to Colm's bedroom. I knocked, but there was no answer.

"He gone over to his mother house, but he coming back to-morrow," Petal said. I kept my head low, trying to hide my face.

"What happen?" Petal kept a steady gaze.

"My poetry book is gone," I said, sharing the details.

"You got to keep a back-up copy of everything from now on, and you can use my laptop whenever you want," Colm said the next day when I told him about my missing poetry book.

Colm bought me a new notebook, but, as the days went by, I often wondered whether it had been Benny or Roxanne who had taken my book. I didn't have any answers.

12.

"YUH BETTER KEEP YUH MOUTH shut when de meeting start," Petal said as we arrived at Arlie's house.

"The girl can speak if she's got something meaningful to contribute," Arlie grinned.

Arlie counted heads. "This is a really big improvement." Some women were sitting while others were standing and chatting noisily about their men and their children. "Bring in some of the folding chairs," Arlie ordered Dante. Petal asked me to help, so I followed Dante behind the house.

As soon as we put one chair down, someone immediately shuffled toward it, and despite bringing in ten, there still weren't enough, so we lugged eight more chairs inside the house.

Arlie addressed the women. "I forwarded our signed petition to the relevant authorities, but so far we've had no response from anyone." But before she could start her next sentence, a voice drowned out hers. All eyes shifted to the speaker, a woman in a buttoned-up shirt, her hair neatly wrapped in a fancy, two-toned headscarf. She stood up and in a gruff tone said, "You sure the minister get the letter?" I'd never seen her before, but I learned later that she'd moved into Flat Hill Village during the week I'd spent at Monty's house.

"Of course, I took it to the M.P.'s office myself," Arlie explained. "He and I had a brief discussion, and then he took the petition. He assured me that we'd have a speedy response. But no one has written or phoned yet."

"They is a bunch of bastards. After they get we vote, they not doing nothing for none of we. My husband and the other men tried to fix the big hole in front we house, but every time rain fall the hole does open up again. Next time, I voting for the opposition," Meena Ramsingh said.

Arlie stood up. "I understand your frustration, and that's why I think the time has come for a public protest. We've got to ask everyone in this village to join us on this one. We've got to mobilize our young men and women."

"The older men and women too." Dahlia's mother, Mrs. Arlington, jumped up from her seat and made a fist. She briefly hopped on the spot. "Some of we older people have a lot of pep in we step." I thought she looked funny, but most of the women cheered.

"I not going on no street wit' no placard in meh hand." Sandra, a top-heavy woman, pursed her lips and folded her arms.

"We got to fight for what we want. No one going to give we nothing for nothing!" Meena Ramsingh shouted at Sandra. The women started bickering; it was an uneven match as they all ganged up on Sandra.

"I going!" Sandra said. "I don't want no part of this," she added vehemently.

All eyes followed her as she bolted toward the door. I was keyed up. I wanted to run behind her and tell her to come back, but I knew better than to move or speak. Petal stood up and clapped, slowly at first and then faster, and, one by one, the other women stood up and began to clap too.

"We trust yuh, Arlie!" Petal exclaimed. "We trust yuh to lead we!"

"Yes! Yes! Yes!" a tall, bony woman shouted in a squeaky voice.

"We can't do this alone. Every villager has to be a team member." Arlie spoke like a preacher. The women applauded. They seemed livelier than I'd ever seen them before. I couldn't stop myself from joining in and I also applauded as loud as I could.

"Have any of you participated in a protest before?" Arlie eyes covered the room, but no one said a word. "I'll tell you a story," she began. "I was eighteen and in my first year at U.W.I. when I got involved in my very first protest. In my final year, a group of my colleagues and I protested again. We were arrested on campus, but all charges were eventually dropped. The police tried to intimidate us, but we didn't allow them to scare us. We had more than a few valid reasons to complain about what those in power were doing, and now we the people of Flat Hill Village have got valid reasons to protest again."

I wanted to hear the details, but Dahlia's mother butted in. "Let we put it to a vote," she said. I didn't see any need for that, but the vote went ahead, and, as expected, everyone in the room voted yes.

"We've got to gauge the public's opinion before formally detailing our plans," Arlie said.

The women agreed to hold an open-air meeting at a place called Flatlands, and to invite all the villagers, including the men.

"Where's Flatlands?" I asked Petal after the meeting.

"Right here in Flat Hill Village," she said, "but way up on top of de hill."

Petal invited Dad to the meeting, but he wasn't interested. I was at a complete loss as to why, since he was one of the most outspoken critics of the muddy, pothole-ridden track. He was usually among the first to help fill in the gaping holes that always appeared after the torrential rains. One day when I asked Dad if he wanted the group to include men, he laughed. "What do you think?" was his response. But when Petal invited Colm to the Flatlands meeting, he eagerly agreed. "I going to design a bunch of flyers," Colm said, and he didn't object when I asked him if I could help him to deliver them.

"I'm sure everyone knows about the meeting already," I said

to Colm just before we left home one Saturday morning to distribute the flyers to the villagers.

"Maybe they do, maybe not." Colm's smile shone through the tired lines on his face and the dark outlines underneath his eyes. He had been sick the day before, but still insisted on personally distributing the leaflets to the villagers. When we got halfway up the hill, I stood still and admired the breathtaking view of the water in the distance.

"It nice, isn't it? Yuh going to get a better view from this spot." Colm motioned me to step closer to him.

"It's really nice up here. If only the roads were better."

"And if only the people up here didn't have to walk so far to get water," Colm cut in. I nodded, agreeing with him one hundred percent.

By the time we approached a tiny wooden house near the top of the hill, our bundle of flyers had dwindled by half. "Anybody there?" Colm shouted.

A woman poked her head out of the upper portion of a wooden door that had been sliced horizontally down the middle. The top half was tightly held in place by a piece of wire fastened onto a thick nail. "We not interested in whatever yuh selling," the woman sneered, leaning forward and resting her elbows on the bottom half of the door.

"I not selling anything, but I have a flyer to give yuh regarding the upcoming village meeting." Colm stepped closer to her.

Suddenly the bottom half of the door flew open and a very short, strongly built man brushed past the woman like a bolt of lightning. "Damn you people! We not interested!" The man spun around in circles. The unravelled edges of his khaki shorts flapped about as he bounced up and down like a madman. He picked up a long, dry branch from the ground that made a swishing sound as he brandished it at us.

"Let's go!" Colm's fingers fluttered nervously as he jumped in front of me like a bodyguard. "Walk ahead!" he said, turning to push me forward.

"What's wrong with him?" I kept looking back at the man's strange antics.

"Speed up!" Colm yelled as the man threw a large stone at us. "That fella's a shitting idiot wit' a big ego, and nothing else to back it," Colm said as we made our way to the next house.

"He didn't have to pelt us," I said.

"There're a lot more like him around, I'm afraid." Colm touched my arm. "Yuh okay? Wanna go home?"

"No, we're almost done," I said. "Let's hand out the rest of them." We slowed down in front of a blue house bordered by a patched-up fence. "Good morning," I called out in my loudest voice.

"Anybody home?" Colm hollered.

Just then, a powerful wind rustled the surrounding trees and their broad branches swayed over our heads. At the same time, a pack of dogs barked in the distance.

"Somebody inside. They just shift the curtain," Colm said, releasing a flyer over the wire fence.

"Why's everyone so unfriendly all of a sudden?" I said as we walked away.

Colm shrugged. "Yuh win some and yuh lose some."

Having trekked up the small mountain, past houses built on the rugged land surrounded by large trees and thick bushes, it felt weird to suddenly arrive on a perfectly flat piece of land that was bare of houses or trees of any kind.

"This is the place they call Flatlands, where the village meeting going to take place." Colm closed his eyes and took a deep breath as if something wonderful in the air had taken control of him.

Two weeks later, I strode up the hillside alongside Colm and Petal. Our neighbour, Shiva Ramsingh, his wife, Meena, and their two children, Suri and Samuel, walked slightly ahead of us. Other villagers were in front of them, while hordes of people followed us. Climbing up didn't seem as daunting as when I'd gone up there with Colm to deliver the flyers. When we arrived at Flatlands, it felt awfully familiar. Arlie, dressed in a bright red pantsuit, stood out from among the twenty or so women mingling close to her.

"A lotta men here!" Petal smiled at Colm before making her way toward Arlie, who was greeting the early arrivals with a firm handshake. Arlie's children, Dante and Carrie, followed their mother. Dante darted toward me and Carrie stuck to him as if she were his shadow.

"How long is this meeting going to last?" Carrie asked Dante with a long face.

"An hour, I think," Dante said.

My eyes searched for Petal, and I found her among the committee members who'd gathered in one spot. They were all dressed in white outfits and blended together like the members of a church choir.

"People," Arlie said, clapping her hands loudly, "it's time to begin." She then detailed the reasons she thought each villager ought to get involved.

"The police should put a *bull-pistle* on allyuh!" a man wearing a baseball cap and a button-down shirt yelled just as Arlie opened the floor to questions.

"They should lock allyuh arse up!" he bellowed. "They should put allyuh in a damn cell and throwway the blasted key!"

"Is him," Colm mouthed.

I nodded, fully aware that it was the same man who'd brandished the stick and thrown the stone at us while we were delivering the flyers.

"Go away!" someone with a throaty voice yelled.

I wished that speaker, who I hoped was as big and as strong as his voice, would step out of the crowd, punch the mischief-maker and make him shut up.

"Keep quiet!" others in the crowd yelled at the man.

Arlie didn't lose her cool, despite the foul language spilling out of the man's mouth. Instead, she raised her voice above his.

"We can't hear you, Arlie!" people shouted.

"I wish my dad were here," I said to Colm.

Shiva and a group of about six men surrounded the mis-chief-maker. "We don't want no trouble," Shiva said in a low voice.

"Is a peaceful meeting we having," he added.

"Jesus Christ, allyuh move outta meh blasted way!" The man barged through the human barricade and hustled down the hill.

Arlie then raised her fist above her head. "We have to be a united force to get what we want." She paused and scanned the crowd. "People, do you agree with me?"

"Yes!" the women's group roared.

A female voice rose above everyone else's. "I wit' you one hundred percent."

"We've got some organizing to do," Arlie said. "If anyone wants to volunteer, please see me at the end of the meeting."

"Why do we need all of this planning? Why can't we just make some posters and start the protest right now?" I asked Colm on the way home.

"It don't ever pay to be in a rush," he said.

About a week later, Colm waved a placard high in the air. I read the words written in thick blue letters out loud. "*We need water to wash up we arse.*"

"Shh," Colm said, placing his index finger over his lips.

"Do they all have the same words?" I asked as he positioned the placard on top of a bunch of others.

"No, each one is unique."

"Can I make up my own placard?"

"Yep, but you gotta finish yuh homework first."

"I don't have any homework," I said as he dragged a card-board box from a stack beneath the house and sliced the bottom out with a pocketknife.

"Yuh sure about that?"

"I swear."

"Okay, go and change and then we can talk."

I hustled into the house, slipped off my school uniform, pulled on some shorts, and rushed back outside.

We made a bunch more posters, and I felt tired from the effort. I climbed into bed after dinner and immediately fell asleep, but awoke around midnight when Moxley and Spider began howling.

"Somebody going to dead." Petal's voice carried from the living room.

"You believe that crap?" Dad teased. "You can't be that superstitious."

"You wait an' see," Petal said. "In dis place when dog start howling is a sure sign we going to a funeral."

"I can't sleep," I said to Petal as I snuck to the living room.

Just then, Dad opened the back door. "Keep quiet!" he yelled at the dogs.

"We got a long day at the demonstration tomorrow," Petal said to me as the dogs finally quieted down.

"Long day?" Dad came toward us. "You didn't ask my permission," he said, staring at me with a blank face. "And, as far as I'm concerned, you're not missing school for that kind of nonsense."

"Why yuh being so hard?" Petal said. "She really looking forward to it just like everybody else."

"The only thing Baby Girl needs to look forward to is the eleven-plus examination."

"But Dad!" I said.

"It's already midnight," he said, "you'd better get back to bed."

The following morning, Dad's voice was even louder than the steady thump, thump his fist made on my bedroom door. "You're going to school as usual today," he said, standing over me with a stern expression.

"It's just one day of school I'll miss. Please, Dad, please," I whined, climbing out of bed and clutching his wrist.

"Your education is more important than holding up a placard on the street. You're not going to be a part of this silly game that Arlie is encouraging the people of Flat Hill Village to engage in."

"But, Dad!"

"Aren't you supposed to be writing your eleven-plus exam in a few months?"

"Suri and Dante are writing exams too, and their parents didn't tell them they couldn't go!"

"If Suri or Dante jumped off a bridge, would you follow them?" Dad said. "Now, you answer me."

"Why are you being so mean?" I cried.

"As matter of fact, I'm going to drive you to school myself today so be ready by eight."

I buried my face in my hands and sobbed.

"You okay?" Petal asked as my sad eyes locked onto hers, but I didn't say anything.

"I real sorry," she continued. "I tried to get him to change his mind but yuh dad more stubborn dan a mule sometimes."

I changed into my school uniform and then trudged outside and stood on the porch. I observed villager after villager entering and exiting Arlie's yard to collect their placards.

"I real sorry, but he's yuh dad." Petal shrugged before making her way down the staircase.

"I going to give yuh a ball by ball commentary of everything." Colm winked, and then shut the gate.

The traffic of people heading down the trail continued for a while, but soon the neighbourhood became a ghost town.

"Time to go," Dad said.

"It isn't even quarter to eight," I said. "I haven't eaten yet."

"Hurry up," he said, as I shovelled down a bowl of raisin bran.

At exactly eight, I followed Dad down the rugged path. We

slipped past an overflowing dumpster and a mangy, brown mutt that was rummaging through the garbage. For the first time in months, memories of the day Dad had brought me to Flat Hill Village came to my mind and a pity party set in. I thought of the twins, convinced they had forgotten about me. Several months had gone by without any contact from either of them. I felt as worthless as a weed that had been plucked out of the ground and discarded.

"We'll never forget you," Lena and Harley had said on their last day of school, just moments before we'd parted.

Yeah, right. I knew for sure they'd dumped me just like everyone else had. I was still a few feet away from the spot where Dad usually parked his car and I should have been able to see his vehicle, but I couldn't. I smirked, hoping my father would get as upset as I was.

"For Christ's sake, hurry up!" Dad was more than a few steps ahead; he gave me a hard look, but I walked even slower.

"Hurry up!" he repeated. "We've got to get to the car on Cuthbert Lane."

"We've got to walk so far?" I pouted, but when we got to the bottom of the hill my face lit up as a sea of white blouses, skirts, dresses, pants, multicoloured flags, and placards of all shapes and sizes greeted us. The group of fifty or so protesters included Dante, Carrie, Suri, and Samuel. I was still a few paces behind my father when I got a clear view of the old pieces of wood, buckets, barrels, bricks, branches, and scraps of iron that completely blocked the roadway to vehicular traffic. It suddenly clicked that Dad must have anticipated the makeshift barricade, and that was why he'd parked on Cuthbert Lane.

"We need water!" Arlie chanted her own made up tune. Then the crowd shouted, "We need good roads too!"

Petal stood alongside Arlie with a big white flag hoisted on top of a rough bamboo pole. *Women's Action Committee* was printed on the flag in big black-and-red letters. Just then, several young men picked up pieces of iron and started a rhythm section. Petal waved the flag with the gusto of a flag woman leading a steel orchestra. A blue Toyota Camry sped toward the protesters but screeched to a halt a few inches short of the makeshift barricade.

"You is a madman or what!" Shiva shouted at the driver.

"It illegal what allyuh idiots doing!" The driver stuck his shiny bald head out the window. Then he reversed and sped away. In next to no time a stream of vehicles made their way toward the barricade, but none of those drivers shouted or screamed at the protesters. Instead, the drivers quietly made a U turn and drove off in the direction from which they had come. I waved frantically, trying to catch Dante and Petal's attention. When they saw me, they waved back energetically. Dante's smile spread from the left side of his face to the right.

"Come on. Let's get out of here!" Dad was at least ten foot-steps ahead. He eyed me like an angry bull; I kept my mouth shut and did as I was told.

13.

I STOOPED FOR A WHILE and then stood up again. I shifted my weight from my left foot to my right, and then I leaned against the brick wall. Ten minutes became twenty and twenty minutes became thirty. Soon I was the lone student in front of the school waiting for a lift home. Could something have happened to my driver, Mr. Wellington? I nervously glanced at my watch. Several minutes later, Dad's car pulled up. "How was your day?" he asked in a tone that was almost too friendly.

He opened the front door and, as I climbed in, he touched my shoulder lightly and grinned. "You're awfully quiet today. You're sure you're okay?" He seemed concerned, but I wasn't in a forgiving mood just yet, so I wiggled away. "Ah, well, I see you're still angry with your daddy," he sighed, positioning both hands on the steering wheel.

Dad's car flew past the spot where the protesters had gathered earlier that morning, but the only evidence left was bits and pieces of trash. He drove up the incline and parked, but remained in his vehicle. "I've got some stuff to take care of," he said as I climbed out of the car. Then he made a U-turn and sped off. I trotted up the rugged path, and the *thud, thud* sound my heart made seemed to get louder with each step.

"Hey you!" yelled one of troublemakers hanging out in front of the abandoned house. I kept my eyes ahead and walked even faster. Soon a joyful feeling came over me and my imagination went wild. My chest rose and fell as I pictured the twins, Lena and Harley, at my heels, trying to catch me. My fingers hooked onto the gate like claws and I tipped forward, gasping for breath. Petal didn't seem to notice me as she chatted with an unfamiliar woman standing on Arlie's side of the fence. "Hi, Petal," I said as I caught my breath.

"This is Leila, Arlie's younger sister," Petal said, slightly turning her neck. Leila smiled at me, and then both women continued their conversation.

I rushed into the house and pounded on Colm's bedroom door. "Colm, are you in your room?" I asked.

"We going to talk later," he eventually said but he didn't sound like his jovial self.

Just then the phone rang. I stuck it to my ear, and a woman in a nervous voice asked, "Is Colm there?"

"Yes, he is," I replied.

"Tell him his mother wants to talk to him."

"What now?" he asked as I knocked his door.

"Your mom's on the phone."

"My mother?" he stuck his head out the door.

"Take it easy, Mom. I'm doing fine. I've got to go. I'll talk to you tomorrow." He hastily hung up. "Don't look at my leg with so much pity. I not dying. It's nothing to worry 'bout," Colm limped toward the sofa.

"What happened?" I asked as he propped up his leg on a soft cushion.

"A beer bottle did this to me." He touched his foot, which was wrapped in a thick white bandage.

"That must really hurt!" I made a face as if I were the one with the injury.

"Not too much," he said. "But my mother is really upset."

"When did it happen?" I asked, closely inspecting his bandaged leg.

"Where else but during the protest," he shrugged. I lowered myself onto the sofa and patted his shoulder sympathetically.

"Yuh want to hear the rest of the story?" he asked, already sounding like his old, perkier self.

"Yeah."

"Quietly, almost sneakily, a crazy driver sped up on the crowd. He jumped out of his car, threw a bottle and it hit me on my ankle before I could dash for cover."

"Stop playing games and tell me the real story!" I climbed off the sofa.

"I not making this up," he said. "Sit down and keep quiet if yuh want to hear the rest of it."

"Okay." I immediately sat down again.

"No one else get hurt, but when the police arrive, it was a different story. The cops said our protest was illegal. The whole thing get outta hand, and they end up arresting Arlie."

"They arrested her?" My jaws froze half open as Petal walked in.

"Two policemen manhandle she and dey slap handcuffs on she hand as if she was a common criminal. Then dey throw she in de back of de police car an' threaten to arrest de rest of we if we didn't move de barricade immediately." Petal shook her head.

"What happened to the man who threw the bottle?"

"The police have him in custody too," Colm said. "The camera captured the whole thing as it was unfolding."

"The camera?"

"Yep, believe it or not, a television camera. I swear to Gawd we going to make de news tonight," Petal said. "Is a good thing de cameraman reach real early."

"Really?" I kept my eyes on Colm, waiting for him to confirm, but he simply shrugged.

Later that evening, I sat in front of the television eating popcorn with Colm, Dad, and Petal.

"If yuh don't fight for yuh rights, yuh don't get no respec'." Petal's upbeat voice filled the room.

"You're getting as feisty as Arlie," Dad said.

I couldn't recall a prior occasion when the four of us had gathered in front of the television eagerly awaiting the evening news. A curly-haired man wearing a dark suit appeared on the screen. He immediately shared details of the prime minister's trip to China.

"He taking we money and travelling all over the world while de small man suffering," Petal huffed.

A news clip featuring the leader of the opposition criticizing the government for wasting taxpayers' money came on next, but of course, he expressed himself much more eloquently than Petal had minutes before. Then the newscaster interviewed a bunch of people regarding the upcoming Tobago House of Assembly elections. I got lost halfway through their question-and-answer session.

"Maybe dey not going to show it because dey don't think we poor people important," Petal said twenty minutes into the hour-long news program.

Bored, I climbed out of my seat to get a drink.

"There's Arlie!" Colm yelled just then, pointing excitedly at the screen. "She standing next to me! Look!"

I made a mad dash to reclaim my seat.

"Take it easy," Colm said, grabbing his injured leg protectively.

"You guys sure did it today," Dad said as we watched two officers slap a pair of handcuffs on Arlie's wrists.

"It real advantageous for two big men to arrest a little woman like Arlie," Petal said. "Now de entire country seeing how dey treat we."

A life insurance commercial flashed on the screen after that so I decided to make my way out to the porch so I could peek at Arlie's brightly lit house.

"Geesan ages!" Petal yelled. "Dat looking like Boyie!"

While rushing back to the living room to look at the television, I tripped, but luckily Dad jumped up from his seat and grabbed me.

"Do you know where this man is?" the newscaster said. "See the details after the break."

"It looks like a mug shot," Dad said during a mosquito repellant commercial.

"Is one of Boyie high school photo dey just show we," Petal corrected my father.

"Mr. Boyie," Dad said, "what are you up to now?"

"Have you seen this man?" The newscaster addressed his viewers as Boyie's photo popped up on the television monitor again.

"Do yuh know her?" Colm asked Petal as the camera zoomed in on a photo of a woman the newscaster identified as Bertha.

"I never see she before," Petal replied.

"Do you want to speak on behalf of your daughter?"

The news reporter then stuck his microphone in front of an older lady he identified as Bertha's mother.

The woman took a deep breath and began: "My daughter Bertha and she boyfriend Boyie was home last night when two masked men force their way inside the house. My daughter hear when the dogs start to bark, but the dogs does always bark when people on the street walk real close to the fence, so she didn't pay no special attention to them. Boyie wasn't feeling well, and that is why he was in bed so early. Bertha was in the living room watching a movie when she hear a loud bang, but she thought the boys and them on the street were bussing bamboo. But then, two men wit' big long guns burst through the door. One of them rough she up and make she keep she head low. The second gunman rush along the corridor and went inside the bedroom an' force Boyie outta the house. I reach home 'round nine-thirty and find Bertha tied up wit' cloth stuff inside she mouth, and tape across she lips. The bandits and them tie she up real tight wit' piece of she father electrical cord. Thank Gawd she still alive. Oh, good Lord, I coulda come home and meet meh daughter dead." The woman then looked skyward and stuck her arms in the air. "Thank Gawd meh grandson wasn't home at the time," she added.

"It's South Trinidad he's been all this time?" Dad said as a video of the house Boyie had been taken from flashed in front of us. Petal gasped as a close-up shot of a bloodstained sheet appeared on the screen.

"You believe that?" Dad's eyes grew bigger than mine.

Then the phone rang and Petal rushed to answer it.

"You live by the sword, and you die by the sword," Dad said to Colm, but Colm kept his mouth shut.

Petal was a bundle of nerves as she put the caller on hold. "Smokey, de news didn't say nobody dead," she said, making her way to the bedroom with the phone stuck to her ear.

"Yep, that's Boyie for you. I guess the next thing they're going to want is a ransom from somebody," Dad said calmly.

"The amount of kidnapping in this country real scary," Colm added. "But I don't understand what Boyie have that anybody might want."

"Exactly!" Dad exclaimed. "Maybe he was involved in banditry. He was surely living a fast life. Everything done in the dark eventually comes to light."

The news ended and a movie came on, but nobody paid attention to it. I remained on the sofa, my lips sealed, and turning my head from left to right, depending on whether Dad or Colm was speaking. *Please keep your mouth shut, Dad,* I thought, uneasy about the negative words spilling out of his mouth. *Boyie's still Petal's brother,*

"We got to do something," Petal said as she walked out of the bedroom in tears.

Dad led Petal to the sofa with his arms around her waist. "There isn't much we can do, except wait for the police to investigate."

The phone rang constantly that evening, and sleep didn't come easily. But after falling asleep, I dreamed that Boyie had returned to Flat Hill Village and told Dad about the day I'd gone to Paradise Land against his wishes. Dad got very angry and grounded me for a whole month.

"Is too much to deal wit'." Petal's was the first voice I heard the following morning.

"Take it easy," Dad said.

I scrambled out of bed when it hit me that Boyie was still missing and I wasn't facing punishment. *Did Boyie plan his own disappearance? Was he an innocent victim? Or could bandits have already killed him?* I asked myself these questions while taking an early morning shower.

Later that morning, Petal sat on the sofa with her eyes shut. She hugged herself tightly and, with her feet firmly on the ground, she became like a stone, except for her twitching lips. In silence I focused on the lines on her forehead, which seemed to have appeared overnight. In the early afternoon, her energy returned and she picked up the broom and swept every nook and cranny as if the house hadn't been cleaned in months.

14.

D AD SAT AT THE DINING TABLE, skimming a magazine.
"That smells real nice." He lifted his eyes off the page
as Petal made her way toward him with a bowl of
steaming chicken soup. He dug in, swallowing one mouthful
after another. When he was done, he dropped the dish, empty
except for a few picked-clean pieces of bone, in the kitchen
sink. "We've got to get going," he said to Petal as he strode
out of the kitchen.

"I coming!" Petal's voice carried from the bedroom. But it
was more than ten minutes before she appeared in the living
room wearing a black skirt and white blouse, her hair piled
up on top of her head. "I ready," she said.

"You're going out?" I said.

"Yep," Dad replied, "but we'll be back early. Finish your
homework and listen to Colm."

"Don't mess up the living room. I just finish cleaning." Petal
followed Dad out the door, teetering on her high heels.

I waited until they were out of earshot before asking Colm
if he knew where they were going. He shrugged. "I swear they
didn't say anything."

I was almost asleep when I heard Petal's voice. They had just
returned and it sounded like they were in the kitchen. "Imagine, a damn twenty-four-year-old pissin' tail woman with a
two-year-old child was living with my teenage brother in she

134

mother house." The loudness of her voice wiped all traces of sleep from my eyes.

"She knows a lot more than she's letting on. I can sense it," Dad said.

"Shame on she mother. She shoulda never let Boyie sleep in she house wit' she daughter." Petal lowered her voice, but, in the stillness, I heard her say, "Smokey, what you really think happen to Boyie?"

"Pets, I really don't know, but somebody's going to talk," Dad said. "This puzzle is going to get solved. And it's going to happen real soon. I can feel it in my bones."

Then I dozed off.

The following morning, Petal mixed some flour with baking powder, butter, and water before sprinkling a pinch of salt and a bit of sugar into the mixture. She then rolled the dough into small balls before flattening and deep-frying them in hot oil. "Yuh know it ready when it look golden-brown." she said when she saw me standing at the door.

Petal pierced the bakes with a fork and tapped them one by one on the edge of the frying pan, allowing the excess oil to drip back into the pan. She put a paper napkin at the bottom of a big white container and stacked them one on top of the other. Then she scooped up several spoonfuls of scrambled eggs from another pan and dropped a fair amount of eggs, as well as two bakes, on three separate plates.

"Here." She handed me a plate and positioned another in front of Colm, who had already pulled out a chair and sat down at the table.

"Umm, these real good." He made a strange sound, somewhat like a dog. "They're almost as good as my mother's. Can I have some more?"

"Help yourself," Petal said as she fried two eggs for Dad.

"Smokey, come and eat!" she called out, placing Dad's breakfast on the table.

"I'm taking a call!" Dad shouted back.

"I not waiting for Smokey, nah," Petal said. "I going to eat before you swallow everything in dis kitchen." She smiled at Colm, who was already halfway through his second serving.

"Yuh okay?" Colm asked as Petal's smile vanished.

"Smokey and me talk to Bertha and de police 'bout Boyie last night."

"Yuh found out anything?"

"The police and dem don't know nothing, and Bertha don't know nothing either," Petal said. "Only three months Boyie was livin' wit' Bertha when dem bandits kidnap him. It real strange dat not even de police could tell we where he was staying before he move in wit' she."

"Really?" Colm dropped his fork on his empty plate and wiped his mouth with a tissue.

"Yesterday Bertha tell Smokey and me dat Boyie never tell she he had a sister. You believe dat?" Petal inhaled. "If Bertha had any common sense, she woulda look for a man who could give she some stability."

"A stable man like me?" Dad stepped into the kitchen with a humungous smile, pulling out a chair next to Petal. He sat down and put his arm around her shoulders, but Petal was having none of it.

"Smokey, dis not a joke, nah." Petal eyed Dad with a long face.

Soon the village became rife with talk about Dad and Petal's conversations with Bertha and the law officers. Petal couldn't blame Colm, Dad, or me for spreading the news, because shortly after discussing the details at the breakfast table, she'd phoned Meena and Arlie and told them too.

"When de youths going to stop killin' one another?" Petal stared at the front page of the *Trinidad Express* newspaper several days later. The agony in her voice was as real as the tears spilling down her cheeks. The headline, in big, bold letters, read: "The Murder Spree Continues: Six Murders in Twenty-Four Hours."

"Dey kill a sixteen-year-old schoolboy not far from here last night. Dey riddle he body wit' bullet after bullet," Petal breathed. "He was a basketball player and he use to sing in the church choir." Then, all of a sudden, as if paying respect to the six dead youths, she fell silent and wiped her eyes.

"Is bad news added on to more bad news," Colm said later. Then he added, "One of the youths they kill is Meena's brother's eldest son."

"What?" Petal's eyes widened.

"He was in the wrong place at the wrong time," Colm said. "He wasn't in a gang or nothing. The bandits grabbed his cell phone, and he made a mistake and challenged them. They got mad, pulled out a gun and shoot his brains out." Colm spoke with as much emotion as if he'd been acquainted with the murdered young man.

"This is ridiculous," Dad said. "Now they're killing people for a cell phone!"

"It's a real crazy feeling I sometimes get when I think about some of the things the youths my age are doing," Colm said.

"De illegal weapons in dey hand does make dem feel like dey have de power of de Almighty," Petal said.

"How these weapons getting into this country? I want somebody to tell me," Colm said and looked at Dad.

"Some businessmen, some crooked police officers, and some high-ranking officials are responsible," Dad said with the conviction of someone privy to inside information.

Even though Boyie had been missing for just over two weeks, none of the detectives assigned to his case had any news to share. Petal couldn't stop cleaning an already shiny house and almost all discussions regarding the demonstration and the Women's Committee had stopped. Instead, theories about what might have happened to Boyie flowed from our neighbours' tongues.

"They buried Boyie's body in a shallow grave in Moruga," Dante told me when I arrived home from school the next day.

"Who said that?" I stood as still as an ice block, waiting for him to share the details.

"It really happened." He tried to convince me, but he was unable to back up his story with hard facts.

"You made it all up!" I yelled.

"I did not!" he insisted.

"Petal's going to get very angry," I warned him.

When I got inside, Petal was curled up on the sofa with one leg on top of the other. For a moment I thought maybe Dante had gotten the story correct. But when Petal looked up at me and sort of smiled, I knew it couldn't be true

As the weeks passed, the widespread gossip regarding Boyie's whereabouts continued non-stop, with alleged sightings of him all over the country. "My cousin say somebody see Boyie in Plymouth, Tobago, driving a Blue Mazda," a lady said to Dad one day while he and I were walking past the standpipe.

"Tell them to call the police," Dad replied bluntly.

Eventually, even I became aware that everyone who'd shared information about an alleged Boyie sighting always referred to a vague "a man" or " woman" who had firsthand knowledge. No one called any of these individuals who claimed to have actually seen Boyie by a specific name. Soon Dad began to refer to these unknown people who'd allegedly seen Boyie as *faceless sighters*.

"The people in Flat Hill village have real creative minds." Colm's mouth twisted to one side as Dad shared the latest rumour—that a drug kingpin might have abducted and killed Boyie. Others were convinced that Bertha had paid someone to get rid of him because he was cheating on her.

"They should do like you and write poetry instead of speculating on whether Boyie's dead or alive," Dad said.

"Did yuh hear the story that Boyie supposedly took a fishing boat and went to the Venezuelan mainland?" Colm said.

I stuffed my mouth with plantain chips, carefully paying attention as they continued to swap tales. But I didn't share

Dante's latest theory—that Boyie had gone to America and joined the U.S. Navy.

One afternoon after school, when I got to the top of the staircase, I was surprised to find two uniformed officers on our porch. When Petal mentioned the circulating rumours to them, the taller of the two said, "Ma'am, everything you've said is pure speculation. There isn't any evidence to support any of it."

As the officers turned to leave, Petal asked, "What allyuh really doing to find meh little brother?"

The shorter officer turned to her and snapped, "The investigation is ongoing. We're not at liberty to share any information which could jeopardize finding the victim alive, or arresting and convicting the perpetrators of this crime."

A few days later, when I got home from school, no one was there. And since I didn't have a key to open the door, I parked myself on the front staircase. It started to drizzle, so I opened my umbrella, aware that if it turned into a heavy downpour I'd be forced to make my way to Dahlia's house. The truth was, I didn't really want to go there. Luckily, moments later, Petal rushed through the gate clutching her big, black leather purse and a plastic bag. "You reach home a long time now?" she asked, breathing heavily.

"Not really."

"Sorry, I late." She wiped the side of her face with the back of her hand. Then she carefully positioned the plastic bag on the bottom staircase, as if there was something inside that could easily break. "Yuh better go inside and change." She dug into her purse and fished out a small bottle containing a coloured liquid. She placed it beside the plastic bag, and then she dug into her handbag again. "I wonder where I put de key?"

"Maybe you lost it."

"No, I don't think so." Petal searched her pockets. "Oh," she muttered as she pulled a bunch of keys from her left jeans pocket. "Here." She handed the keys and her purse to me. She then picked up the tiny bottle and the plastic bag and started to walk toward the gate.

"You're not coming in?" I said as the raindrops got bigger.

"I've got something to take care of," she said.

"In the rain?"

"Shush." She waved me away, so I dashed into the house and changed out of my school uniform. The phone rang; it was a friend from school, but as soon as we exchanged hellos, a call came in on the second line.

"Is Petal home?" Colm's mother, Sandrina asked.

"Hold on," I said, "she's outside."

I dashed for the door, but I froze on the uppermost stair when I noticed Petal slouching forward in the rain clutching a shovel. Her right foot was pressed against the rim of the shovel and she was forcing it into the ground. She scooped out a fair amount of dirt and dumped it onto the wet earth. She then threw the shovel on the ground and untied the same plastic bag she'd earlier placed on the staircase, pulling out a red T-shirt and a tattered pair of sneakers. I kept very still, wondering why she was burying the T-shirt and sneakers inside the freshly dug hole. The hole wasn't very deep, but large enough to conceal both items. Moxley galloped toward her and suddenly dragged the T-shirt from out of the hole.

"Move!" Petal shouted and tugged the clothing from between the dog's teeth; it tore a bit.

"Scram!" she yelled at Moxley. As he wandered off, she flung the torn T-shirt back into the hole, scooped up some loose dirt to cover the opening, then packed it down with the shovel. Then she tossed the shovel onto the ground, pulled a tiny bottle from her blouse pocket, and sprinkled its contents over the spot. Then she dropped the empty bottle onto the soggy earth next to her, patted the top of the freshly covered hole, stood upright, and made the sign of the cross while mumbling some strange words.

"What yuh doing out here?" she huffed, surprised to find me standing next to her.

"It's Sandrina. She said it's important," I called out and ran down the staircase to offer her the telephone.

"My hands dirty." Petal turned her muddy palms inside out to show me. "Hold it up to my ear." She hunched a bit, and I pressed the phone against her earlobe. "Hello, hello," she repeated. "Nobody there, Baby Girl."

I put the phone to my ear, but there was only dead air. "Don't worry, I going to call she later," Petal said. "Let we go inside." She glanced at her outfit, now dripping wet, before scooping up the little bottle from the muddy ground.

I slowed down, and, as she strode past me, I looked at her questioningly, but I didn't say anything. I never discussed the digging incident with Dad, Colm, or any of my friends, but for many days afterwards, I wondered if it was a strange ritual to make Boyie come back. *Could I do the same to make my mom look for me?* Then I remembered I didn't have any of her clothes or shoes to bury.

I began to work even harder at my schoolwork as I prepared to write the eleven-plus examination. I had to do well on the exam as it would determine which secondary school I would be attending. Since arriving in Trinidad, I had consistently placed in the top ten at every end-of-term examination, and I didn't doubt my ability to do well. But when Dad promised to send me to Canada to visit my friend, Makayla, and her mother if I got accepted to one of the top three girls' schools on the island— namely St. Teresa's Convent High School (my first choice), St. Monica's High School, or Bishop's College—I was determined to study even harder.

Several months after Boyie's abduction, the rumours regarding his whereabouts still hadn't died down. "People will be people. They're going to repeat anything no matter how outrageous,"

Dad warned Petal as they discussed the latest alleged sighting of Boyie. "Maybe we've got to accept that he might never be found," he added.

"What if Boyie out there waiting fer me to come an' find him?" Petal sobbed. "I can't give up, Smokey, no, I can't give up on Boyie."

After her arrest, Arlie remained out on bail. But she didn't allow her legal problems to prevent her from continuing her community work. The Women's Committee meetings still took place once a month, although Petal hadn't gone to any of them since Boyie's abduction, and I wasn't allowed to attend in her absence. But Arlie kept Petal up to date regarding every major decision approved by the Women's Committee.

One afternoon, Arlie came to our home carrying a white box. "This is for Smokey's birthday," she said, placing the box on the table.

"You remembered his birthday?" Petal looked surprised.

"Of course, Smokey and my dear departed mother share the same birthday." Arlie dug inside a plastic bag. "Don't be jealous, Petal. I've got something extra special for you too." She fished out a smaller brown envelope from inside a larger one. "They are finally hiring at my workplace. Fill out this application form and return it to me before the end of the week. I'll hand it in for you."

Petal clutched the envelope to her chest. "Thanks so much." Petal had been waiting a long time for this chance.

"I'm not in a position to make any guarantees, but I'll see what I can do to get you in."

"I understand dat," Petal replied.

Arlie turned to leave, but spun around as she got to the door. "So," she paused, "are you coming to the barbecue fundraiser?"

"I don't know yet," Petal said. "It depend on how my body feeling."

"You've got to shake up that body and stop isolating yourself."

"I know," Petal said. "But it real hard to cope not knowing where Boyie is."

"Take care of yourself, please. We're all going to need your help when it's time for another protest," Arlie said and smiled.

"Another one?" Petal asked.

"We vow to keep up the fight, but the truth is we're in no position to mount another one just yet." Arlie waved goodbye.

15.

THE SUN'S RAYS WERE HOT ENOUGH to blister our skin if we dared to expose it as Petal, her two sons, and I made our way to Arlie's place. When we entered Arlie's yard, a group of women was hovering over a makeshift barbecue grill constructed from an oil drum, while other folks were mingling under a big white canvas tent set up for the occasion. The tent provided some much needed shade from the hot sun. Dante brought three chairs from behind the house and stacked them in a pile before going back. I thought he might be looking for more chairs as guests continued to arrive.

Petal joined the group of women, while Warren and Drew ran to a bunch of children playing in the garden. I pulled an empty chair from the pile and dragged it under the tent. I kept my eyes on the roadway, hoping Colm would soon appear. Two days earlier, he'd left for Point Fortin to visit his mom, but he'd promised to make it back in time for the barbecue fundraiser.

"Baby Girl, Colm reach yet?" Dahlia touched my neck. She looked to me like she couldn't wait to see him.

"I haven't seen him," I said, biting into a plump chicken leg.

A few minutes later, Colm arrived, sporting a large smile. "What good timing," Dahlia said, a big grin on her face. She looped her arm in his, and then led him away, giggling about something he said to her.

I finished eating my barbeque chicken, and dumped the bones and the disposable plate in a garbage bag close to Arlie's front staircase. Dante ran up to me and asked if I wanted to play some board games. "Board games?" I made a face. "Why can't we play on the computer instead?"

"Our computer crashed," he said. "The hard drive conked out."

"All right then," I replied. "But who else is going to play with us?"

"Just my sister. She's waiting inside."

"Ludo, bingo, chess, draughts, or snakes and ladders. Which do you want to play?" Carrie asked as Dante and I entered the house. She pointed to a stack of games on the table.

"Bingo," I said.

"Cool!" Carrie uncovered a bright blue box. "I'll call out the numbers!" she said, handing us individual bingo cards.

After Dante had won the first three games, I suggested we play a blackout game. The odds of winning were in my favour since I had more numbers covered than he, but I knew my luck could change at any moment, so I kept my mouth shut. A sudden crashing sound put a stop to the game. The three of us darted out the door, and, when we got to the back of Arlie's house, we saw that a big-boned man with bulging arms had Colm pinned to the ground. As his clenched fist made contact with Colm's face, I flinched.

"Leave my cousin alone!" I rushed forward and tugged at the man's shirt. He raised me off the ground. I flew through the air and staggered toward Dante like a drunk.

"Please, stop!" Dahlia yelled, but her plea fell on deaf ears. One punch turned to two, and two turned to three. A fourth landed in the middle of Colm's forehead and a fifth busted his bottom lip. I nervously rubbed my palms together as blood oozed down Colm's chin.

"Leave him!" I screamed as loudly as Dahlia had.

Why didn't he return a punch or two? I wanted to know.

Colm shielded his face like a defeated fighter thrown against the ropes. He acted as if his one and only goal was to prevent more blows to his eyes, mouth, and nose.

"Oswald, please leave him! Please get off him!" Dahlia pleaded in a tearful, shuddering voice. But Oswald, Boyie's old friend, a known criminal, ignored her.

Shiva scampered toward Colm and Oswald. "Leave the man!" he said, tugging Oswald's arm, but Oswald didn't budge. "Move!" Shiva growled, breathing heavily, and motioning the growing crowd to step back.

Just then, Oswald slammed his leg into Colm's groin, and Colm curled into a ball. Shiva pulled Oswald's shirt, forcing several buttons off and exposing his upper chest. Dante and I stared at each other when we noticed a long, thick scar running from Oswald's neck right down his chest.

"Stop this shit now!" Shiva shouted.

Oswald's feet swept the ground as Shiva and Mickey, who had arrived on the scene seconds earlier, dragged him forcibly away from Colm.

"Move out of meh way!" Oswald yelled, his arms flailing as Shiva and Mickey blocked his path. "I going to kill him!"

"Man, have some respect. This is a family gathering," Shiva said.

Mickey put his hand firmly on Oswald's shoulder. "This is not the place for that kinda nonsense," he said.

"What's going on here?" A stone-faced Arlie appeared just as Dahlia began to mop up Colm's bloodied face with a tissue.

"No, not in my yard!" Arlie exploded, wagging her index finger at Oswald. As Dahlia and I helped Colm off the ground, Oswald howled like an angry dog.

"Don't touch me!" Oswald yelled, dancing back and forth like a champion boxer. Arlie and Oswald's eyes were locked. So dramatic was the difference in their height that from a distance any stranger would have thought they were looking at a big man staring down a child.

"Get off my property!" Arlie snapped, motioning Oswald to leave.

"You ent hear the last of this!" Oswald smoothed his clothes just as Petal and Dad hustled behind the house.

What poor timing, I thought, wishing Dad had got there sooner.

"I'm warning you, Mr. Big Man!" Dad yelled at Oswald. "Take my advice and stop inhaling whatever it is you're snorting."

"Yuh gotta be a shitting, crazy man, to threaten me!" Oswald charged toward Dad, but Shiva and Mickey blocked him.

"One of us is going to die before this day is done!" Dad yelled again.

I held my breath as Petal and Arlie ran to Dad's side, trying to calm him.

"Go home, man. We don't want no more trouble," Mickey said to Oswald.

"I going!" Oswald pulled the edges of his shirt together and stepped out of the yard with a swagger.

16.

I HAD CRAWLED INTO BED only a few moments before a missile landed on our roof. Another one hit, then a third and a fourth. I pulled the covers over my head and imagined I was in the midst of a massive hailstorm.

"What the hell?" Dad yelled from his bedroom. "I'm going to deal with that sucker once and for all!"

The sound of Dad's feet stomping around the house was by no means as loud as the missiles, but his feet made a dull, heavy thud nevertheless. "It's got to be Oswald and his criminal-minded relatives!" Dad bellowed.

"You not going outside?" Petal said. "Please, Smokey, use some common sense!"

I bolted toward the living room. "Dad, please don't go outside!" I clutched his left arm.

"We better call the police," Petal suggested.

"No!" Dad shouted. "I'm going to take care of this myself! When I'm finished with them, they're going to be sorry their mother gave birth to them!"

Dad shook me off, but Petal managed to pull him toward the sofa and make him sit down. I was unsure if it was the ice-cold glass of water I'd gulped down minutes earlier or the tension in the room that had caused my throbbing headache to get worse. But I was relieved that Petal had managed to stop Dad from going outside.

"De Carlin family is a jailbird family," Petal began. "Oswald serve a six-month prison sentence at de Youth Training Center for young criminals, and, by de time he turn eighteen, he had a rap sheet longer dan meh arm."

"I'm not afraid of that!" Dad said, and, even though he smiled, I knew he wasn't joking. I bit my bottom lip, wondering if Petal knew that the cops in Canada had arrested Dad for punching Charm.

"Yuh awake?" Petal asked Colm as he tottered toward us with a black eye and busted lip.

"I couldn't sleep through that," he said.

"Come." She patted the empty space on the sofa.

"Is all my fault," Colm groaned. "I didn't have a clue that Dahlia and Oswald were an item."

"It's not your fault. Nobody has a right to stone this house," Dad said, suddenly sounding weary.

I stood up to go back to bed, but I immediately sat down when something hit the roof again. One, two, three, four, five, six loud thuds, and then the noise stopped.

The following day, neither Dad nor Petal mentioned the missiles. Colm didn't talk about it either, but I couldn't get it off my mind, so I asked Petal, "What's Dad going to do to Oswald?"

"Nothing." She acted as if she couldn't remember Dad's threats.

"Didn't Dad say it was Oswald stoning our house?"

"Yuh dad was jus' angry. He not going to harm nobody."

The creation of a children's soccer club was slated for discussion at the Women's Committee meeting scheduled for seven o'clock that evening. I was bubbling with joy when Petal promised me that she would attend.

That morning, while heading to school, several possible names for our budding soccer club floated in my head. Several villagers had expressed interest, but I wished a woman would get the job.

After school, I barely paid attention to the two police cruisers parked just ahead of where Mr. Wellington usually dropped me off. It had become common for cops to patrol the village. As I trotted upward, the flurry of activity in Flat Hill Village seemed busier than usual. I stepped toward the old, abandoned house where the troublemakers usually hung out to see if I could figure out what was going on. I froze as two uniformed officers drew their pistols.

"Is Oswald they arresting!" a woman shouted from among the large group of curious onlookers. "They get ganja and a weapon on him!"

Another woman in the crowd shouted, "This is overkill. Five of them come here fer one man?"

"Keep back!" One of the officers waved his weapon while two of his colleagues dragged Oswald out of the unkempt yard.

Martha Carlin, her arms and legs bouncing like a half-cooked bowl of porridge, made her way toward the large gathering. "Where they taking him?" she panted.

"Where else but the station!" someone yelled as Martha tucked in one end of a reddish-brown towel wrapped around her head. She trailed the officers, and a bunch of people followed her; I followed too.

"Keep your distance!" one of the officers warned.

I smirked as the officers threw Oswald in the back seat of a police cruiser and slammed the door. I imagined poking my head into the police vehicle and howling at him, but there was no way the officers would have allowed me to do that. And even if they did, would I really have had the guts?

The whites of Martha Carlin's eyes got even whiter as the police car sped off. I was so overjoyed at having seen Oswald in handcuffs that when I turned around and began heading home, I almost passed our house. I hopped up the stairs two at a time, anxious to get my homework done. I didn't want to give Petal an excuse to prevent me from accompanying her to the women's meeting at Arlie's house. I tugged at the front door, but it was shut tight, so I dipped into my backpack and pulled out the spare key that Petal had given to me that time she was late coming home and had found me waiting on the steps when it was raining.

"Keep it safe," she had said when she handed it over. I had slipped it onto the key ring Auntie Hattie had given me. My thoughts strayed, and I wondered if I'd find Petal unconscious inside the house just like the twins and I had found Grandma Wilma. I dismissed that thought almost as quickly as it came, reminding myself that Petal wasn't as old and wrinkly as Grandma Wilma.

As I pushed the key into the lock, my thoughts strayed even more, and I wondered what I would do if I found Boyie splayed out on the sofa reading a book. Relieved that at first glance there was nothing unusual inside, I threw my backpack on the floor, ran toward the telephone's beeping light, and listened to the voice mail.

"Baby Girl, is Petal here. When yuh get home, go to Arlie house and wait fer me there." The message ended.

"Where's Petal?" I asked Arlie when I arrived at her place.

"She had an emergency," Arlie said calmly before ordering her kids and me to do our homework. The three of us shared the kitchen table. Dante helped me to prepare for my Mental Math test, and, in return, I helped him to review a list of words for an upcoming spelling quiz. Carrie sat quietly, completing her English homework by herself. Afterward, we put our textbooks away and settled in front of the television.

Meena was the first to arrive at Arlie's house for the seven o'clock gathering. "Everybody gone to jail wit' Oswald or what?" she joked.

"I'm disappointed," Arlie scanned the room at ten past seven. "I expected more than a few people to show up this evening." Her expression was serious at first, but then she glowed. "I'll start the evening off with some good news," she said. "The charges stemming from my arrest have been dropped."

"Thank yuh Jesus," Mrs. Arlington said several times. The women clapped, but no one asked Arlie to share the details.

Arlie then announced that only three girls had signed up for the soccer team. "Maybe we should have girls and boys play together," Meena suggested.

"No, we can't do that!" a woman named Shirley protested.

"Why not?" Arlie asked.

"My girls wouldn't want to play wit' no boys," Shirley said.

"Hold it!" Arlie's voice went up as the women started arguing. "Let's make a concerted effort to get more girls involved, and then it will be a moot point."

The women then started talking all at once about ways to get more girls signed up, and debating who might be the coach of the team. They passed some snacks around and before long they were discussing the next steps to making improvements in the community.

Toward the end of the meeting, Arlie sighed and said, "I guess you all must have heard the sad news?"

"About Martha's son?" Shirley asked.

"No, about Mr. Charles," Arlie explained. "You must have heard about his passing."

"He never help we, so why we wasting time talking 'bout that?" Shirley sucked her teeth.

"Is a heart attack that kill him," Mrs. Arlington said.

"If we could get a woman M.P., she sure going to do a better job than him," Shirley said.

"Yuh damn right." Mrs. Arlington's eyes met Arlie's. "So why yuh don't represent we?"

Everyone clapped, but Arlie shook her head. "I don't think so," she said politely.

The meeting ended around eight thirty.

"Do you want to sleep?" Arlie asked about an hour later as I started to dozed off on her sofa.

"No," I yawned. "Do you know what time my Dad and Petal are coming home?"

"I'm not sure," Arlie said.

Ten o'clock came and went, and I remained propped up on Arlie's sofa, half asleep.

"Go to Carrie's room," Arlie said, and handed me an oversized T-shirt. I put it on the chair and rushed off to the washroom.

"Did my dad or Petal call?" I asked when I returned, since I'd heard the telephone ring.

"Yes, Petal called, but I told her you could sleep with Carrie tonight."

"But I'm awake."

"Never mind. You can spend one night at my place, can't you?" Arlie smiled.

Even though I wanted to sleep in my own bed, I nodded. I stripped off my clothes and pulled the T-shirt over my head. It fit like a big, long dress. The price tag, still attached, scratched my neck.

"We can easily fix that." Arlie reached for a pair of scissors and cut off the tag. I climbed into a spare bed in Carrie's room and slipped under the covers. I fell asleep without saying my prayers.

I stared at the cream wall. It took a few seconds before I registered where I was. I tiptoed out the door and peeked out the kitchen window at our house, where the lights shone brightly.

"You're up early." Arlie walked up behind me.

"I couldn't fall back to sleep," I said. "Why didn't Petal or Dad come to meet me?"

"Don't worry. I'll escort you home as soon as it's daylight."

When Arlie finally accompanied me to the front gate, Petal was standing there waiting, her face serious. She led me up the staircase. "Meh boys staying wit' us fer a while." She explained that the boys' grandmother had taken ill the previous night and had suddenly died.

"There ent no one to take care of dem in de daytime when dey daddy working, so for now dey back home wit' dey mama," she said.

17.

DREW AND WARREN GREETED ME at the gate. The boys had been staying with us for more than a month without returning to their father's house even once, despite the fact that he'd promised to take them on weekends. Petal pulled out a tiny weed from the front yard. Then she stood upright and, with her hands on her waist, said, "Madam, please clean yuh room. Don't let me have to tell yuh again."

By then I'd gotten used to her constantly nagging me to dust, mop, and sweep my room. But her words always entered one ear and came out the other. I hated sharing a bedroom with two little boys and didn't want to clean up their mess. So on most days I only made my bed.

But I trudged to my room anyway. I picked up a bunch of magazines that I'd left scattered on the bedroom floor the night before. Then I gathered the books lying helter-skelter on the bottom shelf of my bookcase and began sorting them. I was surpised when I suddenly spotted the little address book I'd taken from Boyie's bedroom months earlier and scanned through its pages. I was upset with myself for having forgotten about it. *He knew a bunch of people with strange names,* I thought when I noticed Bop, Thunder, and Growl among the entries listed on its pages.

"Colm, how to draw a car?" Petal's older son hollered from the living room.

"Look at a picture and try until you get it right."

Colm's voice got closer, so I tossed the little book behind the bed, but it landed in plain view at the foot of my bed.

"I going to get my crayons." Warren barged in, leaving the door wide open.

"You don't know how to knock?" I said.

Colm appeared in the threshold holding a postcard. "It hard to share a room with little kids, isn't it?" he asked.

"It was better when they only came on weekends. Now I never have any time to myself."

"Yuh soon going to get yuh room back." He paused. "Yuh in the mood to read some poetry?"

"I've got to put my books back on the shelf," I said, taking in the huge pile of magazines and books on the floor.

"Yuh want help?" He stepped toward the bookshelf.

"Nope."

"You're no fun," he said, picking up the books, even though I had insisted I could do it myself.

"See. I did a good job." His eyes wandered around after he'd neatly lined the books on the bottom shelf.

"What's that?" His eyes caught the little red book sticking out at the foot of my bed.

"Nothing." I leaned forward to pick it up.

"Nice. You've got an address book," he snatched it. "Is your boyfriend's name in it?"

I jumped as high as I could and tried to grab the book, but he held it up so high that I couldn't reach it.

"I don't have a boyfriend," I said. "Please give me my book back."

"Let me see what's in it," Colm chuckled. "Who are all these people?" He turned the pages.

"I don't know."

"This can't be yours?" he asked. "Where'd yuh get it?"

"It used to belong to Boyie."

"What yuh doing with it?"

"I found it."

"Where?"

"In his room."

"When?"

"I don't remember. A long time ago, though." I could feel my face turn bright red.

"Yuh gotta give this to Petal," he advised. "This information might help the police figure out what happened to him."

"You can't tell her I had it."

"I've got to give it to her," Colm insisted.

The room fell silent. My stomach felt like there were worms squirming inside. "Please, don't tell Dad or Petal I had it," I begged. "Dad's going to be really upset and he'll punish me for having kept it."

Colm made his way to the door then turned to face me. "You should have known better, Baby Girl."

My body heated up as I prepared myself for a tongue-lashing from Dad and Petal. "I forgot all about it, Colm, I did. I found it again just now."

"Don't worry. I going to think something up," he paused. "I'll tell Petal I found it under the mattress."

"Thank you," I mumbled as he turned and left the room. I thought my heart was going to jump out of my chest.

18.

P ETAL'S BIRTHDAY FELL ON A sun-drenched Saturday. I
didn't know how old she was; she didn't say, and I didn't
ask. I had a blast at the beach with her, Dad, and a couple of their friends. Drew and Warren had been reunited with
their dad for the weekend. He'd picked them up the previous
day but planned to bring them back to our place on Sunday
because he didn't have a babysitter

Petal didn't usually drink, but she had a couple of beers at
the beach, and when we left the deep blue water behind, her
speech was slurred. "You had fun today?" she asked, turning
to face me as Dad started the car and began to pull away. She
had a big smile on her face.

"Yeah." I brushed away the tiny pieces of chocolate stuck
to my lips. I had especially liked the birthday cake that her
friend had brought to our beach picnic.

"I'm tired like a dog," Dad sighed.

"From sitting on de beach and eating?" Petal chuckled.
"Maybe yuh need some entertainment. Baby Girl, recite one
of yuh poems fer yuh daddy."

"You want me to recite a poem?" I was surprised she'd asked
since it was the first time either she or Dad had asked me to
perform one of my pieces. When Petal and Dad had attended
the Spoken Word Contest I thought they'd come out of duty
and not because they were genuinely interested in poetry.

I decided to recite "No Words Can Help:"

There is a bird in the sky
Flying over my head
I am thinking about you
And what I would do
If I got the chance
to fly over you.

No words can help me
No smiles can cheer me
No flowers sent
No matter how well meant
Will stop me from wishing
for you to come home.

The birds are chirping
But mine is a sad song
You went away
When I was young
I'll never forget you, Mom
And, for you, I will wait
No matter how long.

"Bravo!" Petal clapped heartily afterwards. Her head swayed from side to side. And in that moment, I felt proud.

Petal glanced at her watch as Dad parked his vehicle. "I'm still in time to catch de end of *The Apartment*."

"Don't leave the old man behind," Dad chortled.

"Okay, but hurry up," Petal said.

I edged up the rough trail much more skillfully than when I'd first arrived at Flat Hill Village. I no longer breathed heavily or felt weary, and, having got way ahead of Dad and Petal, I waited for them to catch up.

"Can I stay up and watch *The Apartment* with you?" I looked down at Petal in the dull lighting.

"Just dis once."

As we reached the dilapidated house where the troublemakers usually hung out, a host of male voices echoed from behind the half-broken-down fence.

"They need to have their mouths wash out wit' soap," Petal murmured as swear words spilled out of their mouths.

"Look at de snitch!" one of the youths shouted. Then a choir of male voices giggled in the darkness.

"He's de informer," the same voice called out. "We gonna fix yuh daughter!"

Dad spun around and faced the old house. "Who the hell said that?" he yelled.

"Let we go home," Petal pleaded.

"Please, Dad, let's go," I said, but Dad stood his ground. "Afraid to show yourself, are you?" he hollered.

"Is me who talk." A man emerged from the dark. "What yuh going to do 'bout it?" The man's hand made a *bap, bap* sound as he slapped his chest.

"Forget de man, Claudius," another voice echoed from the shadows.

"Shit!" Petal shouted. "Let we go home!"

"Dad, let's go," I begged.

"You're lucky my wife and daughter are here, otherwise I'd have made you eat your words!" Dad said. I exhaled loudly as Dad stepped closer to us.

"Yuh taking dat threat, Claudius?" another voice said. The men chuckled much louder than before. Petal and I waited until Dad got within arm's length of us before we started to make our way further up the road. A sudden loud thud made me spin around. The men who'd been arguing with Dad scattered east, west, north, and south.

"No!" Petal screamed, then scrambled toward Dad. She got down on her knees and cuddled him as if he were a big rag doll.

"Call somebody!" Petal bawled.

I dug into Dad's pants pocket and fished out his cell phone. "I love you, honey," Dad gurgled and then his eyes closed. I couldn't understand what had happened. Had they thrown something at him? Shot him? I crumpled to the ground next to him.

"Smokey!" Petal sobbed, wrapping her arms around Dad's limp body. I couldn't speak but tears streamed down my cheeks like a mini waterfall.

Mickey appeared almost immediately. Then our next-door neighbour, Shiva, arrived. "This man going to bleed to death if we wait for a slowcoach ambulance." Mickey ordered several men to carry Dad downhill and to put him inside his car.

"Go to Arlie's house." Petal waved me away before climbing in next to Dad.

I stood under the streetlight trembling and wondering if Dad would live or die. The crowd of about twenty or so villagers formed an almost perfect semi-circle. But I was so out of it that I couldn't make sense of what they were discussing.

Meena stepped forward from among the crowd, and took me by the arm. "I'm going to Arlie's," I whispered when she offered to take me to her house.

"Yuh dad going to be all right," she said, escorting me up the trail. But with each step, the fear in me swelled as images of Dad's blood-soaked clothes flashed in my head. I couldn't stop trembling and by the time I got to Arlie's house, I could hardly breathe.

"I just got the news." Arlie's voice cracked as she hustled toward Meena and me. I was way taller than her, so she tilted her head upward to see my eyes.

We made it up her staircase, and no one spoke as we stepped into the living room and stood under the fluorescent lights. "You've got a few traces of blood on your hands," she said, and pointed to my fingers.

I whimpered like a newborn puppy when I saw the blood, my dad's blood. Arlie led me to the bathroom, where she washed and then dried my hands as if I were a small and helpless child. My jaws snapped shut when Dante and Carrie came out of their rooms, their sad eyes glued to my face.

"You don't have to talk," Arlie assured me. "You don't have to explain anything to anybody."

I buried my face in her chest and wept.

"Petal wants to talk to you," Arlie said later that evening. A lump formed in my throat and my body wobbled as I kept my hands at my side, refusing to take the phone she was handing over to me. "Don't you worry. Everything's okay." Arlie held the phone against my earlobe.

"Yuh dad lost a lotta blood but he conscious now," Petal said in a soft, crisp voice.

"He is?" I grabbed the receiver and my breathing slowed. *Did I hear right?*

I felt weary and wanted to lie down, but I remained propped up on Arlie's fluffy cushion, waiting for Petal to return. I needed to look into her eyes. Only then would I truly believe my dad was going to survive.

"Why don't the police lock up the entire Carlin family and throw away the key?" I asked Arlie.

"Claudius Carlin is going to jail for a rather long time, believe me." She brushed my cheeks with her hand. "And, if your dad was the one who reported Oswald's drug activity, then I'm damn proud of him."

Arlie sat on the sofa with a magazine. I had only that very second noticed her small ears and the tiny mole on her neck. Dante sat at his mother's left, Carrie at her right. I sat on a chair facing them.

"You want to hear a story?" Arlie lifted her eyes from the magazine. "I was a shy ten-year-old when I met my dad for the first time," she began. "I will never forget the moment that short, strapping man with a permanent smile told me that I was his child. I must say, even though he was a bit messed up in the head, he was a really good man."

"Is he still alive?" I asked.

"No, he died when I was twenty-two. Lung cancer claimed him," she said. "It happened the same year I got my Bachelor of Arts degree at U.W.I."

"What did you study?"

"History. I was a history buff all through secondary school, but I did my Master's in Politics. Political Science, that is. I wanted to be a politician in my younger days," Arlie giggled. "But I'm quite happy to be a plain social activist in my old age."

"You're not plain, and you're not old. You're too good to be living in Flat Hill," I blurted.

"Too good?" Arlie smirked. "Education doesn't make one person better than another, only a little bit wiser, maybe."

"I wish—" I started, then held back.

"Wish what?" Arlie prodded, and the room fell silent as she waited for me to finish what I had been about to say.

"Nothing," I said, biting my lip. I couldn't admit that I wished she were my real mother.

FLAT HILL VILLAGE STABBING

Nathaniel Sparks, 35, a former resident of Ontario, Canada, sustained life-threatening injuries after he was stabbed in the presence of his wife and daughter. Claudius Carlin, 21, a resident of Flat Hill Village, was arrested and charged with attempted murder. The accused man, who was on probation at the time of the alleged crime, had his application for bail denied.

I lay on my stomach, pressing both palms against my cheeks, allowing my arms to take the weight of my upper body. With bended knees, I stuck my feet up in the air and pointed my toes toward the ceiling. I re-read the article a couple more times. *Why was Claudius out on bail? If he'd remained in jail, he wouldn't have been able to hurt Dad.* I climbed out of bed, grabbed a pair of scissors and cut the article out of the

Trinidad Express newspaper.

"It hurts like hell." Dad screwed up his face as I stepped toward his hospital bed.

"Don't," I said as he tried to sit up. I kissed his stubbly cheek and he shifted, trying to get a better glimpse of my face. He grimaced as if a two-ton truck had hit his chest.

"That's better," he sighed when Petal adjusted his pillow and helped him sit up. "How's my little girl?" He touched my arm and I wrapped my fingers around his.

"I'm okay, Dad, but I miss you," I said.

Then he asked Petal about the boys. "I leave dem wit' Miss Arlington," she replied.

I pulled a chair next to Dad and handed him a scrapbook I'd starting making. "You're famous," I said. I had pasted in the article from the newspaper.

"Shit!" Dad's face drooped. "Where'd you get this?"

"In the *Express*."

"My face is probably all over the blasted Internet," Dad scowled, shoving the scrapbook at me. "I didn't ask for any of this."

"I'm sorry, Dad. I thought you'd be glad to see it." I was confused and hurt. So when Arlie walked in and asked me to go and get some drinks with her, I jumped at the offer.

When we returned, the tension in the room was thicker than before we'd left.

"When will you be leaving the hospital?" I asked Dad.

"Tuesday or Wednesday, I hope. At least one of my ladies wants me home," he winked. That made me feel better, but then he held his chest as if the pain was too much.

A nasty cough kept me from Dad's hospital bed for several days, and I was anxious to see him again and make sure he was okay. The day before, Dad's blood pressure had skyrocketed, and the doctors had had difficulty controlling it. Also, complications stemming from the injuries to his internal organs meant he was likely to remain hospitalized longer than we'd originally thought. When Petal and I got to his bed, his eyes were shut and his cheeks had lost a lot of fat. I touched his chin; it wasn't as prickly as when I'd previously kissed him.

A few days later, a thin, tall woman I'd never seen before stood at Dad's hospital bed. She wore a sleeveless print dress and brown leather sandals. Her grey hair was cut short, almost like a boy's. "This is my wife, Petal, and my daughter, Baby Girl," Dad said to the smiling woman.

"I'm Aunt Cleo." Her palm felt damp as our hands met in a firm handshake. I rubbed my fingers against my cotton dress in case my hand was also sweaty. Aunt Cleo shook Petal's hand next, but her eyes were fixed on my face.

"You look so much like my niece, Darlene. Well, except Darlene was a little bit darker than you, sweetheart," Aunt Cleo paused. "Is this your mom?" She looked at Petal briefly and then her eyes landed back on me.

"No, my mom's not here," I said.

"She's still in Canada?" she asked.

Dad gave me a hard look, so I knew it was time to shut up. Was she really Dad's aunt, or simply one of his mother's long lost friends? I sensed Dad would be mad if I questioned her, so I didn't. Before she left, Aunt Cleo jotted down her phone number and gave it to my father.

"Who's that lady?" I asked Dad.

"She's who she says she is: Aunt Cleo," he replied.

"Is she really your aunt?"

"No."

"But she said she was."

"She's my mother's cousin. A very distant cousin." He stressed the word "very."

"How'd she know you were here? Did you call her?"

"Me? Call her?" He made a face. "She saw the shitting

newspaper article about the stabbing, recognized my name, and had her police officer son do some investigating. That's how she found me. I hope she doesn't ever come back here again."

"She seemed nice," I said. "Why don't you like her? Do you think she's too old and wrinkled up to be our friend?"

"We all have to get old one day," Petal laughed.

"I wish she'd come back," I said. I wanted her son to act as my private investigator and help me locate my real mother.

"I don't want her here. She's a busybody who asks too many questions. She doesn't need to know every detail about my past, and, furthermore, I don't need extended family at my age," Dad said. "It's way too late for that."

When Dad was discharged from the hospital, his doctors ordered him to take things slowly. Money was tight since Dad's paid sick leave had run out. A couple of his work colleagues came to our home and gave him a cheque, but I don't know how much money they gave him. But the relief that Dad and Petal felt was palpable after his friends left.

"De mail over dere." Petal pointed to a stack of letters on the kitchen table.

"Bills and more bills." Dad skimmed though them. Then he held up a yellow envelope, turned it over, and examined the back. "What's this!" he shrieked. He tore the envelope and pulled out a buttery-coloured piece of paper. His eyes narrowed as he read it. Then he scowled and stuffed the letter in his pocket. I was so curious, but I didn't ask anything about it. I could tell he wouldn't tell me anything.

A few days before Dad returned to work, Petal got the position she'd interviewed for at Arlie's workplace. "You've got to help out more around the house now that Petal has a job," Dad said to me on Petal's first day. I nodded, but if helping out more meant scooping up dog poop or tugging out weeds from the front of the house, I wasn't planning on doing any of that.

That same day, Dad handed me the two big envelopes containing all his old photos. "Hold on to this," he said.

"For me?"

"You're a big girl now. I'm sure you'll take good care of them." I was well aware that the photos of Dad's parents, grandparents, and other relatives meant a lot to him, and I was stunned that he trusted me to be their custodian, so I put them in the top drawer of my desk, which was the safest place I could think of.

At Sunday dinner, Colm asked for our attention. I looked up at him and his face was serious. When he said he had an announcement to make, I promptly put down my fork at the side of my plate. "Now that Drew and Warren are here indefinitely, yuh going to need more space and is more than time I make my own way, so I moving out."

"Where to?" Petal said.

"I going to share an apartment with one of my workmates. He's got a two-bedroom place and is looking for someone to split de expenses with." No one but me seemed to mind this very much. And it was happening all too soon; Colm explained that he'd be going the very next day.

The next morning when I got up I saw that Colm had already lined up all his bags in a row, waiting for his workmate, Joe, to come and pick him up.

"Are you going to come back to visit me?" I asked Colm as I rushed toward him and we hugged.

"Of course," he replied with a giant smile, patting my head affectionately. "Just promise me you're never going to stop writing poetry."

After his friend arrived, they packed up the car and he said goodbye to all of us. I could tell he was excited. As he stepped out the gate, I was convinced that unlike my biological mom, my stepmom, Charm and her daughter, Clara, Auntie Hattie, Lena, and Harley, Colm would keep in touch with me. Just before he got into the car, he turned to look at me, and he waved and smiled brightly.

Not long after Colm moved out, I got my eleven-plus exam results. My heart sank when I saw Maitland Comprehensive on my results slip, but when I learned that my friend, Satish, had also passed for Maitland, the heavy weight on my chest lifted a bit.

"I passed for Queen's Royal College. What about you?" Dante shouted from across the fence separating his yard from ours as I made my way up our staircase.

"I'm going to Maitland," I said softly.

"Maitland?" he said.

"Maitland is a good school," I replied, even though I didn't really believe that.

"Suri also got her first choice, she's going to Bishop's College," he added.

"I see." I spoke even softer.

Idiot, fool, stupid, dumb were some of the words I used to describe myself. I felt like the odd one out among my Flat Hill Village friends. I waddled up the staircase, hoping Dad would still buy me an airline ticket to Canada to visit Makayla and her mother.

19.

THE INSTANT I ENTERED the room, I was drawn to his eyes. They were a distinctive brown, similar to my father's. The two men were roughly the same height and the same size; they could easily have been mistaken for brothers.

"Melody or Baby Girl, which do you prefer?" he asked as if he'd been briefed about me.

"Baby Girl," I said, sticking my hand out to meet his.

"I'm Stanley. Meet my wife."

"I'm Marguerite." She greeted me with an easy smile and a firm handshake. My eyes locked onto her bulging legs, as round as tree trunks holding up her tall, strapping frame. "And this is our daughter, Nichelle." Marguerite gestured toward a girl who couldn't have been more than a couple of years older than me.

"Nith to meet you." Nichelle's lisp was obvious.

"Nice to meet you too," I replied.

I was in awe of her beauty. She was much prettier than most girls I knew, and her skin was as smooth as a newborn's. Nichelle glanced at her watch as if she was running late for an important date. Then she rubbed her palms together before slipping off her backpack and placing it on the floor. Our three guests accepted Petal's invitation to sit.

"You have only one daughter?" Petal asked Marguerite.

"No, we've got another girl. Nona's three years older and studying to be a physician at U.W.I. in Mona, Jamaica."

"Nona's the brains in the family," Stanley said. "Mind you,

Nichelle's got brains as well, but she's the artistic one. She sings, paints, and plays the piano."

"Dat's great," Petal said.

"When Aunt Cleo told me about Nathaniel, um, I mean Smokey…"

"Yeah, we all call him Smokey," Petal cut in.

"I was in the Bahamas when Aunt Cleo phoned to tell me she'd seen him. I could hardly wait to reacquaint myself with my long-lost cousin after so many years." Stanley's eyes met mine. "But instead, I'm lucky to meet you, his little girl." His gaze moved back to Petal. "Mind you, I don't usually appear at anyone's house without calling first, but I wanted this to be a surprise. After all, we're family."

"A surprise is good sometimes." Petal remained standing, even though everyone else had found a seat by then.

"It's a pity we weren't able to see Nath … um, I mean Smokey today." Stanley turned to face me. "Family's very important. I have fond memories of your dad as a young boy. In those days we called him Natty and his twin brother, Howie. When we were, um … let's see… about four or five, I guess, we spent a lot of time at our grandparents' place, but after a while we didn't see them again. And when I asked Mom why, she said they'd moved away."

"Smokey is yuh first cousin?" Petal asked.

"Yes, his mother and my father were siblings, but my father died shortly after I turned two, so I don't remember my dad at all, I'm afraid."

"Aunt Cleo was my father's first cousin and your grand-mother's first cousin too," Stanley said to me. "I guess your dad must have told you about his childhood?" He paused momentarily. "When my girls were younger I'd often share tales about the elders, but they're not interested in any of that now."

"My dad used to stay in El Socorro, and his mother had a zabocado tree," I said, proud to let him know that I wasn't clueless about my ancestry, and that, unlike his kids, I wanted to learn more.

"Ith's called a zaboca tree, or an avocado tree," Nichelle corrected me.

Everyone in the room laughed, but I felt really silly and would have hidden my face in a paper bag if I'd had one handy. Luckily an idea quickly hit me. "We've got some family pictures," I said. "Do you want to see them?"

"Sure," Stanley said.

I marched to my room and returned with the two big envelopes Dad had given me. "Do you know any of these people?" I eagerly showed him the photos of the people Dad had never been able to identify.

"I don't think so," Stanley squinted. "Just a second." He took a pair of wire-rimmed glasses from his pocket and shoved them on. His face lit up only after he'd got through half the pile. "This is Malcolm Sparks. Good old Malcolm. He was a boy back then. Malcolm was my great uncle, so that makes him your great-great uncle. And this is Bella."

"Who's Bella?" I asked.

"She was your great-great aunt, Uncle Malcolm's wife."

He pressed his lips together as he examined the last photo. "Sorry, I can't identify anyone else, but I'm sure Aunt Cleo could do a much better job than me or anyone else. She's our matriarch with the memory of a teenager."

"I've got more," I said, dragging out the rest of the photos from the two envelopes.

"You've got quite a collection here." Stanley held the stack like a deck of cards and made more than a few funny faces as he examined them. "The old house," Stanley said with his eyes glued to a wooden house on stilts. "Nich, this is the old house." He shifted toward his daughter, nudging her to look at the photo.

"Uhh, your family lived there?" Nichelle's contorted expression made me want to slap her.

"This was my grandparents' house. Ma and Pa didn't have a lot of earthly riches—no indoor plumbing, no electric lights—but they had more than enough love to go around." His face was suddenly covered by an intense glow. "This is definitely a treasure trove of photos you have here. Aunt Cleo's house is on this spot."

"In El Socorro?" I asked.

"Yes, the old house is gone, but the memories remain in my heart."

Nichelle dug into her backpack and pulled out six books. "I brought these for you," she said as she handed them over to me.

As I positioned the novels on the coffee table, a couple slipped onto the floor. Before I could bend to pick them up, Stanley had already caught all of them except for one book titled *An Angel Returns*. "There you go," Stanley said.

Nichelle picked up *An Angel Returns* and stacked it on top of the pile. "Thith is one of my favourites. I'm sure you'll love ith."

By the time Stanley, his wife, and daughter had left, I felt as light as a feather and full of joy knowing that I had blood relatives who wanted my father and me in their lives. As I scribbled Malcolm's and Bella's names on the backs of their photos, I could hardly believe I'd learned more about my family's history in the last couple of hours than I'd learned in my entire life.

It turned out that Stanley was a Presbyterian minister and a university lecturer; his wife Marguerite was a high school principal. And even though their younger daughter, Nichelle, didn't have any interest in poetry, sports, or our family's history, and I didn't have any desire to learn how to paint or to play the piano, it didn't matter. Despite our differences, I desperately hoped she and I would bond over time.

When Dad walked in, I was so anxious to tell him about Stanley's visit that I could hardly get the words out. "Slow down." Dad edged closer and put his hands on my shoulders. He was listening intently. "A pastor and a professor, eh?" he said after I'd shared the details. "Hmmm ... I need a smoke." He pulled the cigarettes out of his shirt pocket and ambled out the door.

I followed him eagerly, practically jumping out of my skin. "How come you never took me to see them?" I asked, settling on the staircase next to him.

"To see who?"

"My cousins."

"In name only." Dad looked me straight in the eye with a serious expression. My body tensed, frustrated by his frosty response. He lit a cigarette and a cloud of smoke encircled us.

"Why don't you want to be friends with them?"

"You've only met those people once," he said. "You really don't know two hoots about them."

"I know that Stanley is a minister and Marguerite is a teacher!" I yelled. "Why don't you like them? I like them! They're family and I want to know them!" I shouted and darted back inside the house and into my room, flinging myself on the bed. I couldn't understand why he was being so cold about them.

"Come here, Baby Girl!" Dad rushed after me. "It's time we have a chat." He sat on the edge of my mattress and nudged my arm gently.

"My mom and dad were estranged from these people. In fact, my parents weren't close to any of their so-called relatives."

"Why?"

"It stems from Howie's death. Mom blamed a family member for it."

For the first time ever, Dad told me the story about the day his mother had fallen ill and left him and his twin brother, Howie, in the care of one of their relatives.

"Who?"

"Who else but Aunt Cleo," he said.

"The same Aunt Cleo who visited you at the hospital?"

"Yes, her," Dad said. "While under her care, Howie drowned in the river. The authorities ruled it an accident, but my mother never forgave her. She said Aunt Cleo was negligent. Mom never got over Howie's death. She always felt the rest of the family had more sympathy for Aunt Cleo than for her, even though she was the one who'd lost a child. They're cruel people, Mom always said."

Dad faced the window, but he continued to speak. "We moved to Canada soon after the tragedy. When Mom and Dad died, I was only ten, but I'd heard so many negative things about my mother's relatives that I didn't want to live with any of them. My dad was an only child. There weren't any aunts or uncles on his side to go to. My mom's friend, Aunt Mona was kind to take me in. After Aunt Mona died, I had to learn to take care of myself."

Dad hugged me and softly said, "Even though I mess up as a parent sometimes, I really mean it whenever I tell you that I want you to have a much better life than mine."

20.

S INCE BOYIE'S DISAPPEARANCE, Petal hadn't attended any of the women's meetings. On the day she'd finally planned to go, her sons' grandmother had died, and shortly thereafter Dad had been hospitalized. Then she got her new job and complained about being too tired.

"Arlie is busy, and she's at every single meeting," I said scornfully one day when Petal decided to pass on another meeting, even though days earlier she'd promised to attend, and of course, to take me with her. I wanted to go so badly.

"Arlie don't have two little kids to take care of. Her kids big!" Petal snapped. "But if yuh would do yuh share of de housework, dat might help."

"But I just washed all the dishes."

"So why yuh leave a puddle of water round de sink fer me to wipe den?" She mopped the damp area with a thick cloth. "If yuh pick up de clothes off de line and pass de broom in de kitchen, dat would make a big difference."

I tucked my tail between my legs and headed into the blinding sunlight. I picked up the clothes flapping noisily in the strong breeze and bundled them into a bulky pile. I began to sweep the kitchen, but Petal grabbed the broom. "Dis is how to do it properly," she muttered irritably.

"You're always finding fault with everything I do. That's why I never want to help you!" I shouted, and then ran to my room.

"I sorry." Petal came after me. "Look, I think I going to de meeting after all. Yuh coming wit' me?" This was a typical day in our new normal life, Petal and I often disagreeing about little things, but making up in the end. I knew life would never go back to the way it was before Boyie's disappearance, even if he turned up alive.

"I need to know if he dead or alive," Petal would often say to my dad. I wanted her to be happy again, but the thought of Boyie coming back to live with us made me cringe. I surely felt older and a little bit wiser than I had when I'd first arrived at Flat Hill Village.

Colm had covered for me and given the red address book that was in my possession to Petal stating that he'd found it under his mattress just like he said he would. Petal had given it to the police the day after she received it, thinking that it might offer new leads, but so far it hadn't. But Petal had not given up hope of finding him one day.

The moment Petal and I got to the top of Arlie's staircase, Mrs. Arlington shook my hand so hard that I thought my entire arm would separate from my body. "Glad you here, girl." She energetically shook Petal's hand as well.

"Is really you or is Halle Berry?" Meena eyed Petal's new shorter hairdo. Petal gave her a big, pleased grin. I could tell she was happy we were here now. Several of the Women's Committee members were gathered on Arlie's porch, chatting and laughing. I went inside to see what Arlie was doing. She was in the living room sorting through a bunch of documents.

"Do you believe in angels?" I asked thinking about a movie I'd watched with Dad and Petal the night before.

"Yes," Arlie said, her smile absent-minded. She gathered up her documents then made her way to the porch and ushered the women into the living room.

"People, we've got to get started!" she said, and began to address them: "As you ladies are aware, we, the voters in this constituency, need to elect a new Member of Parliament in the upcoming by-election, and, as is the norm, the potential candidates will soon be campaigning for our votes. It's not my place to tell you whom you should vote for, but please pay careful attention to the promises each and every candidate makes. Remember, if you don't vote, you don't have a moral right to complain. Please exercise your civic duty and take the time to choose wisely."

"But a general election is only months away," Petal said. "Why dey wasting time and money to have a by-election now?"

"The constitution states that a by-election must be held within a specific time frame, so the rule of law must prevail," Arlie said.

"You have any of the candidates' names?" Meena asked.

"Joseph Wilson from the PMP party, Harold Singh from the URC party, and Margaret Jones from the DOC party," Arlie read from a piece of paper.

I was anxious for Arlie to discuss the children's sports club, but the women just asked questions about the by-election, so I closed my eyes and tried to compose a poem about the previous night's movie that had impressed me.

The movie had begun with a woman dressed completely in white approaching a teenage girl. So, the first line, *She appeared, dressed in white,* came quickly, but then I hit a brick wall. With my eyes still closed, I summoned up the details of the movie, hoping they would inspire me.

"I've been looking for you for fifteen years," the woman had said.

"Why would you be searching for me?" the girl asked curiously.

"You're the reason I didn't give up on life," the woman replied. "Why were you hiding?"

"Me, hiding?"

"I've looked for you all over the world and couldn't find you."

"But," the girl paused, "who are you to be searching for me?"

"I gave birth to you," the woman said.

"My mother's dead. She died during childbirth. That's what Dad said."

"He's not telling the truth."

"My dad wouldn't…"

"Please hear me out," the woman replied and stepped closer to the girl. "I'm standing before you now. I'm alive. I don't look dead, do I?"

"No, but…"

"I'm not some crazy woman trying to mess up your life. Look at my face, the shape of my nose, my eyes, and my mouth. Look at your fingers. They're long and slender just like mine. And you've got that triangular birthmark below your belly button."

"How'd you know about that?" The girl immediately touched her stomach.

"I couldn't have made this all up. Could I?" The woman smiled. "There's no way I could have known."

Maybe, one day, my real mom and me could have a conversation like this, I thought.

"Yuh sleeping? Petal nudged me.

"No, I'm not." I swiftly opened my eyes. "I was just thinking."

"Thinking? Is time to go home, Baby Girl."

"Already?"

"De meeting finish."

"But what about the sports club?"

"We talked about dat already," she said and looked at me with a puzzled expression. "Yuh sure yuh all right?"

I grinned when Petal confirmed that twelve girls had registered for the soccer team.

"Mickey is going to be de coach," she said.

I don't know how she was able to arrange it, but one month after the by-election Arlie announced that our newly elected Member of Parliament, Joseph Wilson, was coming to Flat Hill Village.

"This is a golden opportunity," Arlie said. "We still don't have good roads or a reliable water supply, so let's take this opportunity to enlighten Mr. Wilson regarding our plight and—"

"If he don't give us no help we going to know what to do next time," Meena cut in.

"Yuh, sure right," Petal said.

"Dem politicians too damn disgusting!" Sandra added.

A handful of women giggled. Arlie scanned the gathering as if she were a teacher seeking out the naughty children. "When you're asking someone for something, you've got to do it with respect," she said.

"Is basic human rights to have water in we pipe. Is not no favour nobody doing for none of we," Meena said.

"Come on people, when the minister gets here please treat the man with dignity," Arlie said. Then she adjourned the meeting. Petal and I left Arlie's house under a light drizzle.

"We could make it." I begged Petal to at least try to outrun the dark clouds heading in our direction. I didn't want to go back into Arlie's house as she had suggested, preferring to risk getting soaked rather than to listen to one more negative word about Mr. Wilson's planned visit to Flat Hill Village. As far as I knew, nobody special had ever come to Flat Hill Village, and I was looking forward to meeting a VIP.

"Is Mr. Wilson going to come up to our house?" I asked as we hustled home.

"I don't think so," Petal responded as she held a plastic bag over her head. The billowing wind slapped big drops of water down on us, and, despite Petal's best efforts, her hair still got wet. I darted up the staircase but came to a sudden stop on the mat, trying to catch my breath. Then I heard a familiar voice.

I could feel the smile lighting up my face. "No glasses?" I said as Colm poked his head out the door.

"I'm wearing contacts," he said.

"Wow, you look so different."

"Yuh getting taller and prettier."

"And wetter." I glanced at my wet socks and squishy shoes.

"I met my real cousins," I said to Colm after I'd changed into dry clothes.

"So yuh found someone to replace me." He smirked.

"No one can ever do that," I said. "And no one can help me with poetry like you can."

The thick clouds made it impossible to spot the hilltop in the distance. The drizzle turned into a massive downpour, causing a channel of dirty brown water to sweep the roadway and creating a giant chocolate waterslide. I was sure that if anyone got too close to the mad rush of water, the current could easily sweep him or her away.

Moxley and Spider were barking louder than usual as I recited some of my newer poems to Colm. But when the first round of thunder exploded, the dogs, as well as I, went completely silent. A massive rock suddenly loosened from the earth with a loud swish, tumbling down the roadway, and one of the coconut trees came crashing down, narrowly missing Arlie's house. The heavy rainfall continued to lash against the roof, and, when Petal turned up the radio, I was grateful to be in a safe place, away from the widespread flash flooding the news reporter was announcing.

"Set de alarm clock," Petal told Colm later that evening, insisting he should spend the night with us. Colm put on a pair of my dad's pajamas and slept on the sofa. I liked that he was back in the house with us.

On a very sunny Saturday, Flat Hill Village Girls' Soccer Club held its inaugural meeting at Meena's house. Dahlia's two sisters, Carrie, and I were among the thirteen girls who showed up. We settled on three benches in a large room on the lower level of the house. Our new coach faced us on a wooden chair. "I drafted some rules," he said. "Girls, you need to be on time for practice and you shouldn't be absent without a valid reason. We can't have a successful team if we're not disciplined."

"How often are we going to meet?" Carrie asked.

"Once a week," our coach said. "We'll meet in the afternoons from four to six. This time will eventually change to Saturday mornings in a couple months when my work schedule changes."

We didn't have anywhere else to practice but at Flatlands. None of us minded having to trek up the hill to get there. It would have been much more convenient if Flat Hill Village had a nice community center with a large open space where we could practice drills. But we were not as fortunate as some of the other communities on the island.

On my way home, I couldn't help but think about how much my life had changed since I'd left Toronto, and I wondered if it would soon change again. When I got home, Dad was puffing a cigarette on the staircase. "You had a good time?" he asked, moving over to make room for me to get by.

"Most of the girls have never played soccer before, but everyone wants to learn," I said as I climbed up two stairs at a time.

But before I reached the top, Dad yelled, "We're going to Cousin Stanley's house next weekend!"

I think my heart stopped for a minute. Then I turned and gave him a big smile.

21.

"WHAT TIME ARE WE LEAVING?" I asked Petal when she said we'd be visiting the Emperor Valley Zoo. Earlier that day, Dad had postponed our trip to Stanley's place because he had to cover for a work colleague who'd fallen ill. Petal's boys had never been to the zoo before, but I'd been there twice with Vena and the twins. I was disappointed we weren't going to visit our cousins, but I liked going to the zoo.

"We going to leave home at one o'clock," Petal said, but at around midday two uniformed police officers, one way taller than my father and the other not much taller than me, arrived at our gate. "Your mother's home?" the shorter officer said.

"I don't live with my mother," I said.

"We need to speak to Petal Sparks," the taller man said in a serious tone.

"She's inside." I turned around quickly, preparing to zip up the staircase, but the dogs barked loudly, alerting Petal that someone was at the gate. "Who out there?" Petal's voice floated toward us.

"Police!" I yelled.

She appeared at the door in bare feet, clutching a red-and-white tea towel. "Something happen to Smokey?" Petal's face was contorted, as if she'd just tasted a dish with a very sharp taste.

"No, ma'am, but can we speak to you in private? It's very important," the taller man said.

"Baby Girl, put de dogs in dey house," she said as she invited the officers onto the porch.

I secured the dogs in their kennel as the dull, heavy banging of a jackhammer wafted from the Carlins' house. I peered uphill trying to spot the workmen who'd recently started to rebuild Martha Carlin's dwelling, but I didn't see anyone. So far the builders had erected the brick walls, but the roof was not yet in place. Since the house had been destroyed by fire, Martha and her children had lived in a makeshift one-room shack; I often wondered how they all fit in such a tiny space.

Petal hadn't argued with Martha since Dad had assumed the chore of cleaning up behind the house. Not even after Martha's nephew, Claudius, had stabbed my father. In truth, the Carlins had been dumping far less garbage on us than in previous months.

Martha's son, Oswald, and her nephew, Claudius, remained in custody. Both had a string of charges filed against them, and no one expected either to be released for many years.

Suddenly, Petal started to bawl so loudly that I scampered up the rear staircase and lost my flip-flops in the process. When I got to the living room, the two officers were gone, but Petal was sitting on the sofa, her face buried in her hands. Her two boys huddled beside her, their eyes fixed on her face. "Call yuh Dad," she sniffled and momentarily looked up.

That day I knew for sure that Boyie wasn't ever coming home. He was dead, killed by a gunshot to the head. His body—or, more correctly, his bones—were found in a shallow grave near a citrus field in Tabaquite. The police suspected he'd been killed the very same day he'd been abducted. "Why dey do dat to meh little brother?" Petal screamed. "He was only nineteen..."

"Can I get you anything?" I asked, stroking her arm. She just cried louder, so I fussed over her and made sure the two boys were occupied, waiting for Dad to come home and take over.

Our home bustled with activity as our neighbours popped

in to express their condolences. They only made Petal cry louder too. But some of them told funny stories about Boyie, and now and then Petal would give them a weak smile before she started sobbing again.

I was relieved that Boyie wasn't ever coming back, but I was sorry his death had brought Petal so much sadness.

The strong scent of spices clogged my nostrils, so I poked my head into the kitchen to see what Arlie and a couple other women who'd gathered there were doing. The energy in the house was so strong that I felt as though we were preparing for a big family celebration. Unlike the people who'd attended Mr. Arthur's wake, no one at Boyie's wake wore long dresses or fancy head ties. There weren't any sad faces except for Petal's.

Dahlia's mother, Mrs. Arlington, handed Dante a plateful of *pelau* before serving Carrie and then Suri. Just as she offered Samuel a dish, the lights flickered and the house fell into complete darkness, but in a few seconds the lights came on again. The electricity had been turning on and off for several weeks now, and everyone had been complaining about it.

Mickey, Shiva, Mr. Wellington, and Dad sat in the front of the house on collapsible chairs we'd borrowed from Arlie. I poked my head over the balcony, listening to them. "Where did they find Boyie's body?" Mr. Wellington asked Dad.

"In Tabaquite," Dad said. "The police got an anonymous tip about illegal activity at a house there. The officers stormed the residence. They shot and killed two thugs who fired at them. They also captured a woman who eventually led them to the shallow grave in the citrus field where Boyie's remains were found."

Once again the lights dimmed but quickly brightened. "Is Boyie who doing that!" blurted Suri, who was seated on the porch next to Dante, Carrie, and Samuel. Just then the lights blinked again, and Carrie's plate slipped.

"Dead people have no power," Dante insisted.

"Yes, they do," Suri said. "My papie threw a book off my daddy's shelf, and Papie was already dead."

"Chile, get de broom and clean-up dis mess." Mrs. Arlington observed Carrie's upside-down paper plate and the bits of rice, peas, and chicken scattered at our feet. I hesitated for a moment, but her ugly expression made me pop out of my seat and head straight to the kitchen.

Our visitors belted out a hymn, and, as I picked up the broom, I heard Mrs. Arlington's loud, raspy voice above everyone else's. While I cleaned Carrie's mess, my friends giggled at Mrs. Arlington's unusual antics. Suri almost fell out of her seat as Mrs. Arlington swayed from right to left.

"She going to do a cartwheel any time," Dante whispered, but, even if she had the skill, there wasn't enough space on the porch for that. As the people sang "Blessed Assurance," Dad's cousin Stanley and his wife walked in.

"Greetings!" Stanley addressed everyone in a gigantic voice. His wife Marguerite smiled prettily.

"Good to see you, man," Dad said to his cousin.

"Where have you been hiding?" Stanley grinned.

"I've been around, but working long hours."

"So you're making all the dough."

"Long hours, yes, but there isn't anything in these." Dad slapped his pants pockets.

"You've probably got it stashed away in an offshore bank."

"No such luck, but I'm glad you came to support us."

"Marguerite was hesitant to come after dark, but we got here quite safely, thank God."

"You can't be too wary of the Flat Hill Village youth," Marguerite said. "I was convinced a young man at the standpipe had a rifle in a paper bag tucked under his arm."

"But it was only a long loaf of bread," Stanley laughed.

"Well, Flat Hill Village surely has its problems," Dad said, glancing at me, "and sometimes I do worry about our safety."

"How are you?" Stanley's voice lowered a notch as his eyes met mine.

"I'm okay," I said. Marguerite greeted me with a snug embrace. "Where's Nichelle?"

"She's hitting the books—she's got an important test on Monday. But she sent this for you." Marguerite handed me a plastic bag.

"It's heavy." I put the bag down at my feet and peeked inside. There were a bunch of books. "Thanks so much."

By two-thirty in the morning, everyone except Colm's mom, Sandrina had left. I switched on my nightlight, opened my bedroom door, and climbed into bed. I tried not to think about the story Suri had shared about her dead grandfather throwing a book off a shelf, but I couldn't get it out of my head. I shut my eyes really tight. Moments later, someone knocked.

"Yuh mind if Sandrina sleep wit' yuh tonight?" Petal asked.

"No," I replied.

Sandrina climbed in, and I began moving around to make myself comfortable. When that didn't work, I cushioned my back with two small pillows.

"You can't sleep?" Sandrina asked, lifting her head.

"No," I said. "Do you think that Boyie would haunt the people who killed him?"

"When a man is dead, he's dead," Sandrina said. "It's either he's going straight to Heaven or Hell. No dead man has ever come back to hurt nobody."

"Is Boyie going to Hell?"

"That depends on what was in his heart when he died."

A mental picture of a tall, skinny man pressing a gun to Boyie's temple filled my head, and I wondered how scared he must have felt. Then I tried to imagine how it would feel to be dead.

Can dead people listen to music? The song Boyie had been

blasting the day Dad and I moved into Flat Hill Village came to mind. I hoped Boyie could play some music wherever he was.

After learning of Boyie's death, Petal lost all desire to cook or clean, so I was relieved when Sandrina offered to stay at our place until after the funeral to help with the household chores. But Sandrina's idea of helping was to give me instructions. "Get the broom and sweep the floor," Sandrina ordered, staring at me with eyes as bright as a full moon. I'd washed and dried the breakfast dishes minutes earlier, and I needed some quiet time to put my thoughts on paper. I wanted to tell her to leave me alone, but the dirty look on her face made me clamp my mouth shut.

On the day of the funeral, Colm picked up his mother in a gently used Ford hatchback he'd recently purchased, and, shortly after they left, I slipped on a dark blue dress. About half an hour later, Petal, Dad, the boys, and I headed down the dusty track, and I felt our neighbours' eyes on us as we climbed into Dad's car.

"Where are we going?" Drew asked.

"To your Uncle Boyie's funeral." I fastened his seat belt.

"Funeral?" He squinted, putting his tiny fingers over his eyes to block the glare of the sun.

"Yes, we're going to Boyie's funeral," I said. "Do you know what a funeral is?"

Even though he nodded, he looked confused. I didn't know how to explain it, so I said nothing.

When Dad parked in front of Mt. Hanley's Presbyterian Church, there was already a crowd packed in the front of the building. I searched for Boyie's girlfriend, Bertha, but didn't see anyone resembling her. Some uniformed police officers climbed out of their vehicles and scattered among the large gathering. When the hearse pulled up, the air grew still. Arlie clutched Petal's right arm and Meena her left. "Watch the boys," Dad said to me, and he joined Colm and the other pallbearers.

"Let we go in." Petal's voice shook a bit.

At the cemetery, a woman dressed in white barged through the crowd. "Wait!" she bellowed, her voice sounding half human and half animal.

"I need to say goodbye!" She cradled the casket for what seemed like forever. A man I'd never seen before eventually led her away. The woman was a lot skinner than the image I'd seen of Bertha, but later I learned it was indeed her. Two men lowered the casket into the ground, using long pieces of rope. Then they dumped mounds of dirt on top of the shiny box. A strong wind raised the powdery earth. I closed my eyes and held my breath. Petal put a bouquet of white flowers on the grave. Warren pulled out a tissue from his pocket and mopped up the tears rolling down his mother's cheeks. Then I cried, even though I wasn't sure why.

Dad took us to Stanley and Marguerite's place the following weekend. When we got there, it seemed odd that there weren't any trees, flowers, or grass in front of the house. But just like most dwellings on the island, fancy wrought iron shielded the windows and doors. A sign posted on the gate read *Beware of the Dog*, so when Marguerite invited us in, I hesitated until she said that their dog had recently died and they hadn't yet decided whether to get another pet.

As we entered the house, a strong wind rattled three large photos on the wall; I examined the portraits of three very young children. "They're my three babies," Marguerite said when she noticed what I was staring at. The pictures made an even sharper knocking sound as the wind bounced them around again. I settled in a chair facing Petal and Dad, somewhat confused since, on a previous occasion, Marguerite had only mentioned having one other daughter, Nona.

"Sorry I'm late. I had an emergency to take care of." Stanley rushed in just as Marguerite finished telling us about their dog, Jimmy, who at twelve years old had lost his battle with cancer.

"With my type of work I get urgent calls at any time." Stanley mopped his brow with a handkerchief. "Whew, it's hot. Is Nichelle back yet?"

"No, but she'll be here any minute," Marguerite said as her husband turned on the air conditioner. Shortly after, Nichelle walked in with a tall, skinny girl.

"You're finally visiting." Nichelle introduced her friend Natalie, a classmate. I was tempted to follow them along the corridor, but I wasn't sure they would welcome my company, so I pulled out several magazines from a large pile and skimmed through them. I couldn't find anything to grasp my attention though and I was starting to feel bored. Dad and Stanley moved to the far end of the room, chatting about an upcoming soccer match between their national soccer team and the United States.

"This year will be fifteen years since I started working at St. Teresa's." Marguerite eased closer to Petal. "Ten years as both an English and Geography teacher, and five as principal."

"You're de principal at St. Teresa's?" Petal said. "Dat's one of de best schools on de island." She paused. "It was her first choice." Petal looked at me, but I kept my eyes on the pages of the magazine I had spread open on my lap. In reality, I was stealing glances at them every few seconds.

"When I was in primary school, a girl in meh class pass for St. Teresa's," Petal said. "She went away to university on a scholarship, but I don't have a clue if she ever came back."

"Well, our girls work extremely hard, and that's why we do so well in the scholarship department," Marguerite said. "Nichelle is at St. Teresa's now, and my older girl, Nona, went there as well."

Dad pulled out two cigarettes, and he and Stanley headed to the back of the house.

"So, how are you coping with everything? Marguerite asked Petal.

"Hanging in."

"It's going to take a very long time for the pain to heal. I've had my share of loss too, so I know."

"You lose a brother too?"

"No, not a brother, but Jenny, my second child. She was just a few weeks old when she died. If she'd lived, she would have turned seventeen this year. She's the baby in the middle picture over there."

"I real sorry to hear dat," Petal said, her eyes filling with shiny tears.

"No," Marguerite said, "don't feel sorry for me. God took her and I've learned to accept that she's in a better place.

Turning her attention to me, Marguerite said, "So, Baby Girl, you're at secondary school?"

I nodded. "Yes."

"Which one?"

"Maitland Comprehensive," I said.

"It's one of the newer ones, isn't it?" Marguerite asked. "There are so many new schools now that I've lost track."

"Yes, she going to de same school Boyie use to go to," Petal said.

"I see." Marguerite's eyes shifted to my face.

"Do you like it?"

"Not really." I made a face. "Last week a boy at my school slapped a teacher in her face and the police arrested him."

"That's not good," Marguerite said, shaking her head. "That's not good at all."

"Maybe if she had tried a little harder she would have done a little better, heh, heh, heh." Dad said in mid-stride, but no one else laughed or even smiled.

I felt like a bonehead. I wanted to jump up and say, *Dad, I did my best* over and over until he believed me, but I didn't. I just squirmed in my seat, and hung my head. Stanley glared at Dad as if he wanted to scold him and an uncomfortable silence filled the room.

"Smokey, dat not funny at all." Petal rolled her eyes. "Baby Girl real smart, and she does write real good poetry too."

"I'm sure she's a very intelligent girl," Stanley said moments before Nichelle walked in and announced that Natalie's father was on his way to pick her up.

After Natalie left, Nichelle helped her mom serve us snacks and drinks. Then she invited me to the back of the house. I was surprised that, unlike the front of the dwelling, the backyard overflowed with masses of flowering plants, big green bushes, and fruit trees. My eyes caught a tiny blue bird perched on top of a clothesline strung between two coconut trees. The little bird flew away, and, moments later, my eyes locked onto a mango tree laden with clusters of the plump yellow fruit.

"I couldn't believe whath your Dad said," Nichelle said as we settled on a bench under a sprawling plum tree. "Does he always hurth your feelings like thath?"

"Not really," I said, embarrassed she had heard Dad's words. Did she think I was just another dumb comprehensive school kid who wouldn't amount to anything? I kept my eyes on a gang of black ants crawling on top of a busted mango. I wondered how I might change the topic of conversation, but Nichelle took care of that.

"You know whath," Nichelle said, "loths of girls at my school are stuck up. Some of them only got accepted because their parents have lots of money and influence and not because they're brighter than anyone else. At first I didn't wanth to go to St. Teresa's. When Mom transferred me there, I was mad as hell."

"You didn't pass for St. Teresa's?" I finally looked up.

"No, I passed for a comprehensive school too, but Mom was right, St. Teresa's is a better school and I'm getting a much better education than I would have if I'd stayed at my old school. I'd love for you to come there. You want me to ask Mom?

"To ask her?"

"Yes, to get you a transfer."

"To St. Teresa's?"

"Why not?"

"But you said the girls are stuck up. I don't want to go there anymore if the girls are like that."

"Not all of them are. My friend Natalie is nice. You just have to choose the people you lime with carefully."

I didn't say much to either Dad or Petal as we travelled back to Flat Hill Village, but the desire to attend St. Teresa's Convent High School, which I'd put to rest, had suddenly woken up, and I imagined myself decked out in the school's uniform. I silently wished I could trade places with Nichelle, because she was much prettier than me, had perfect parents, lived in a nice house in one of the better parts of the country, and attended one of the best schools too.

"Why yuh so quiet?" Petal asked.

"Nichelle's going to ask her mom to get me into St. Teresa's," I blurted out.

"She said dat?" Petal frowned as if she didn't believe me. But I nodded my head, and I secretly hoped it would happen.

22.

M EENA AND MRS. ARLINGTON sat on Petal's porch discussing Mr. Wilson, our new Member of Parliament, who was scheduled to visit Flat Hill Village at three o'clock that afternoon. Arlie had confirmed earlier in the week that he was finally coming, after two previous cancellations. It was the first time the committee members had congregated in a place other than Arlie's house. This was because workmen were in the midst of constructing an extension to her porch, and it wasn't going to be completed for another couple of weeks.

"If the rain fall and wash him away, he going to see how we does live when it raining," Mrs. Arlington said to Meena Ramsingh.

I thought she was having a pie-in-the-sky dream, since it was one of those boiling hot days when I wouldn't have chosen to go outside if I had a choice. I aimed the fan at my upper body, but only hot air hit me. The warmer I felt, the more I wished our house had air conditioning like the big white house on Paradise Lane. All the while, the fan's whirring remained a backdrop to the women's conversation. I slipped into a strapless top before searching the closet and pulling out the tiniest pair of shorts I possessed.

"Yuh not leaving dis house dress like dat," Petal exclaimed, giving me such a harsh look that I promptly returned to my bedroom. It was around two-thirty in the afternoon when I made my way back to the living room in a strapless blue cotton dress. Petal, dressed completely in white, served orange juice, soda, and chocolate cake to her guests. The women continued to trickle in, but due to a shortage of chairs, Sandra settled on the uppermost stair.

"Bring some of our folding chairs over," Arlie said to Dante and Carrie.

"Yuh want to help dem?" Petal asked me.

I really didn't want to, but with at least twenty eyes on me I felt compelled to comply. We made several trips in the boiling sun, lugging the chairs from Arlie's to Petal's house. Dad and Meena's husband, Shiva, mingled with the women for a short while. They then made their way to the kitchen, where they sipped cold beer and examined some photos Dad had snapped of the big crater that had resurfaced again after the last downpour. I gulped back a glass of ice-cold water and made myself invisible next to the refrigerator.

"We're going to give him these," Dad said to Shiva, after separating a few pictures from the bunch.

I returned to the porch when Arlie called the meeting to order. She held up a sheet of paper. "Here I have a list of the topics we're going to discuss with our M.P. when he arrives." She began to call out the items. "The shortage of pipe borne water, the unpaved road, the crime in our community, the lack of any recreational facilities."

"The young people need jobs, jobs and more jobs," Mrs. Arlington interrupted.

"I'm getting to that in a moment." Arlie lifted her eyes from the sheet, pursing her lips. "One thing I am requesting is that we don't show our frustration," she continued. "We've got to be calm and collected."

After reading the entire list, she sat down and Petal stood up. "I want to thank Arlie for all de work she's done to bring de Minister to Flat Hill Village." Some of the women applauded.

"Allyuh sure he going to show up?" Meena rose from her seat.

"Of course, he is," Petal said.

"Well, time will tell," Meena said and sat.

Arlie stood again, She adjourned the meeting glancing at her watch. "It's time to eat," she said. Mrs. Arlington offered the women orange juice and cake that she'd prepared.

"Go inside and chat wit' yuh friends," Petal said after I'd received a big piece of cake. So I made my way into the living room. Carrie, inspecting Mr. Wilson's photo in the newspaper, said, "He's a tall, fat man with a big head."

Every couple of minutes we'd take turns poking our heads out the window in search of our Member of Parliament. Samuel pointed to a beefy man who was walking up the trail with a black briefcase. "Mr. Wilson's coming—that's him with the hat."

"Mr. Wilson's not that fat. When I saw him on TV, he looked as skinny as Baby Girl's dad," Dante said. "And TV makes you look ten pounds fatter than your real size." I thought Dante had made an excellent point, but decided not to add my two cents' worth.

Suri, however, expressed my thoughts exactly when she said, "We're going to see how fat Mr. Wilson is when he gets here."

I imagined Mr. Wilson dressed in a business suit with sneakers on his feet. That made me laugh out loud. "What's so funny?" Carrie asked.

"Nothing," I said, aware that it was unlikely our M.P. would come to Flat Hill Village on official government business in running shoes. Four o'clock turned to four thirty, and still there was no sign of him. Finally, at ten minutes to five, Mickey shouted from the roadway, "The Minister and his people are finally coming up the hill!"

"I'm going to escort him up." Arlie sped out of the door as if she were rushing to catch the last bus of the evening. We followed her out of the house in a single file toward the street.

When Shiva stepped onto the dry, sandy roadway, the wind grabbed his baseball cap off his head. A pile of dust hit my face, momentarily blinding me, so I closed my eyes until the wind died down and the dust settled. A few of the women were mopping the dust from their faces with crumpled hankies.

"He's not fat and he's not tall. You're both half-right," I said to Dante and Carrie when I got a clear view of Mr. Wilson. A stocky man with a harshness to his face that comes with age approached us, accompanied by a tall, thin woman. Both held wary gazes as if preparing to spring on a potential attacker at short notice.

"He's as young as my elder sister's son." Meena's eyes glowed like a young girl's in the presence of her favourite teen idol. And Meena was right—Mr. Wilson wasn't much older than the guys who usually hung out near the abandoned house, but I was sure he had more brains than all of them put together.

He wasn't in a formal business suit, but a lily-white shirt with black pants and a red tie with white dots all over it. When I got within arm's reach of him, I scanned his face quickly. *How odd!* I thought when I saw a dimple smack in the middle of his right cheek, but couldn't find a matching one on his left. My eyes examined his feet, and I knew it would be possible for me to see my face in his shoes if I tried. They were that shiny, despite having climbed up our dusty, sandy hill. Another strong wind hit, and a tuft of black, straight hair at the top of Mr. Wilson's head fell forward. But it wasn't quite enough to completely hide the discoloured bump on his forehead.

Mr. Wilson mopped up the sweat trickling down his face and scrunched his handkerchief into a ball before tucking it in one of his back pockets. Then his eyes shifted from one woman to the next as Arlie introduced the Women's Action Committee members. I wormed my way into the line directly in front of Mrs. Arlington.

"This is Melody," Arlie said when I got to the top.

"But everyone calls me Baby Girl," I blurted.

"Baby Girl?" he repeated. "That's really nice."

I smiled back at him before stepping aside and mingling with the women who'd already made their introductions. Petal and a bunch of other women remained in an orderly line, like church parishioners waiting to greet their spiritual leader after Sunday service. He shook their hands and greeted them one by one.

When he was done, Mr. Wilson addressed the crowd in a big, bold voice. "I'm glad to meet my constituents. I'm here to address your needs, your concerns, and to answer your questions. I want only the best for every man, woman, and child residing in this neighbourhood."

"We need a better water supply!" a voice in the back of the crowd cut in.

"And better roads too!" a woman with a grainy voice shouted.

"When it raining we drowning, and when the sun hot the dust suffocating everybody!" another female voice yelled.

Mr. Wilson grew pale and his face tightened, a mass of lines suddenly appearing on his forehead as a chorus of complaints from both men and women continued to hit him. And for a while I could no longer hear what he was saying, even though his mouth was moving.

"Excuse me!" Arlie's voice was as big as a man's. She spun around. "Let's give the Minister time to speak, then you'll all have your chance."

The crowd went quiet and once again I could hear Mr. Wilson's voice. But less than a minute later Shiva pointed to four people charging in our direction. "What wrong with them?"

The skinniest waved a long, thin item that I thought could be used as a weapon. As they got closer, I saw that they were part of the gang of youths who hung out by the derelict house at all hours of the day and night.

"Oh no, they're not coming here to cause trouble!" Arlie looked at Smokey and then at Mickey, as if expecting them to act quickly. As if on cue, Dad, Mickey, and Shiva stepped out from among the crowd. Three other men soon joined them, but, despite the distraction, Mr. Wilson continued to address everyone. The man at Mr. Wilson's side shoved his hand inside his pocket, and I thought he was going to pull out a gun, but instead he fished out a pen and scribbled something in his notebook.

"I understand your frustration. I know everyone wants a better standard of living for their children. I would..."

"No, Dad!" I yelled, as my father stepped at least two feet ahead of the other men that were about to confront the four youth. He remained in the dead centre in the path of the approaching men. As they got closer, I realized the skinniest of them was indeed holding a long stick. Right then Dad sprang back to join the other men. Then I saw it. A greenish, brownish lizard, more than four feet in length, race toward Mr. Wilson's shiny shoes. I shrieked and almost jumped out of my shoes as the reptile crawled within inches of my feet. The crowd parted, leaving more than enough space for the lizard, and the four young men who were trying to catch it, to get through. Theo, Martha Carlin's youngest son, eased through the crowd holding the stick that I now realized had a noose secured by duct tape at the end of it and, in the wink of an eye, he expertly slipped this makeshift apparatus over the iguana's body. Then he twisted the noose, pinning the reptile to the ground.

"Grab it!" the crowd chanted. Mr. Wilson stared at the lizard and hollered along with everyone else. Then he lunged forward, trying to get a better look at the creepy-crawly that had upstaged him. The lizard wiggled as Theo held it up in the air like a trophy.

"We going to skin it and cook it." Theo exposed very white teeth.

"If I didn't have a pressing engagement I might have stuck around," Mr. Wilson said with full lips pulled upward and outward. Theo, along with his companions, smiled back at him. Then they all disappeared in the direction from which they'd come, carrying their prized possession.

"Let's get back to business." Mr. Wilson addressed us for a while longer. Then Dad gave him the pictures of the recurring crater he had snapped after the last rainstorm.

When we arrived home, sweat trickled down my back and I felt as if I'd been sprayed with a water gun. Petal rushed to take a shower. I sat under the fan waiting my turn and wishing we had an extra bathroom. After I showered, I changed into my fourth outfit of the day. Petal's eyes were glowing when I walked into the living room. She rushed toward me and folded me into her arms, holding me tight. "Marguerite called. Congratulations! Yuh going to St. Teresa's."

"I'm going to St. Teresa's?" I could barely get the words out, she was holding me so tightly against her chest.

"Yes, Marguerite phoned when yuh was in de shower. She said dat one of de girls at St. Teresa is moving to America fer good, so yuh going to get she place."

This was the best news ever. I'd never been as excited about anything in my life since Dad and I had moved to Trinidad.

23.

SPORTING WIDE SMILES, Suri and Samuel waved at me as they climbed into their dad's Ford Escort. When the car pulled away, I remained in my regular spot waiting for Mr. Wellington. I really didn't care to write the test our mathematics teacher had scheduled first thing that Friday morning, but I was eager to know whether either of my two poems entered in the National Secondary Schools Poetry Competition had made the cut.

I was due to be transferred to St. Teresa's Convent High School the following Monday, and days earlier Petal had accompanied me to Port-of-Spain to purchase new school supplies. Although I was excited about wearing my brand new school blouse, skirt, and tie, I felt a little bit uneasy about having to make new friends.

Arlie and Carrie walked ahead of Dante. "Hurry up, boy," Arlie said, just before she and Carrie slipped inside her blue Audi.

Dante picked up the pace, and, as soon as he got in, he and Carrie waved at me just as energetically as Suri and Samuel had done minutes before.

"You okay?" Mr. Wellington's car pulled up about five minutes later.

"Yes," I said, noticing one side of the collar on his stiffly ironed shirt stuck out further than the other.

"Then why you so serious?"

"I'm just thinking," I said, settling in the back seat and throwing my backpack on the empty space next to me.

"I thought maybe you were upset because the weatherman said it's going to rain like peas by mid-morning." He glanced at me through his mirror, and then he shifted his gaze to the front passenger seat. "By the way, Jasmine and Cherise phoned last night. They're starting their new school today," he said, after which he began to shuffle through a stack of papers. However, he continued to talk about his two daughters, who'd travelled to Texas days earlier to join their mother. As I wound down the window, I was a tiny bit jealous of his two girls, but I consoled myself with the thought that I'd soon be a St. Teresa's Convent High School girl.

At least ten people, including Dahlia's two younger sisters, strode past Mr. Wellington's car. Dahlia's sisters entered a red Mazda at the bottom of the hill, and, just as the vehicle moved off, Mr. Wellington climbed out of his car and stuffed the papers he'd been sorting into the trunk. He slipped back inside, and, as he prepared to drive off, Martha Carlin's son, Theo, stepped in front of us, blocking us. Two youths whom I'd never seen before stood on either side of him, like bodyguards.

"Why are they standing in the middle of the street like they're not afraid of iron?" Mr. Wellington tooted his horn three times, and Theo and his companions shuffled aside. Just then an SUV screeched to a halt at the bottom of the hill.

"Keep yuh head down!" Mr. Wellington yelled at me at least five times as a series of crackling sounds rang out as loud as tree limbs snapping during a powerful storm. I remained in the cramped space just behind the driver's seat while tiny pieces of glass rained down on me. Suddenly, the popping noises stopped and tires screeched. Then someone hollered, "Theo, on the ground!"

"You okay?" Mr. Wellington asked.

"Yeah," I said, but I was shaking all over.

"You sure?"

"Yeah."

"Trigger-happy gunmen," Mr. Wellington said as I sat up and stared through his shattered windshield. "You didn't see that car, you hear me?" he said in a tight, firm voice.

I didn't answer.

"Christ, stay right here!" He slipped out of the car and joined the fast-growing crowd.

As I dusted tiny pieces of glass from all over me, a woman yelled, "He bleedin' like hell!" I poked my head out of the window, but the crowd was blocking my view, so I climbed out of the vehicle.

"Get back in!" Mr. Wellington shouted, but his words came too late. I'd already seen the blood pouring out of Theo's mouth and nose. The left side of his head had been blown to bits, and he lay on his stomach with both arms spread like an eagle's wings. I covered my eyes with my hands and jumped back into the vehicle.

As if in a trance, I stared at the tiny pieces of glass scattered on the rubber mat beneath my feet, and I didn't look up until a woman shrieked. "Not Theo, not meh son, not meh baby, not meh chile!" Martha Carlin's breasts and legs shook wildly as she and her daughter, Marlene, whose body was as thin as a dried-up stick, raced downhill. She carried a shoeless child in her arms.

"Oh Gawd, not Theo, not meh little brother!" she hollered.

"Let meh hold him." A woman snatched the infant from Marlene. Martha went down on all fours, holding both sides of her head. Then Martha dropped down beside her. Both were wailing. A crowd tightened around both women, and I could no longer see them.

An ambulance pulled up and a convoy of police cars parked helter-skelter on the roadway. "Move aside!" several officers bellowed. The crowd parted.

Then I heard tapping on the window. Slowly, I raised my head. "Are you all right?" a female officer asked. I nodded.

"Come out," she ordered, not too politely.

I stiffened. I kept my eyes low, making sure not to catch a second glimpse of Theo as I climbed out of the vehicle, clutching my school bag.

"What's your name?" she said in an unexpectedly softer tone.

"Melody Sparks." I spoke in my throat.

"What?"

"I'm Melody Sparks."

"Did you see what happened?"

"I didn't see anything," I said.

"What's your mother's name, dear?"

"Jada Shoemaker."

"She's here?"

"Here?"

"Is she over there?" The officer pointed to the crowd of people gathered a few feet from Mr. Wellington's vehicle.

"My mom's not here. I don't live with her." I wiped my nose with my sleeve. "I live with my dad."

"What's his name?"

"Everyone calls him Smokey, but his real name is Nathaniel, Nathaniel Sparks, and my dad's wife is Petal...."

"I'm the person you should be talking to." A grim-looking Mr. Wellington slipped between the officer and me.

"You're her father?" the officer asked.

"No."

"A relative?"

"No, this is my vehicle." He touched the door but kept his eyes on the officer's face. "It's my job to drive her to and from school every day." While the officer questioned Mr. Wellington, I stumbled toward Meena.

"Yuh all right?" Meena put her hand on my back. Everyone kept asking me that.

"Uh-huh," I said, but truthfully, I wasn't sure. I still felt scared.

Two more police cruisers sped up the hill. The lady officer stepped away from Mr. Wellington and headed toward her newly arrived colleagues.

"I'm going home," I said to Mr. Wellington, and distanced myself from the crowd.

I'd gotten almost halfway home when I saw Petal.

"Yuh okay?" She came toward me with a fearful look on her face.

"I didn't get hurt or anything," I said, "but I saw Theo. I saw his body. His head is all bashed up as if someone hit him with a big bat."

"I know," she said slowly. "Meena just phone me."

"You came to meet me?"

"Yes," she said, "but I also need to talk to Mr. Wellington."

She took a few steps in the direction of the crowd. "Yuh not coming?" She turned around.

"No, I don't want to."

"You want to go home and wait for me there?"

"I don't want to go home alone. Can I wait for you right there?" I pointed to a tall coconut tree about halfway between where we were standing and where the shooting had occurred.

"Fine." She tangled her fingers with mine and, in silence, we headed in the direction of the scene of the crime.

"I'll wait here," I whispered and then slipped my fingers from hers as soon as we got to the coconut tree. I dumped my backpack on the ground and leaned against the trunk of the tree, keeping an eye on Petal as she walked away. I watched her speak to Mr. Wellington for a while, and then the female officer who'd questioned Mr. Wellington and me spoke with her briefly.

Mr. Wellington climbed into his vehicle, but he couldn't drive off because the police cruisers remained smack in the middle of the road, blocking his car and all the others. Suddenly a knot formed in my stomach as the reality of what I'd witnessed hit me. My knees buckled and I slumped onto a rock beside the tree.

"Theo get kill and Baby Girl see de whole thing, but she all right." Petal said to Dad on her mobile phone when she got back to me. "Yuh want to talk to yuh dad?"

"No," I said, but she shoved the phone in my face.

I refused to take it and instead brushed off the dust stuck to the bottom of my bag. Petal told Dad that the two youths who had been with Boyie when he was killed had disappeared, and that no one had been able to identify them. As we headed home, I thought of Boyie's murder at nineteen and Theo's at seventeen. *What if Theo's killer makes me number three?* I got an eerie feeling when we passed the ramshackle house, fully aware that Theo would never hang out there again.

"Let we hurry!" Petal said as the first drizzle hit. She rushed ahead, but even though the drops got heavier, I lagged behind and didn't take my umbrella from my bag. Water poured from the sky like big, cloudy sheets, and by the time I arrived at home I was soaking wet. I headed to the bathroom and stared in the mirror. A serious, sad girl, with dripping wet hair and more than a few pimples stared back at me. The wind roared like a mini hurricane.

Are the rain gods crying for Theo? His bashed-in face flashed on the wall, on the ceiling and on the top of my bed. Then my thoughts strayed to our M.P.'s visit, when Theo had proudly held up the wiggling reptile.

By the time Dad arrived home, the sun had come out of its hiding place, but he'd barely made his way up the staircase when two police officers arrived at the gate. "Did you know the murder victim?" The officers stood in the verandah while they spoke to Dad and Petal. I remained in the living room, hiding behind the door, listening.

"Of course, he lives with his mother in the unfinished house up there," Dad said.

"Where were you when the shooting happened? Do you know who shot him? Do you know the names of the two people who were with the deceased?" The officers bombarded Dad and Petal with a host of questions, but they answered mostly in the negative. "We need to talk to your daughter," one of the officers said.

"Why?" Dad asked.

"She may have some crucial evidence."

"I don't think so." Dad's tone was blunt.

"This is serious business," the officer said. "She was at the scene of the crime."

"She wasn't the only one present, and she's only a child," Dad said, but the officers persisted, so he gave in to their demand. I panicked and scampered to my bedroom. I collapsed on the bed and scrunched myself into a ball. Dad tapped on the door.

"Please make them go away," I sobbed.

"Just tell them you didn't see anything, and I promise they won't bother us again," Dad said.

It took some coaxing, but finally I followed Dad to the porch where the officers were waiting. "I heard a loud bang and the windshield shattered. That's it." I glanced at the taller of the two officers before lowering my head again.

"You're sure you're telling us everything?"

"Yes," I said.

"What colour was the car?"

"C-c-c-car?" I stuttered. "I don't know about any car. I didn't see anything," I said.

"She's only a child. There were at least a dozen people on the street when it happened," Dad said. "Why aren't you questioning them?"

"We've been doing that, sir. We plan to knock on every door in this village."

After the officers left, guilt rode my chest like a spoiled lunch and I felt horrible about lying to them. Even though I couldn't identify the shooter, I had seen the car. But I didn't admit that even to Dad.

I sat on my bed trying to finish a poem. I hadn't completed any new ones in weeks, but had four that were half done. I'd been working on them all afternoon, trying to keep my mind off the awful things that had happened recently.

"What is it?" I calmly asked Petal as she knocked on the door.

"A call for you." She pointed to the receiver.

I beamed with joy as Mr. Daniel, my English teacher at Maitland Comprehensive, shared the good news that one of my poems had won third place at the National Secondary Schools Poetry Competition. The joy was short-lived because, a few minutes later, Dad barged through my door.

"It's not safe for you to stay here. You're not sleeping in Flat Hill Village tonight."

"I didn't see anything, Dad," I said.

"I've already made arrangements."

"I'm not going back to Monty's house." I pursed my lips, preparing to cry. "I'm not going there, not for even one night."

"You're going to Stanley's place," Dad said. "We're taking you to Noel Gardens tonight."

I remembered the tone of Mr. Wellington's voice when he barked at me and told me not to tell anyone about the car I'd seen. I hadn't said anything to anyone, so what was going on? Why was Dad afraid for me? I shivered uncontrollably, and mutely packed my things.

24.

I CHECKED MY BAGS a couple of times to make sure I wasn't leaving behind my notebook full of poems, the two big envelopes stuffed with the pictures Dad had given me, and the key chain made of coconut shells, a treasured gift from Auntie Hattie. Petal took the boys to Arlie's place, and, right after they left, Dad put his hand on my shoulder and calmly said, "As soon as things settle down you'll be coming home."

He didn't explain what "settle down" meant, though.

"It's time we head on out," he announced the moment Petal returned. I took a deep breath as he picked up the blue suitcase in which I'd shoved a bunch of my clothes.

Petal slung a large brown bag with a broad strap over her shoulder. The bag contained my new school uniform, shoes, tie, and other school supplies. "If yuh forget anything, we going bring it fer yuh," Petal said.

I picked up my backpack and followed her and Dad out the door.

The people of Flat Hill Village had become part of me, but I was leaving them and the village behind. And even though my absence was supposed to be temporary, I wasn't sure what would happen if Theo's killers weren't found and the days turned into weeks and the weeks turned into months. Would Dad force me to remain at Stanley's house for months and months?

I'd lost faith in everything and everyone, and I sensed miserable times ahead. I had slowed my pace without realizing it, because when I looked up, Dad and Petal were way ahead of me. As I struggled to catch up, I tried to focus on the coming weeks, not months, but the sudden thought that I might not get along with the family made me sick to my stomach. I cringed at the thought of living with folks I didn't know very well.

Nichelle and I had gotten closer since our chat at the back of her parents' house, but the reality was, besides books, we didn't have any of the same interests.

Father God, please let the police find Theo's killer and allow my life to go back to the way it was before his murder, I prayed, trying even harder to wipe away the negative thoughts that had begun to devour my insides. No one spoke as we went around the crater that had opened up again in front of Suri and Samuel's house.

"Dey have no respec' fer de dead." Petal's face twisted in disgust when a soca tune at full volume hit our eardrums. A man with a big, round belly filling a bucket of water nodded at Dad, and just then, two half naked, snotty-nosed tots ran right in front of us. The three of us had to shift to the right to avoid walking into them.

As I got to the streetlight next to Dad's parked car, I noticed a brown, muddy paste stuck to my sneakers like glue. But with so much going on in my head I suddenly didn't care that they were filthy.

When we arrived at Stanley's house, no one mentioned Theo's slaying, and instead Petal, Dad, and Marguerite discussed the upcoming general elections for a while. I sunk into a chair, struggling to wipe the vivid images of Theo's bloody body from my mind, but I couldn't. Dad and Petal got up to leave and Marguerite trailed them.

"Stay inside," Dad ordered as I attempted to follow them.

I stuck my head out the window and saw Dad, Petal, and Marguerite huddled beside Dad's car. I tried to read their lips but it was too hard to figure out their words, so I quickly gave up. Just as Dad drove off, Stanley pulled up and Nichelle climbed out of her father's SUV with two bags. She walked inside ahead of her father, and, at her mother's request, led me to my room.

"Thith is your private space," she said as we entered and placed the brown bag containing my school supplies close to the door.

I put my blue suitcase beside the queen-sized bed and dropped my backpack next to it.

"Sorry, I've got to take thith call." Nichelle pressed her cell phone against her ear and left.

I pushed a half-open door leading to a neat little bathroom. I stood between the toilet bowl and the bathtub and examined several tiny flowers on the tiles that seemed to be the same shade of blue as my suitcase. Then I stepped toward the bed and sat on the mattress, which without doubt felt thicker and firmer than mine. My eyes moved from the walls to the windows to the closet, taking in a clock radio, a full-length mirror, a desk, and a matching chair. But I didn't stand up again until I noticed a laptop on an oak desk. *Was this to be mine?* I'd never owned a computer. Then I stood in front of the full-length mirror and stared at my tall, lean body. I ran my fingers up and down one of my skinny arms before doing the same to the other. When my eyes caught a whitehead on the tip of my nose, I raised both arms, preparing to squeeze it. But just as my fingertips reached my nose, Nichelle asked, "You're settling in?" poking her head through the door and making her way to the foot of the bed.

"Yeah." I dragged my new school skirts from my brown bag and slipped them onto individual hangers. I dipped into the bag again and pulled out five school shirts.

"They need ironing," she said.

"I know. I'll do it tomorrow," I said. "Will you show me where the iron is?"

"No," she said with a blank expression.

I froze, not knowing how to respond, but then she snickered. "I'm pulling your leg."

I kept my eyes on the door as someone knocked. "What are you two doing?" Marguerite walked in.

"Nothing," Nichelle said.

"Do you like your room?" Marguerite's eyes met mine.

"It's nice," I said. "I really like the computer. May I use it?"

"Of course," Marguerite said. "You're free to use it whenever you want."

Nichelle sat on my bed, making herself comfortable. Maybe she wanted to tell me something, I thought.

But Marguerite turned to her and patted her on the head. "The clean dishes aren't going to come out of the dishwasher by themselves," she said rather sternly.

After shoving my school clothes in the closet, I joined Nichelle in the kitchen and helped empty the dishwasher and put the dishes away in the cupboards. Marguerite pulled a Styrofoam container from the fridge and put it inside the microwave oven. "I'm going to warm this up, and we'll eat soon," she said, stirring another pot on the stove.

During dinner, I sat at the dining table alongside Nichelle and her parents. "You're not going to try even a little of it?" Marguerite eyed the untouched food on my plate. By then everyone else had almost finished everything on their plates.

"I really don't ever eat goat meat, I'm sorry," I eventually said.

"In future, just tell me ahead of time. I don't have horns, you know," Marguerite smiled.

"I'm sorry," I repeated and lowered my head.

The incident left me uneasy, and all I wanted to do was curl up in my room and stick my nose into a good book. But I didn't want to appear rude, so I joined the entire family in the living room and watched *Law and Order* with them. When the show ended, Nichelle and her parents spoke for what seemed like an eternity about a host for some upcoming church activities. I was bored and almost fell asleep on the sofa, but I opened my eyes quickly when Nichelle said goodnight to her parents in a voice close to that of a two-year-old child. *How odd,* I thought, jumping up from the sofa. I echoed her good night and finally went to my room.

That night I went down on my knees and prayed harder than I'd ever prayed in my entire life, asking God to help the police solve Theo's murder so I could return home to live with my father. I slipped under the covers and closed my eyes, but couldn't get Theo out of my head. I eventually climbed out of bed, pulled the drapes to one side and gazed for a long time at the half moon and countless stars in the sky.

On Monday, I awoke early and took a quick shower before slipping into my brand new school uniform. A wide smile stayed on my face as I adjusted my tie, even though it took several tries before I was satisfied. "Can I ask you something? I said to Nichelle, resting my backpack on the back seat of her mom's vehicle.

"Shoot," she said from the front seat, keeping her eyes in a book.

I had wanted to ask her how it felt to attend a school where her mother was the principal, but I held my tongue when Marguerite eased into the driver's seat.

"Whath do you want to know?" Nichelle turned.

"How does it feel to go to an all-girls school?" I said, changing the question.

"You'll concentrate better. Boys are often a big distraction," Marguerite answered for her daughter.

"Oh, Mom, Baby Girl was talking to me, not you," Nichelle exhaled. "Girls can cause distractions too, buth don't you worry. St. Mark's is just across the street, and I'm sure you'll meet some really cute guys soon."

"What are you telling the child?" Marguerite smiled.

My heart pounded when Marguerite swerved into the school-yard and parked in the principal's spot. Nichelle flew out of the vehicle before I'd unbuckled my seatbelt. "Stay with me," Marguerite said, and then led me through the main door to an open area. "Wait here." She signalled me to sit and then walked away.

I put my backpack on my lap, cuddling it as if it were a stuffed toy. Then I hunched forward and remained very still while resting my chin on top of the backpack. A woman in a grey suit walked past my chair and ignored me completely. Another woman, shorter and thinner than the first, smiled at me briefly before entering a nearby office. I felt like a very important person when it hit me that I, Melody Sparks, better known as Baby Girl, was living under the same roof as the principal of one of the best high schools on the island. But fear instantly took over when I thought of the possible negative reactions I might get from my new classmates if they knew I'd previously attended Maitland Comprehensive. I decided to keep that fact to myself.

My first day at St. Teresa's ended just as it began, without incident. I even made a new friend—a girl named Rose Bishop who was born in England to Trinidadian parents.

Two days later, when Marguerite's car pulled up in front of her Noel Gardens home, Dad was standing on the roadway next to his vehicle. I climbed out of Marguerite's car and greeted him. "Now you can call me whenever you want to," he said, handing me a tiny package.

I pulled off the wrapper. "No overseas calls, please," Dad joked as I inspected a red cell phone.

"How long before I can come home?" I asked.

"I don't know yet, but everyone's been minding their P's and Q's since Theo's death."

During the next couple of weeks I spoke to my father on a daily basis, but eventually our calls lessened to about once a week. Over time, whenever Stanley had time to spare, he'd regale me with stories about his grandparents, aunts, uncles, and cousins, stories I found endlessly fascinating. One night he informed me that one of our ancestors had once been the mayor of Arima! I was suitably impressed and this seemed to make Stanley puff up. When Stanley shared a story about his mother, my eyes watered. He noticed. "Is there something you want to tell me?" he asked gently.

"I must be a fool for wanting to meet my real mom, since she doesn't care two hoots about me," I said, mopping the tears from my cheeks.

"Don't be so hard on yourself," he said. "You certainly deserve to know who you are and where you came from." I picked up the glass of water next to me and began to sip from it, but almost spilled the glass when Stanley said that Nichelle wasn't his or Marguerite's biological child.

"She's not?"

"My dear," Stanley said, "blood isn't everything. Nichelle's a very dear daughter to Marguerite and me." As he spoke, just like a jigsaw puzzle that comes to life when the last piece is fitted into place, I finally figured out why Nichelle never took an interest in her parents' ancestry. I understood now that it really wasn't her history.

"You're doing your homework?" Nichelle poked her head through my half-open bedroom door, just like she did most evenings.

"I'm finishing an English essay." I looked up at her smiling face and beckoned to her to come inside.

"You study way too much. You're just like my sister, Nona. No social life, only school work and more school work."

"I want to get an English degree, so I have to work hard to graduate from high school with good grades."

"Girl, you're crazy. I'm the one preparing to write exams soon, noth you." Nichelle chuckled, stepping closer to me.

"Look, I know Daddy told you about me. I just want you to know I'm cool with it."

"You're not even a little upset?"

"Upset?" Nichelle paused. "Oh no, it's not a secret. Almost everyone knows I'm adopted. Ith's not a big deal, really."

"You don't feel like you were abandoned?"

"Mom and Daddy are the only parents I've even known. And even though Mom and I don't get along at times, well, I love her 'cause I know she wants the best for me. She and Daddy are the greatest parents I could have asked for."

"You make it sound as if it doesn't matter…"

"Thath my birth mom gave me up?" Nichelle said. "My birth mom was seventeen when she had me. Thath's just two years older than I am now. She died when I was still a baby, and Mom and Daddy stepped in. Mom and my birth mom were sort of cousins, you know."

"You're lucky."

"Thath my birth mom died?" Nichelle's piercing eyes remained on my face.

"That's not what I meant," I said. "Your real mom didn't choose to die, but my mom chose to leave me."

"I'm sorry," Nichelle said. "I kind of assumed, thath, well…"

"My mom left my dad and me when I was real little. But I still want to find her. I want to ask her why she walked out and left me with a man."

"Oh no, don't say thath. Your mom didn't leave you with just any man. Your mom left you with your dad."

"It hurts," I said, my voice quivering. "When I first started to write poetry, the pain kind of eased off and I didn't think about her a lot, but lately…"

"She's been on your mind?" Nichelle cut in. "Maybe you spend too much time talking about all thath family history stuff with Daddy."

The bond between Nichelle and me strengthened more than I ever expected, and the boys at St. Mark's school, located on the opposite side of the street from St. Teresa's, became a regular topic for us. We'd giggle uncontrollably about which St. Teresa's girl liked which St. Mark's boy. One day I almost peed myself when I couldn't stop laughing when Nichelle admitted she was attracted to her biology teacher's son, Justin, who was also the captain of his school's cricket team. And Nichelle almost died laughing too when I confessed that I really liked her best friend, Natalie's younger brother, Mason.

A couple days after my birthday, Dad and Petal came to visit me. "I've got some news," Dad said, looking at me and then at Petal. By then I'd been at Noel Gardens for several months and I wasn't in a hurry to return home any more. I loved my Dad and wanted him in my life, but I didn't need to be stuck to his coat tails as much. Dante was the last Flat Hill Village friend I'd shared a phone conversation with, and our most recent chat had been filled with long periods of uncomfortable silence.

"You want to guess what the good news is?" Dad grinned.

"The police found Theo's killer?"

"No," he said, "try again."

A huge smile took over my face as I wondered if by some miracle Dad had located Jada Shoemaker, my long-lost mother. But I sensed Dad would get annoyed if I mentioned her name, and my smile melted. "Are you there?" Dad waved his hand in front of my face.

"I can't guess," I said as my heart rate sped up. I settled on the sofa with my hand over my chest.

"You're no fun at all," Dad said. "The good news is that you're getting a little brother."

"Or a sister," Petal said.

By the time Dad and Petal left, jealousy dug deep into my chest. I felt as if Dad would no longer need me as much since he was going to have a brand new baby with his wife. But why was I resentful when I didn't want to move back to Flat Hill Village myself?

Only a few weeks later, the headline in the Guardian newspaper read, *Twin Brothers Killed during Shoot-Out with Police.* "The detectives in charge of Theo's case have very strong evidence that they were Theo's killers," Dad said.

I remained silent, trying to think up a good enough excuse to be allowed to remain in Noel Gardens a while longer. "You heard me?" Dad added.

"Yes," I nodded. "Can I remain here until school closes for the holidays?"

"She's welcome to stay as long as she wants," Marguerite said.

I hugged my father, but I was careful to watch my words, since I didn't want to be branded as someone who'd chosen another family over her own just because they lived in a nicer house in a more affluent part of town. Nichelle had become the big sister I always longed for and I'd miss her more than anyone else. I'd also miss the quality time Stanley and I shared. But above all, I was scared that when I returned to Flat Hill Village I'd no longer feel as safe as I'd felt at my cousins' home. I'd grown used to a life without drama and I didn't want that to ever change.

25.

MOVING DAY ARRIVED SOONER than I had wished, but I kept my feelings about not wanting to return to Flat Hill Village to myself. "You've got a lot of stuff." Nichelle said as she put a box much smaller than all the others in the back seat of my father's vehicle. It seems I was going home with more stuff than I came with. I waved at Nichelle and her mom and felt sad as Dad swerved onto the street.

"It's good that we're going ahead with the new room," he said.

"New room?"

"Workmen are going to start constructing a new bedroom for Petal and me later this week," he said. "You can have our old one and the baby could eventually get yours." He paused for a moment. "By the way, it's a girl."

I had mixed feelings about my unborn sister, but, by the time we had gotten halfway home, I convinced myself that it would be cool to have a baby sister. I'd only seen Petal a couple of times in the past couple of months, but we often talked on the phone. She'd kept me posted regarding the latest happenings in Flat Hill Village. Dahlia had graduated from high school and, with Arlie's assistance, secured a government job. Arlie still headed the neighbourhood Women's Committee, and the membership had been opened up to men, but Dad hadn't joined. Also, the girls' soccer club had been disbanded due to falling membership.

"Dad," I asked, "are you ever going to send me back to Canada to visit Makayla?"

"I'm sorry, it's not going to happen this year," he said. "The baby and the addition to the house are stretching us to the max."

"Why don't we move to a better area?"

"Petal wouldn't agree to leave," Dad said. "Her childhood home means a lot to her."

"We could get a much nicer house, like that one." I pointed to a two-storey dwelling resembling Vena's Paradise Lane home.

"You know how much that costs?" Dad smirked. "You've got expensive tastes, just like your mother, and it could get you into trouble."

"My mother?"

"Never mind." He swerved up the hill, but didn't park in his usual spot. "I can drive straight to our yard now," he said.

"This is really awesome." I stuck my head out the window as my father's car glided up the smooth, asphalt-covered road, past houses on one side and some massive greenery on the other. "Who lives in that new house?" I pointed as Dad drove past a pea-green two-storey house with a black, arched iron gate. The emerald home stood on the same spot where the abandoned house once was. "The Coopers, you wouldn't know them. They're new to the area," he said.

A man filling a bucket of water at the standpipe waved at Dad. Dad slowed down and waved back. "I don't know him," I said.

"He's also new to the neighbourhood."

Dad pulled up in front of our house. I climbed out of the car and unlatched the gate. He swerved into a brand new garage, which had been constructed during my absence. I stepped past a fair amount of moss beside the staircase, dropped my backpack on the porch, and inspected the changes in the neighbourhood. It looked like a lot had happened in the months I had been away.

"Up there hasn't changed a lot," Dad said, looking at the houses on the hillside facing us.

"Yeah." I nodded, noting that only one house looked considerably different. That house had larger windows and had been repainted cream instead of its former dusty brown.

"The man we passed at the standpipe lives there," Dad said. "He's Arlie's distant cousin."

As Dad mentioned Arlie's name, I glanced at her house; it looked exactly the same.

"Baby Girl!" Drew yelled. "You're back?"

Just then Warren, his nose running, sped toward me.

"Yes, I'm back for good." I kicked off my shoes and hugged the boys. Everything in the living room looked the same, except for a fair amount of dust on the television and stereo system. I felt tiny grains of sand beneath my feet but continued full speed toward my room.

"I'm going to say hi to Petal," I said to Dad as he brought the first box into my bedroom.

"Can I come in?" I said, standing in front of Petal's half-open bedroom door.

"Sure." She gingerly moved to a seated position, with both hands cupping her round belly. "I glad yuh home. Your dad trying, but as yuh see, he not doing a very good job with de housework," she said.

I half smiled, wary about being stuck with household chores on a daily basis.

"Tell me how yuh doing." Petal patted the mattress.

"Everything keeps changing," I said.

"Dat's how life is," she said. "Nothing ever stays the same."

Moxley and Spider started to bark, so I raced down the rear staircase to check on them. I unlocked the door to their kennel, and Moxley's hind legs bumped into my midsection. They both jumped up and licked my face. After the dogs calmed down, I refilled their water bowls. Then I looked up at Martha Carlin's house. The roof was in place, but the exterior walls still needed painting.

The fence separating our property from the Carlins' stood up much straighter than before, though it appeared to be a little curved in the middle. The huge rip at the bottom of the wire fence had been repaired, and there wasn't any garbage streaming downhill, except for a single newspaper leaf fluttering in the wind.

Despite my initial reluctance to return to Flat Hill Village, I immediately felt at home, and a week after my return I accompanied Petal to the committee meeting at Arlie's house just like old times. The organization had been renamed the Flat Hill Neighbourhood Association.

Mr. Wellington had moved away, and I convinced Dad that I was old enough to travel to school on my own. He allowed me to start taking public transportation.

One Saturday, Dad inspected the freshly painted bedroom that had taken longer to complete than originally expected. "It looks good, doesn't it?" he said as my eyes circled the bare space. I was glad the roof, walls, windows, and doors were finally in place, and I no longer had to listen to Dad's daily rants about the delay. I followed him into his and Petal's old bedroom, which was soon going to be mine. "Where do you want your bed?" Dad asked.

"In the middle."

"Our new room going to be too full up if we put de desk in there with de baby crib." Petal sat up. "Yuh want de desk to stay here?"

"Yeah, it would be cool to have a bigger one," I said.

The next morning Dad had to rush Petal to the hospital. "She's going to have the baby early," he said, visibly excited.

Arlie invited the boys and me to spend the day at her place. We arrived at her house at about eleven o'clock that morning, and made ourselves right at home. Carrie and I started chatting about girl stuff right away. It was as though we couldn't get the words out fast enough. Dante barely said a word, though, and that felt kind of weird, but Carrie and I had a lot to talk about.

The day before Petal came home with the new baby, the boys and I helped Dad move his and Petal's clothes and other small items to their spanking new room. Mickey and Shiva lugged the larger pieces of furniture, and, after they left, I sat on the floor in my soon-to-be new room and pulled out the bottom drawer of the oak desk. I had intended to wipe it clean with a wet rag, but to my surprise a shoebox lay inside. I scooped it out and placed it on the floor.

"Baby Girl!" Warren rushed in, waving a sheet of paper.

"Look, I made a picture of my baby sister!" he said with a gap-toothed smile.

He rushed at me at full speed and bumped into the shoebox, knocking it on its side. A stack of envelopes and some loose sheets held together with a red rubber band toppled out.

"Here." He handed his drawing to me with a big toothy smile.

"It's nice," I complimented him, even though the head and limbs were out of proportion.

Warren passed me the stack of letters and loose sheets he'd knocked over and plucked the rubber band securing them as if he were strumming a guitar. Then the rubber band burst and the letters scattered onto the floor and the loose sheets floated across the room.

"Look at what you've done," I said as I grabbed two of the sheets, only to realize I was holding Boyie's death certificate and Dad and Petal's marriage certificate. Warren lingered in the same spot, glancing first at the letters spread out on the floor, and then at me. "Start picking them up, please!" I said.

In silence, he started to gather them up and handed them to me a few at a time. Soon I had the entire pile. "Go and play with your brother now," I ordered.

As soon as he left the room, I inspected Dad's name and address scribbled in black ink on the uppermost envelope.

It had been postmarked almost two years earlier and mailed from Kingston, Ontario, Canada.

Just like Dad and Petal to keep a heap of old letters, I thought as I searched through the stack and realized that they were all addressed to Dad. Then it suddenly clicked that the handwriting on all of them was identical. I flipped one over, curious to identify the sender. The name "Shirley Roe" was printed very neatly on the back of the envelopes I'd randomly selected to examine.

Who is Shirley Roe? I placed the entire stack on the ground and pulled out a yellow sheet of lined paper from one of the envelopes. Three torn holes on the right side of the paper gave the impression that someone had hastily pulled it out of a binder. I held the note and read.

> *Dear Smokey,*
>
> *I have been trying to locate you for quite some time. I am sorry you got injured in that terrible incident, but it must have been God's way of leading me to you. The truth is, I am writing to ask you to allow me to have contact with my granddaughter, and Mushy needs contact with her too; after all she's her firstborn. We both know Mushy has done wrong, but please don't punish her any more. She's suffered enough and has been paying her debt to society for her misgivings all of these years. I am not looking for your pity, but I need to let you know that I have cancer and chances are I might not be around for much longer, so please reply promptly.*
>
> *Regards,*
> *Shirley*

I held the note between two fingers, not sure what to make of it. Why did Dad have a stack of letters from someone in Canada named Shirley Roe, a woman I'd never heard of before? And who was Mushy? My mind was full of confusing thoughts. I took a deep breath before shoving the note back in its envelope. But I couldn't stop myself from peeking inside a second envelope. I yanked out its contents, the paper inside equally yellowed. This note was much longer than the first. My eyes almost popped out of my head the moment I read the first few lines.

This can't be right, I thought.

"Petal wants to talk to you." Dad's voice bounced off the wall as he barged in. I looked up at him with anguish, and my hands shaking visibly.

Everything moved in slow motion as Dad's eyes shifted from the note in my hand to the stack of letters piled up on the floor beside the empty shoebox. But I was more concerned about what I'd just learned than about being caught reading mail addressed to Dad.

"Shit!" he yelled. A look of fear, anger, and guilt took hold of his face. "Why the hell are you reading these?" He snatched the yellow sheet of paper.

"Wa-wa…Warren knocked them to the ground," I stuttered.

"You should know better than to read other people's letters!" he yelled, but, despite his loud tone, I heard Petal's voice drifting out of the receiver.

"What going on there?" Her voice was full of concern. "Smokey, please talk to me!"

Dad handed me the phone. He went down on one knee and scooped up the letters, shoving them back into the shoebox, and sped away with the box under his arm.

"Dad is mad." I clutched the phone. "I was only trying to help. I was only cleaning out the desk."

"Yuh read yuh dad letters?" Petal moaned.

I kept silent.

"Answer me, Baby Girl? Did yuh read yuh dad letters?"

"I only read two of them," I eventually admitted.

"Damn it," she said, "let me talk to Smokey."

I found Dad sitting on the edge of his bed with his hands pressed against his forehead. "Petal wants to talk to you," I said. Dad lifted his head. He seemed to stare straight through me. I extended my arm, and he took the phone without saying anything. I went back to the bedroom and sat down at the oak desk. A few minutes later, Dad pushed the door open.

"You shouldn't have read any of them." His voice sounded calmer. "I've been trying to protect you all these years. This is not how I wanted you to find out."

You lied! I wanted to say, but I couldn't speak.

"We need to have a talk." He came closer, extending his right arm to touch mine, but I didn't want him to stroke my arms, my legs, or any part of me, so I sprang off the chair and ran out of the room and then out the front door. I sped through the gate and went straight to Arlie's place.

"What's wrong?" Arlie glanced at my face and then at my feet. "No shoes?" she said as tears streamed down my face.

"Come and talk to me." She led me to her bedroom. "Sit down." She handed me a tissue. Then she locked the door. "It's just you and me now. Tell me what's troubling you."

I had been at Arlie's house more times than I could count, but had never stepped inside her bedroom until that very moment. I was too distressed to inspect the unfamiliar space except to notice that it was pleasant and comfortable and safe.

"Talk to me, Baby Girl," she said, trying to coax me to speak, but I couldn't stop myself from sobbing. "Look at me." She put her hand under my chin. "I'm here for you." She sounded genuine, but I was too ashamed to look up.

"Baby Girl's dad is here!" Carrie knocked the door.

"I don't want to talk to him!" I said. "I don't want to see him!"

"Tell Smokey I'll escort Baby Girl home," Arlie said to Carrie.

"My real mom's alive. They called her Mushy and my grandmother is Shirley Roe," I eventually sputtered, as Arlie kept prodding.

"So why the tears?" Arlie said. "That's good news, isn't it?"

"No, it's not," I said. "I wish she were dead." I sobbed even louder. "I hate her. I hate both of them!"

"I know it's painful not to have had your mother in your life. But I'm sure there must be a very good reason why she hasn't been with you all these years. Maybe she had a very mixed up life." Arlie paused. "Maybe your mom had the same sort of life as my dad."

"It's really bad." I inhaled. Then I blurted out, "My mom's in jail." I looked Arlie straight in the face.

"What?" Arlie grimaced. "Who told you that?"

"I read it in one of Dad's letters," I said. "Dad's been lying to me all these years."

"Maybe he was only trying to protect you." Arlie hugged me as I sobbed into her shoulder.

Eventually, my sobs turned into sniffles. Arlie didn't pry for specifics. She must have worried that any thing she might say could trigger more tears. We remained in her bedroom for almost an hour before I said, "I'm ready to go home now."

"I promise not to share any of this with anyone." Arlie opened the door.

I moved along Arlie's corridor very slowly, and the pitiful look on Dante and Carrie's faces brought back memories of Lena and Harley's pained expressions on the day Dad took me out of Paradise Lane against my will. How I wished I were a little girl again so I could once again daydream about finding the mother I always wanted: a superwoman, angel, and princess all wrapped into one. *Why did she have to be in prison?*

Arlie unhinged the gate and motioned me through. "I can go in by myself." I made my way up the staircase hoping Dad wouldn't try to sugarcoat the story.

"Are you okay?" He rested a beer bottle on the window-sill. "I couldn't share all that ugliness with you. I couldn't look you in the eyes and tell you that your mom was serving time. She's been in prison since you were three years old. But in truth she left us just before your first birthday. I have to accept some of the blame. I wasn't the ideal father or the ideal husband," Dad said. "Your grandmother began writing to me before we left Canada, and she hinted that Mushy, your mom, was going to seek visitation when she got out of prison. Mushy was up for parole the year we left, and to be honest, that's what made me want to come back to Trinidad. I wasn't going to let her confuse you." Dad explained that my biological grandmother, Shirley Roe, had made contact with him again after his picture was posted on the Internet following the stabbing incident.

"I found out a few months ago that your grandmother died, but your mother is almost certainly going to be out on parole by this time next year, and, if that happens, she'll likely move back from the States to Canada. She was born in the U.S., but she is a Canadian citizen. Both of her parents are Canadians."

"Why did she go to jail?"

"Attempting to traffic drugs across the U.S. border," he said. "Here is her address. You can write to her when you are ready."

"No, I don't want to write to her." I bit my lip.

"You can go back to Stanley's place if you want to," Dad said. "I spoke to Stanley about the whole situation, and he and Marguerite have welcomed you with open arms. You can stay with them for as long as you wish."

"I already promised to help Petal with the baby," I said, as Dad hugged me.

The following day, I rushed home from school anxious to hold my baby sister, Raven-Anne, for the first time. Her face was as wrinkled as a dried-up prune, but she was of a lighter complexion than any prune I'd ever seen in my life. "You want to be her godmother?" Petal asked.

"Me?"

"You're her big sister, and I know yuh always going to look out fer her."

"You're sure?" I questioned.

"Don't worry. I sure yuh going to make de perfect godmother."

Raven-Anne's baptism service was held at Stanley's church three months later, and afterward invited guests gathered at our Flat Hill Village home to celebrate the event.

"Annette, meet Baby Girl." Colm introduced me to a petite girl with pretty brown eyes. Then Stanley, Marguerite, and Nichelle arrived. Arlie and her kids came through the gate shortly before Dahlia, her two younger sisters, and their mother. It wasn't long before the tent Dad and Shiva had put up for the occasion was packed with guests.

"Seems everyone here except Meena and de kids," Petal said as Colm's mom, Sandrina hustled through the gate. Petal offered a lazy smile. "You're okay?" she asked
as I stood next to her.

"I'm fine," I said, but, in truth, I desperately needed time to myself, so I disappeared behind the house and hurried up the staircase. My mind wandered to a host of different people who'd touched my life, all whom I hadn't seen in ages: Charm and Clara; my Canadian friend, Makayla; Vena and the twins, and, of course, Auntie Hattie. A vivid image of my mom cooped up in an eight by ten cell came to mind, causing me to tear up. As much as I wanted to get in touch with her, fear had kept me from writing the letter.

"What are you doing here all by yourself?" Dad came forward, gingerly carrying my baby sister in his arms. I hastily dried my eyes with my sleeves and made my way toward him. "Raven-Anne wants you to hold her," Dad said, sounding somewhat relieved as he placed the baby in my arms. We walked to the front of the house, but before I got there, I heard her voice.

"Baby Girl! Hey, Baby Girl, are you there?"

I couldn't believe it! Makayla, my childhood friend whom I hadn't seen in more than two years, stood beside her mother and her younger brother.

"Makayla!" I screeched as she rushed toward me. We wrapped our arms around each other, and jumped up and down excitedly. I was still holding the baby close to my chest, but she didn't seem to mind all the excitement at all. Makayla then pulled out a tiny camera and snapped a picture of Raven-Anne and me.

The following night, I sat at my oak desk thinking of all the people who'd been present at Raven-Anne's baptismal celebration. Out of the blue it felt like the right time, so I picked up a pen.

Dear Mushy,

I am sorry that I am already a teenager and we don't know each other. My dad has been a very good father. He loves me and I love him. I want to love you too, and I hope we can get to know each other better by writing letters. Hopefully, Dad will send me to Canada to see you when you come home next year. Can you send me a picture?

Your daughter,

Melody Sparks (better known as Baby Girl)

I wrote her real name, Jada Shoemaker, her assigned prison number, and address on an envelope. I placed the note and a copy of one of my most recent poems inside it. I licked the flap and sealed it before attaching a stamp on the upper right-hand corner.

On impulse, I slid open the bottom drawer of my desk, took out the stack of very old photos Dad had given me and scanned them quickly. I froze when I got to the only photo I had of Dad and his deceased twin brother, Howie. I pulled the battered photo of the two young boys posing under the zaboca tree from the pile and propped it up on my desk. I was thankful I had it, but also grateful I already had a bunch of pictures of me and my baby-sister, Raven-Anne, that I had also propped up on my desk. I smiled at my family in photographs on my desk, and at the thought of all the other family I had come to know over the past while.

I decided to mail the letter to my mother on my way to school the next day. I smoothed the envelope and tucked it neatly into my backpack.

Acknowledgements

Thank you God for restoring my health and allowing me to achieve this milestone. Mommy and Daddy thank you for being the best parents ever. I miss both of you so much. I am consoled to know that you are with me in spirit.

A shout out of gratitude to my former work colleagues, Anne Mackenzie and Phyllis Depoe for taking time out of your busy schedule to read my manuscript and to offer valuable feedback. A special thank you to my sister, Caroline Guevara for offering advice on several manuscripts at short notice and without expecting anything in return. To my mentor at the Humber School for Writers, Rabindranath Maharaj; the knowledge I gained from you is invaluable. Allister Thompson, thank you for providing editorial advice on this and other projects.

Thanks to everyone at Inanna Publications involved in the production and publication of this book, especially Luciana Ricciutelli, Editor-in-Chief.

Glynis Guevara was born in Barataria, Trinidad and Tobago. She holds a Bachelor of Law (Hons.) degree from the University of London, England, and is a graduate of Humber School for Writers creative writing program. She also successfully completed a technical writing certificate, an information technology post graduate diploma, and a teacher of adults certificate. Glynis was shortlisted for the Small Axe Literary short fiction prize in 2012 and the inaugural Burt Award for Caribbean literature in 2014. She currently works as an adult literacy instructor in Toronto. *Under the Zaboca Tree* is her debut novel. Her second novel, *Black Beach,* is forthcoming from Inanna Publications. Her website is www.glynisguevara.com.